CAROLE WILKINSON

 HYPERION BOOKS FOR CHILDREN

NEW YORK

First published in 2003 by black dog books
15 Gertrude Street, Fitzroy Vic 3065 Australia.
Copyright © 2003 by Carole Wilkinson

For information address Hyperion Books for Children,
114 Fifth Avenue, New York, New York 10011-5690.
First U.S. edition, 2005
1 3 5 7 9 10 8 6 4 2
Text design by Michael Yuen
Map by Julian Bruère

Library of Congress Cataloging-in-Publication Data on file.
ISBN 0-7868-5581-9
Reinforced binding

Visit www.hyperionbooksforchildren.com

FOR JOHN
WHO FIRST INTRODUCED
ME TO DRAGONS

AND LILI
MY RESIDENT EDITOR
AND SOUNDING BOARD

CONTENTS

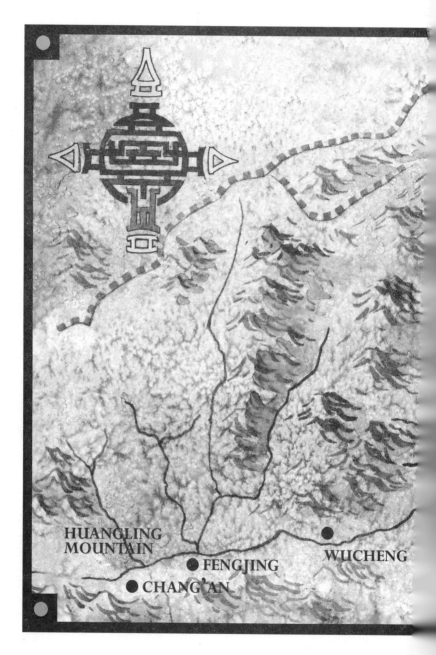

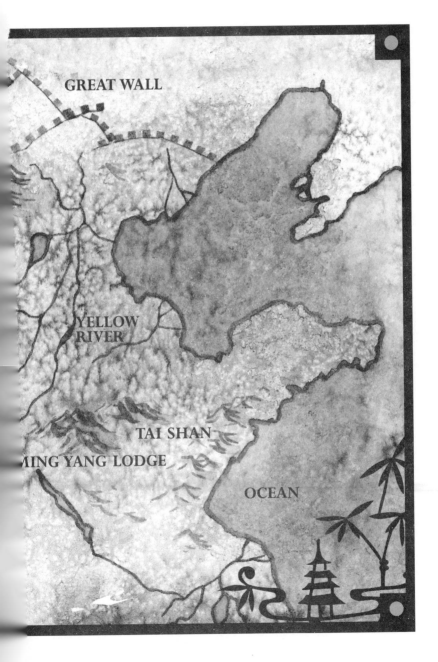

CHAPTER ONE

THE EDGE
OF THE EMPIRE

A bamboo bowl flew through the air, aimed at the slave girl's head. She ducked out of the way. She was very experienced at dodging flying objects—from inkstones to chicken bones.

Her master slumped back onto his bed, exhausted by the effort of throwing the bowl. "Feed the beasts, wretch."

"Yes, Master Lan," the girl replied.

Lan scowled at her with the distaste he reserved for rats, spiders, and maggoty meat. The only time he smiled was when he was laughing at her stupidity.

"Don't take all day either."

"No, Master Lan."

She slipped out of her master's house as an empty wine jar flew toward the door.

It was a bitterly cold day. Snow crunched beneath the slave girl's straw shoes as she hurried toward the animal pens. The sky was the color of ashes. It looked like it would soon snow again.

The slave girl didn't have a name; she didn't know how old she was. She had lived at Huangling Palace since her parents had sold her to Lan when she was a small child. The previous summer, Lan had shouted that she was thickheaded for a girl of ten years. As she could only count to ten, she didn't know how old that made her now.

Huangling Mountain was a barren hill in a range of many barren hills that marked the western boundary of the Han empire. Throughout winter it was waist deep in snow and blasted by freezing winds. In the summer the air was so hot it was like breathing in flames. The Emperor's father had built a palace in this faraway place so that the world would know how vast his empire was. Unfortunately, it was so far from anywhere that few people ever saw it.

The palace was surrounded by a high wall of rammed earth. In the eastern wall was the entrance gate. The Emperor's residence occupied more than three-quarters of the palace grounds. The animal pens, the stores, and the servants' houses were squashed together in the remaining quarter. In all the slave girl's time at Huangling, there had never been an imperial visit. The palace's graceful halls and sitting rooms, its gardens and pavilions were always empty. Slaves weren't allowed in the palace. Master Lan said he would beat her if she ever went in there. He went into the palace from time to time, but he always came back angry. He grumbled about the wasted space, the unused bed chambers, the cloth-draped furniture, while he had to sleep in his humble house with one room and a roof that leaked.

Compared to the corner of the ox shed, where the slave girl slept on a pile of straw, Master Lan's house was luxurious. There was a rug on the earth floor, and on the wall hung a painting of a dragon on a length of blue silk. The fire burned all through winter and a clever system of pipes carried heat to warm his bed. Even the goat had a better home than the slave girl.

It wasn't the goat that she was going to feed, though. It wasn't the oxen, mooing sadly in their stalls. It wasn't the pigs or even the chickens. In the farthest corner of the farthest palace in the empire, behind the servants' quarters, at the back of the stables and sheds, there was another animal enclosure. It was a pit in the ground, a dungeon hewn from the raw rock of Huangling. The only entrance to this pit was a hinged grate, not made of bamboo, like the other animal enclosures, but of bronze.

The slave girl wore trousers that were patched on the knees and too short for her, and a threadbare jacket with many mends. These were her only clothes. An icy wind blew across the courtyard and straight through the worn fabric—even at the front where the edges overlapped and wrapped around her. She looked into the pit, but could see nothing in the darkness below. She slid a latch across, lifted the grate, and went down a staircase cut into the rock. The girl shivered. Not because of the cold. Not because of the darkness. Not because of the smell of stale air that came up to meet her from the dungeon. There was something else that she couldn't put a name to that made her uneasy. The pit always had that effect on her, as if there were something waiting in the darkness—something dangerous and frightening.

It wasn't the creatures that lived in the pit that unsettled her. Even though they were big and had sharp teeth and claws, she wasn't afraid of them. They were an unnatural sort of beast. Different from the farm animals she cared for and, as far as she could see, of no use to anyone. They were dragons.

It was dark and smelled of urine and rotting straw.

It had been a long time since the pit had been cleaned. The girl moved out of the square of pale, banded light beneath the grate and into the darkness. She shuffled forward, wishing she could bring a lamp. Master Lan had forbidden such a waste of lamp oil. Her eyes grew used to the darkness. The patch of light beneath the grate now seemed bright.

The dragons slept in the darkest corner of the pit. There were only two of them now. The girl could just remember when there had been four. Lao Ma, the old woman who kept the palace clean, could remember the day the dragons first arrived. She had been no more than a girl herself. Lao Ma said there were a dozen or more of the creatures then. The slave girl wondered what had happened to all the others.

The creatures didn't move as she approached. They had never tried to hurt her, but she had a feeling that they were hiding their true nature. The painting of the dragon in Master Lan's house showed a magnificent golden creature, snaking and shimmering among clouds. In the dim light of the pit it was hard to make out exactly what the two imperial dragons looked like. They certainly weren't magnificent. They looked dull and gray. Their scales did not shimmer. They did not fly. Their long scaly bodies lay all day, curled up like piles of thick rope, in the dirty straw.

Master Lan was the Imperial Dragon Keeper. His seal of office hung from his waist by a length of greasy ribbon. It was a rectangle of white jade with characters cut into one end and a carving of a dragon on the other. It was Master Lan's job to feed and care for the imperial dragons. The girl was just supposed to feed the farm animals and take care of Master Lan's personal needs—cooking his meals, mending his worn silk robes, keeping his house clean. But the Dragon Keeper was lazy. As the girl had grown older, he'd given her more and more of his duties. He spent more and more of his days lying on his bed, eating, drinking wine, and complaining.

It was the Emperor's fault, he said. The imperial dragons really belonged at the imperial palace in Chang'an. That's how it had been for thousands of years. A shaman should examine them daily, divining the Emperor's future from the dragons' behavior. If the dragons frolicked happily in the pleasure gardens, it was a good sign for the empire. If they sulked and didn't eat, it was a bad omen. Many years ago, one of the dragons had bitten an emperor, the father of the current emperor, when he was a child. The child was scared of the beasts. As soon as he came to power, he had sent the dragons as far away as possible—to Huangling Mountain. There wasn't a day went by that Master Lan didn't complain that he should have been at Chang'an.

The slave girl put down the bowl of mashed taro and millet she had prepared for the dragons.

"Dinnertime," she said.

One dragon stirred. She could barely make out its shape. It lifted its snout to sniff the food, then turned its head away.

"Ungrateful beast," she muttered.

The bowl of food she had left that morning was still there, untouched apart from where rats had nibbled around the edge.

The slave girl had been feeding the dragons since Master Lan had decided he had bad knees and couldn't climb up and down the dungeon stairs every day. That must have been nearly a year ago. The oxen mooed whenever she went near their shed. The goat wagged its tail when she fed it. Even the chickens fluttered expectantly when she brought them food. The dragons had barely glanced at her in all that time.

"I was going to change your straw," she grumbled. "But now you can wait."

She picked up the bowl of fresh food. No point in wasting it on such surly beasts. They could finish the morning's mash first.

There was a rustle in the straw. A nose poked out. It sniffed the air. Beneath the nose were two large yellow teeth. The nose was followed by a brown head, a fat, furry body, and finally, a long tail.

The girl's frown turned to a smile. "Is that you, Hua?"

It was a large rat. She picked it up and hugged it, holding it up to her face and feeling its soft fur on her cheek.

"We'll have a good meal tonight," she told the rat. "I've got taro and millet; if I can steal a little ginger from Master Lan's dinner, it'll be a feast."

The rat glanced nervously at the dragons.

"Don't worry about them," the girl said. "They won't hurt you."

The girl tucked Hua inside her jacket next to the square of bamboo that hung around her neck. It had a worn character carved on it. Lao Ma had told her she was wearing it the day she arrived at Huangling. The girl didn't know the meaning of the character. She couldn't read and neither could Lao Ma. She hurried back up the stone steps.

The slave girl was cooking her master's evening meal in the servants' kitchen when he crept up behind her, startling her.

"I found rat droppings in my bed," the Dragon Keeper shouted. "I told you to kill that pest."

"I did, Master Lan," the girl said, hoping Hua would stay still inside her jacket. "Just as you ordered."

"You're lying," her master snarled. "If I ever find it, I'll boil it alive."

He picked up the bowl of lentils that were soaking for the girl's own dinner and hurled it out into the courtyard. The lentils scattered in the snow.

He sniffed the stew. "If there's no onion in my dinner, you'll get a beating!"

The girl hadn't put an onion in her master's stew. There were none left in Lao Ma's food store.

The slave girl ran to the gate. Not the big wooden gates with the bronze hinges which were always locked, but a small gate made of bamboo poles behind the goat shed. Outside the palace walls were the orchard (some stunted apple trees and half-dead cherry trees), the vegetable garden, and the rest of the world. Most of the garden was covered with snow, but there was one corner that the gardener kept clear. Underneath a pile of straw, the girl found a few frost-bitten onion plants sticking out of the soil. She hacked at the frozen earth with her blade, but it was as hard as stone. She cut off the limp leaves and hoped they would provide enough flavor.

She sat back on her heels. There was a dark orange blot on the horizon. Somewhere beyond the clouds the sun was setting. She wondered what she would have been doing right now if she hadn't been sold as a slave. Would she be happy? Would she be sitting in a cozy house with her parents? Brothers and sisters? Would she have a full stomach?

She'd thought about running away from Huangling many times. It would be easy enough. But where would she go? She scanned the horizon in every direction. There was nothing but snow-covered mountains gradually fading from white to gray in the twilight. There were no villages, no remote garrisons, not so much as a tree in sight. She watched a lone snow eagle glide into the distance and came to the same conclusion as she had all the other times she'd thought about running away. Unless she grew wings, she'd have to stay at Huangling. She got to her feet and went back to finish preparing her master's meal.

After she had served the stew to Master Lan, she retrieved her own dinner from the snow. It took more than an hour of kneeling in the cold and dark to find even half the lentils. She was glad she'd stolen the dragons' taro and millet. Without them, her dinner would have been very meager. She added the lentils to a pot of boiling water.

A leather pouch hung from her waist, suspended from a length of frayed hemp rope. As well as her rusty iron blade, it contained her secret possessions—a hairpin given to her by the man who delivered to the stores twice a year, a piece of weathered wood shaped just like a fish, and a white eagle feather. She took out the blade and chopped up the piece of ginger she'd saved from her master's dinner. She added that to the pot with the taro and millet.

She went to collect the dirty dishes from Master Lan's house. He was sprawled on the bed snoring. As well as the upturned bowl and wine cup, she took a bronze lamp shaped like a ram from beside her sleeping master's bed. Back in the kitchen she pulled a small clay jar from behind the stove. It was full of lamp oil. She filled up the lamp.

"Come on, Hua," said the slave girl, picking up the rat and tucking him into her jacket. "While we're waiting for our dinner to cook, let's go and explore the world."

Master Lan would have beat her if he found out that every time she lit a lamp for him, she saved a little of the oil for herself. She took no more than a drop or two each night, but slowly she collected enough to fill a lamp.

Outside she shielded the lamp with her jacket, just in case any of the other palace staff were around. It was very unlikely. The men were all as old as Lao Ma. They liked to be tucked in bed early. The girl ducked through a hole in the tangled vine that shielded the palace from the servants' quarters, the animal sheds, and other unsightly buildings. It also hid her secret visits to the palace from the other servants. She glanced up at the dark sky. She hoped the clouds would hide her from the gods. She walked through the dark gardens and opened the door of the Jade Flower Hall. The lamp lit a small circle of light on the floor. She followed a dark corridor. This was her secret pleasure, exploring the palace while everyone else was sleeping.

Master Lan was always saying that Huangling was tiny compared to the palaces in Chang'an, but to the slave girl it seemed huge. Each time she went on one of her night-time excursions to the palace, she visited a different room. Once she had gone into the Emperor's own chamber. She had even dared to sit on his bed, which was as big as a wheat field. This time she went to a small hall where the palace women, if there had been any, would normally spend their days. It was one of her favorite rooms. She held up the lamp. The circle of light moved from the floor to the wall. It lit a painting of a mountain with a tiny building on its peak. The mountain loomed above a flat plain, impossibly high, its slopes scattered with tiny trees that were twisted and gnarled but still looked beautiful.

She held up the rat so that he could see the painting.

"Do you think this is what the world looks like, Hua?" she whispered.

The rat twitched his whiskers.

She shone the lamp farther along the wall where it fell on a silk wall hanging. This had a painting of a garden. In the garden there was a lake with a bridge zigzagging across it. The garden was bursting with flowers: pink, blue, pale purple, bright yellow. The girl didn't know the names of the flowers. She had never seen anything growing on Huangling that had such bright colors.

"Do you think there really are such flowers?"

In summer, a few peonies struggled into flower in the neglected gardens of Huangling, but they looked limp and pale alongside the gorgeous flowers in the painted garden. She liked to think that somewhere in the world there were things so bright and beautiful, but she doubted that they really existed.

"It's how painters would like the world to be," she whispered to the rat. "There aren't real places like these."

Her stomach rumbled.

"Let's go and eat," she said.

Back in the kitchen, the girl made sure that the oil in the lamp was at exactly the same level as it had been before. Master Lan had a habit of checking. She spooned her dinner into a wooden bowl. Then she tiptoed into her master's house to sit by the fire. Hua came out from his hiding place inside her jacket.

"Here you are, Hua," the girl said, setting down a second smaller bowl of food on the hearth.

The rat ate greedily.

Hua hadn't always been the girl's pet. She had first made his acquaintance when she found him stealing a chicken leg (which she had stolen from Master Lan). She was furious and tried to hit the rat with a piece of firewood. He was quick and escaped easily. Then she woke one night to find him nibbling her fingers. She determined to catch the pest and built a trap out of thin bamboo canes. Once she'd caught the rat, though, she couldn't bring herself to kill it. She decided that he was quite a pretty creature with his glossy brown fur, pink ears, and whippy tail. She called him Hua, which meant Blossom. She started to train him. The rat responded well. Before long he had become quite tame and was the girl's best and only friend.

When Master Lan discovered she was keeping a rat as a pet, he ordered her to kill it. She had to keep Hua out of his sight. That's when she'd got the idea of keeping him hidden in the folds of her jacket.

She settled by the fire to enjoy the food and warmth in peace. This was her favorite time of day.

"Life's not so bad, is it, Hua?" The rat was lying contentedly in front of the fire.

"We've been out to see the world, we've got a meal inside us, and we can warm our toes by the fire." The rat rolled over so that she could scratch his full stomach. "And we've got each other."

CHAPTER TWO

AN EVIL NIGHT

The following day, the slave girl felt guilty about taking the dragons' food. She trudged through the snow to the shed where Lao Ma had just finished milking the goat. The old woman's eyesight was poor. She didn't notice the slave girl dipping a bowl into the bucket of warm milk as she chatted about the weather.

The girl went down into the pit and put the bowl of milk in front of the coiled dragons. The larger dragon lifted its head. Two yellow eyes stared at her. It was the first time she'd seen the creature so close. It lapped up some milk and then lowered its head again. The slave girl was turning to leave when one of the dragons let out a roar. She'd never heard the beasts make any noise before. This was a terrible sound, as if someone were crashing copper bowls together.

Loneliness, the slave girl thought, though she didn't know why.

She put her hands over her ears to try and block out the mournful noise.

Misery.

The dragon continued to roar. Hua scrambled out of the girl's jacket and ran away, squeaking.

Despair. The word echoed in her mind, though she didn't really know what it meant.

A light appeared at the top of the steps. Master Lan stumbled down. Hua darted between his legs. Lao Ma was right behind Lan, but she was afraid of the dragons and wouldn't go down the steps.

"What have you done, brat?" Lan shouted.

"Nothing," said the girl, which was true. "I gave them their dinner last night as usual," she said, which was not true.

Master Lan approached the dragons timidly. He held the lamp in one hand and a bamboo stick in the other, ready to defend himself. His worn silk slipper squelched in dragon droppings. The beast roared again, a sound that made the girl want to curl up in a ball and weep.

"It's an evil omen," moaned Lao Ma from the top of the steps. "It could be the end of the world."

In the lamplight, the slave girl could see the yellow-eyed dragon sitting on its haunches. Its head was raised to the roof of the pit as it howled. The other dragon hadn't moved. Master Lan prodded it with his bamboo stick, but it still didn't stir.

"It's dead," he said.

The dragon howled louder still. Lao Ma wailed too.

"This is your fault," Lan swiped the girl on the side of the head. "You haven't been looking after the beasts properly."

Master Lan surveyed the dragon's corpse. "What a waste. That animal would have been worth five thousand gold *jin* to the right buyer."

"I did my best, master," said the girl, though she knew she could have done more.

"You're a useless wretch. Don't just stand there," he shouted. "Help me drag it out."

The slave girl was frightened by the metallic sounds that the other dragon was making, but she was more frightened of her master. She crept toward the dead beast. The sight of its lifeless body filled her with sadness—with guilt too. She should have realized it was ailing. Master Lan grasped the dragon's tail. The girl took hold of one of its taloned feet. It was the first time she had touched a dragon's scaly hide. It was rough and dry, like leather that had been left out in the weather for too long. Now that it was stretched full length, it was bigger than she had realized. They dragged the creature to the foot of the stairs, but it was too heavy for them to haul up even one of the steps.

"Fetch the other men," ordered Lan.

The girl ran to collect the rest of the palace staff. There were only three of them—the gardener, the carpenter, and the painter. They tied a rope around the dead dragon's neck and all four men hauled on it. They dragged it up five steps. The sound of the dead body smacking against the stone made the girl feel sick. The other dragon howled with every blow. The men heaved and strained. Despite the cold, sweat ran down their faces as they strained to drag the body up the steps. The girl had never seen her master work so hard. As much as they tried, they couldn't get the dragon all the way up the steps. In the end, the carpenter had to build a device with a wheel and a rope. With the help of this pulley the men hauled the dead beast out into the courtyard.

The gray day was giving way to a darker gray twilight. A shower of rain turned to sleet. Icy drops, blown by a strong wind, stung the girl's face and hands like sewing needles. It had taken all day to get the dead dragon out of the pit. The whole time, the remaining dragon had continued to make its clashing metallic sounds that set the girl's teeth on edge. She began to think that she'd have to listen to that awful noise for the rest of her life.

"Build a fire," shouted the Dragon Keeper.

"What are you going to do?" the girl asked.

"Don't question me!" Lan snapped, his robes flapping in the wind. He turned to Lao Ma. "Bring out your biggest pot."

The girl had no idea what her master had in mind.

Lao Ma seemed to know, though. She shook her head and chanted prayers of forgiveness.

"What's going on?" the girl asked as she watched her master order the men to fetch wood and bring coals from his fireplace. Before long, despite the snow that was starting to fall, there was a fire blazing in the courtyard. The men placed a huge cooking pot on the fire and filled it with snow.

The dragon kept howling from the pit. It chilled the girl more than the wind and snow. She wanted to crawl away and hide in the dark. But there was worse to come, much worse. Master Lan sent the girl to get an ax. The flames grew higher. He took the ax, raised it above his head and brought it down. The blade dug deep into the flesh of the dragon. Thick purple blood oozed from the wound. Lan cut out the dragon's heart and liver and put them in a bowl. From the pit the howl of the other dragon grew louder. The slave girl covered her ears and prayed for the soul of the dragon.

"Bring me ginger and vinegar," Lan shouted. "I need eggplant and squash."

Lao Ma shook her head.

Lan growled like an animal. "Do as I say." He grabbed the old woman and shoved her in the direction of the food store. "You go with her, rat-girl," he shouted. "You'll both obey me or end up in the pickle, too."

"Pickle?" The girl couldn't make sense of what was happening.

"Why is he making pickle?" she asked Lao Ma as they hurried into the food store. "Has he gone mad?"

Lao Ma passed her a string of garlic and a jar of vinegar.

"He wants to get rid of the evidence. The earth's too frozen to bury the corpse. He can sell the heart, the liver, and the bones, but he has to get rid of the rest. The Emperor doesn't like the dragons, but if he finds out that Lan has failed in his duty to care for them, he'll be executed just like his father."

"But why doesn't he—"

"Just do as he says, girl."

They hurried back with the ingredients. Heavy clouds hid the moon, and the girl was glad. It meant she could see little as the Dragon Keeper hacked up the dead dragon, cackling as if it were the most amusing thing he'd done in a long while. He threw hunks of flesh into the steaming pot, scooped up the thickened blood from the snow, and added that as well. He made the girl chop up the vegetables and throw them into the hideous mixture with the vinegar and garlic. Her fingers were stiff and clumsy from the cold. She tried to focus on the snowflakes settling on her sleeve. The beautiful white flakes were visible for a moment as perfect star shapes, each one different, before the heat from the fire melted them. But they couldn't distract her from the gruesome sight of Lan butchering the dragon flesh. The spicy smell made her empty stomach rumble, but she felt sick at the thought of eating. Things were never going to be the same at Huangling.

Wild animals beyond the palace walls howled, joining the dragon in a horrible chorus. The flames licked around the pot, lighting up Lan's blood-flecked face and reflecting in his wild eyes. As he stirred the pot, he looked like a demon. If they weren't executed for treason, the girl felt sure they would all go to the worse regions of Hell for the awful crime of pickling an imperial dragon. How Hell could be a worse place than Huangling on that terrible night, she couldn't imagine.

CHAPTER THREE

THE IMPERIAL BANQUET

The girl opened her eyes. During the night, she'd been waiting for thunderbolts to fall down from Heaven or imperial guards to come crashing through the gates. Nothing had happened. She hadn't expected to see another morning, but a bloodred stain on the eastern sky proved her wrong. She had fallen asleep by the fire, which was now nothing but a circle of smoking ashes. She was icy cold. Her clothes were stiff where the snow had turned to ice. The cooking pot was lying empty on its side. Next to it was a jagged, snow-covered shape that she couldn't identify in the early morning light. She got stiffly to her feet. As the sky grew lighter, she realized it was a pile of broken, bloody bones. Mercifully, the dragon had stopped howling from the pit.

All that day the girl prayed to the immortals for forgiveness, promising to take good care of the remaining dragon. Master Lan rode down the mountain with the dragon's heart and liver in a jar, the bones in sacks. The jars of pickle disappeared into the kitchens. The next day passed, and still no heavenly vengeance arrived to punish them for their sins. At the very least she was expecting regular beatings from Master Lan, but when he returned, all he did was make her shovel the animal manure for the gardener. He didn't mention the night of the pickling.

"I should have paid more attention when I bought you, rat-girl," Lan said as he watched the slave girl pick up the empty wine jars scattered around his bed. His hair, which was supposed to be in a tight knot on the top of his head, was falling over his eyes. His robes were stained with spilled wine. "I didn't realize you were cursed."

The girl tried to pick up the jars with her right hand.

"Your wretched parents should have told me you were left-handed."

The mention of her parents made the girl fumble. She dropped a jar. It smashed into pieces.

"Idiot," snarled Lan. "No wonder you were so cheap. I've had nothing but bad luck since you arrived."

The Dragon Keeper threw the nearest thing at the girl—a bronze lamp shaped like a ram.

The girl tried to convince herself otherwise, but she couldn't shake off the horrible feeling that it was her fault the dragon had died. She hadn't taken as much care of the dragons as she had the other animals. She was fond of the big-eyed oxen. The goat's antics made her laugh. She talked to the pigs and they grunted back. The dragons had always made her uncomfortable. She promised the gods she would be kinder to the remaining dragon.

The first thing she did was clean the dragon's pit. It took many trips up and down the steps to take out the stinking straw and to carry down buckets of hot water to scrub the floor. The dragon showed little interest until she reached the farthest corner of the pit. Then it suddenly became very agitated, or at least the girl thought it was agitated by the sounds it made—like someone rapidly beating a gong. The girl had smuggled the oil lamp into the pit so that she could clean properly. The lamp provided only a pinpoint of brightness as the dull black rock sucked up its light. She was surprised, then, to see a faint reflection in the back corner of the dungeon. She moved the lamp closer to investigate.

The anxious gonging of the dragon grew faster. Wedged in a recess at the back of the dungeon was something oval and about the size of a melon. It was smeared with dragon's droppings. The girl picked it up. It was cold to touch. She wiped a patch with her sleeve and held it close to the light. She gasped. It was beautiful. A large, purple stone with swirls of milky white disappearing into its depths. An image appeared in her mind—a wide expanse of blue. She didn't know what it was. The image came and went in a flash.

A noise startled her. It was a deep rumbling sound, like someone pounding a drum made of beaten metal.

"Don't touch stone!" She looked around, but the voice seemed to be inside her mind, as it had been on the night of the pickling. This time it wasn't sad, it was angry.

The girl turned. Behind her there was a terrifying monster rearing up on its haunches. Its yellow eyes were narrowed to slits. Its huge teeth were bared. For the first time, the girl was afraid of the dragon. She put the stone back in its alcove.

"I wasn't going to take it," she stammered, though she didn't know who she was talking to. "I have no use for it."

The dragon settled down onto its four feet and slunk back to the bed of fresh straw. The girl sat still while the pounding of her heart slowed and her hands stopped shaking. Lao Ma had told her stories of dragons that guarded hoards of gold and jewels. Perhaps this was all that was left of the dragon's hoard. She tried to remember the image that had flashed into her mind. The more she tried to recall it, the more indistinct it became, until she couldn't remember it at all.

"What do you think dragons like to eat, Hua?" she asked the rat that evening.

She had tried different combinations of vegetables in the dragon's meals to encourage him to eat more. He still ate little. Hua was gnawing on a chicken bone he'd found.

"You're right!" the girl exclaimed. "He might be different from the other animals. He might like to eat meat like you."

She took a bowl of her own chicken gruel to the dragon. He didn't eat it immediately, but when she returned the next morning, the bowl was empty.

After that, she brought meat whenever she could and stole milk as often as she dared. It was hard to tell in the dim light, but she thought that the dragon's appearance was improving. With time and patience, the dragon might come to trust her and look forward to her visits as much as the oxen and the goat did.

A week passed and then another. It snowed less. Occasional patches of pale blue sky showed through the clouds.

"What the dragon really needs is some fresh air," the slave girl said to Hua one morning. "He'd better not try to run away, though."

The other men were away hunting. Lao Ma was working in the palace somewhere. When Master Lan was having his afternoon nap, the girl went down into the pit. She tied a length of rope around the dragon's neck and gently led him to the stone steps. The dragon lifted one foot onto the first step. Then he placed another foot on the second step. His limbs were stiff from lack of use. Each step seemed to cause him pain.

She coaxed the creature up one step at a time and eventually he came up into the courtyard. Sunlight seeped through gaps in the cloud cover like water from a cracked bucket. The dragon covered his eyes with one paw. It was some minutes before his eyes grew used to the daylight.

The girl slowly led the dragon around the courtyard. Startled chickens squawked and flapped out of their way. When there was a larger break in the clouds and sunlight lit a patch of the courtyard, the dragon moved to stand in it.

"It must be a long time since you felt the warmth of the sun," the girl said, patting his scaly neck.

For the first time, she could see the dragon clearly, and she couldn't help staring. He was bigger than she'd imagined. From nose to tail he was the length of three men, but his body curved and coiled like a snake's, so that he could appear to be much smaller if he wanted. At the shoulder he stood no higher than a young ox. When he raised his head to its full height, he was eye to eye with the girl. In the sunlight, his scales were greeny blue, the color of water in a deep spring. His head was crowned with two long, curved horns with needle-sharp points. He had long whiskers, not of hair but of sinewy strands that hung down on either side of his bulbous nose. His body narrowed to a snakelike tail. Tufts of long hair sprouted from behind his knees. His stocky legs ended in feet like large cats' paws with soft pads beneath them. Each foot was armed with four long, sharp talons. Unlike cats' claws, they didn't retract: they were always out and dangerous-looking. His teeth were also large and frightening, but the dragon's soft red lips made it look more like he was smiling than baring his teeth when his mouth was open.

She took the dragon up into the courtyard every day. After a week, she let him walk around untethered. She discovered a soft, unscaly spot under his chin where he liked to be scratched. He made gentle metallic noises, the same sounds that he made whenever she brought him milk. They sounded like the wind chimes that hung outside the palace entrance hall to ward off evil spirits. It was a melancholy sound, but the girl thought it meant he was pleased.

A rasping voice disturbed the peace of the courtyard.

"Where are you, wretch?" Master Lan was awake.

"You can stay out here in the sun for a while if you like," the girl said to the dragon.

She tied the dragon to a water trough and ran to her master before he came looking for her.

"I'll have pork for my meal tonight," the Dragon Keeper said when she arrived out of breath. It was only midafternoon, but the floor was already littered with wine jars.

"With some of that excellent pickle I made some weeks back. The flavors should be nicely matured by now, and very tasty."

It was the first time Master Lan had referred to the pickle. He seemed to think it was a great joke, laughing so much he fell off his bed.

"Get me more wine," he demanded as he crawled back onto the bed.

"There is no more," replied the girl. "You drank it all. You'll have to wait until the spring provisions arrive."

"I need more wine now!" shouted the Dragon Keeper. "Get some from the Emperor's store. The old woman will tell you where it is."

"But I'm not allowed to go into the palace."

"I give you permission."

"I can't!" she gasped. "Stealing from the Emperor is a crime, punishable by death!"

"I won't tell him, if you don't." The Dragon Keeper chuckled at his own great wit. "Do as you're told, or you'll get a beating."

The Emperor was the son of Heaven, just one step away from being a god. The girl was sure that he must know everything—about her secret night visits to the palace, about the time she'd sat on the imperial bed, about the dragon pickle. He'd chosen not to punish her for her previous crimes, but adding another seemed to be trying the imperial patience. She had no choice, though. Lan was her master. She had to obey him.

"Go on, wretch," he shouted, hurling an inkstone in her direction. He missed.

She'd been inside the palace plenty of times before, but never in daylight. As she approached it, she could feel eyes on her—the eyes of Heaven.

The girl ducked through the opening in the wisteria vine. For a brief time each spring the wisteria was covered in purple flowers, but the rest of the time it was a tortured tangle of bare twigs. A path led to the Jade Flower Hall. The wind chimes tinkled in the breeze, sounding like the dragon when he was happy. The girl didn't feel happy at all. She could see that the doors were painted with images of the two door gods. On the left door was the pale face of the handsome Yu Lei; on the right his brother, Shen Tu, with a fierce, red face and popping eyes. Shen Tu's door was hanging off its hinges. The slave girl pushed open the left door and stepped in. The afternoon light seeped in through the intricate latticed shutters of the six-sided windows. The palace looked dingy and neglected in the daylight. Huge, dusty lanterns hung from the carved wooden ceiling. Narrow tables against the walls displayed delicately carved ornaments made entirely of green jade— and draped with spider webs. Withered potted plants stood on the stone floor.

The rat's nose was protruding from her jacket, sniffing the air.

"I'm glad you're here to keep me company, Hua."

The girl walked through the hall to the doorway on the opposite side. This led to a large courtyard garden.

Two bare trees and a pond of dark frozen water were all that were visible, the rest was covered with snow. There was a red and green pavilion that would once have been pretty, but the paint was now faded and peeling. Around the edge of the courtyard was a roofed walkway, open to the courtyard on one side. The supporting columns were carved with swirling clouds and also in need of painting. She made her way along the western corridor.

The main palace building loomed in front of her, making her feel the size of a cicada. The roof of Master Lan's house was so low she could almost touch it. The palace roof reached up to the sky. The corners turned up in elegant curves. On either end of the roof ridge was the carved head of a snarling dragon. As she gazed up, a sheet of melting snow slid off the roof, revealing curved terra-cotta tiles glazed shiny black. The snow crashed at her feet. The polished doorway was huge, as big as an entire wall of Master Lan's house, and carved with long-legged cranes. She didn't enter the doorway. She was sure the Emperor's wine wouldn't be in there.

She walked around the main building and followed another covered walkway. A circular entrance appeared on her right. She stepped through and found herself in a passageway. On one of her earlier visits she had stumbled across the darkened imperial kitchens. That would be a sensible place to start looking for wine. The corridors were hung with faded silk wall hangings. Everywhere the girl looked, there were signs of neglect. Lao Ma did her best to keep the palace clean, but it was too big a job for one old woman. She worked constantly, but as soon as she turned her back on a cleaned room, the dust would settle again. It took Lao Ma weeks to work her way around the palace and back to where she started. The old woman's eyesight was poor. She couldn't see the spiderwebs draped over the lanterns or the dust collecting in corners. The gardener, the painter, and the carpenter were less conscientious. They had long ago given up doing their work. The girl turned a corner and then another. She stood still. She had no idea where the kitchens were.

The slave girl was beginning to think that a beating from her master would be better than offending Heaven, when Lao Ma appeared at the other end of the corridor. She was waving her arms and wailing in the dialect of her home village. The slave girl couldn't understand a word she was saying. The old woman disappeared through a doorway. A group of men suddenly appeared around a corner. The slave girl stood and stared. There were more than ten of them. She wondered if she were dreaming. Who were these men? Where had they come from? The first two were guards wearing short red tunics, trousers, and leather vests. They were carrying two-bladed spears. One blade stuck straight out from the spear handle, the other was at right angles to it. The other men were all wearing flowing silk robes with wide sleeves. Long colored ribbons fluttered from their waists. They wore winged headdresses. They strode toward the girl in step. One of them was banging a gong. She knew these men must be very important.

"Bow down before your Emperor," shouted the man with the gong. The slave girl stood frozen to the spot. The man with the gong was now close enough for her to see his long beard and his fiercely angled eyebrows.

"Bow down or you will be beheaded, slave," he shouted.

The girl threw herself to the floor, lying flat on her stomach. The men marched past her, kicking dust into her eyes. She waited for them to pass, but heard the sound of more footsteps approaching. Another person was coming along the corridor. She blinked the dust from her eyes and glimpsed one slippered foot and the hem of the most magnificent gown she had ever seen. The fabric was shiny, black satin. Characters and pictures of dragons were cunningly woven into it in gold threads. The dragons were slightly raised, as if real tiny dragons had been sewn into the fabric. The silk slipper was embroidered with fine stitching, also in gold, forming spiral patterns that reminded the girl of high wispy clouds.

Her heart was thumping so hard she thought it would burst through her chest. The wonderful hem and the beautiful slipper belonged to the Emperor himself.

He knew all about the crimes committed by his servants at Huangling. He had come personally to witness their punishment. He had waited until they thought they had gotten away with their crimes, to make the punishments more painful.

The slave girl got to her feet and ran down several corridors, trying to retrace her steps. Now that she wasn't looking for them, she found herself in the kitchens. The palace had suddenly come alive, like an animal waking from its winter sleep. The kitchen was full of shouting strangers. Servants were bringing in baskets and boxes. Fruit and vegetables were piled onto benches. Chickens and pheasants were strung from hooks.

The girl had never seen so much food. Cooks unpacked knives and spoons from long chests. Kitchen hands lit stoves and heaved pots onto them.

"Get out of my way, girl." A large man carrying a side of beef almost knocked her off her feet.

The front of her jacket started to wriggle.

"Be still," she whispered to the rat. "I know it smells good in here, but we have to get out."

The girl tried to go back out into the corridor, but a woman with a cleaver pushed her aside to give herself room to chop up six chickens. The girl was pushed and bumped, elbowed and knocked, until she was jostled out of a door into another room.

This room was twice as big as the Jade Flower Hall,

much quieter than the kitchen. There was no one in it except for a servant who was sweeping the floor. Several patterned rugs, a scattering of embroidered cushions, and a lacquered folding screen were the only furnishings. The girl stood and stared at the craftsmanship in the screen. The bottom section was inlaid with mother-of-pearl, skillfully arranged to create a picture of a garden. The open latticework at the top of the screen was carved into a pattern of birds and blossoms on twigs that were so fine, she was sure just a touch would snap them. She heard footsteps coming from another direction and the sound of the gong getting closer and closer. The servant hurried out of the room. The girl's legs trembled. There were only two doors. One led to the crowded kitchen. At any moment she was sure that the Emperor would emerge through the other. There was only one place to hide. She managed to get her wobbly legs moving and ducked behind the carved screen.

The girl watched through the spaces between the birds and the twigs as her fears proved true. The two guards marched in and stood at attention at either side of the doorway. The Emperor and his ministers entered the hall. She tried not to look at the Emperor's face, as she knew it was forbidden, but she couldn't help it. He was a sour-faced man with a turned-down mouth and tiny eyes surrounded by heavy wrinkles of flesh. His face was fat, his body huge. She could be beheaded for such thoughts, but she couldn't stop them. One minister, who had more ribbons than the others and a gold seal of office, was talking to the Emperor with his head bowed. With the help of two other ministers the Emperor lowered himself onto a pile of embroidered cushions. The ministers all took their places behind the Emperor.

She felt a sudden sense of dread. It weighed heavy in her stomach. Two other people entered. One was a thin woman, dressed lavishly like the Emperor, with sleeves so wide they almost touched the floor. She sat down next to the Emperor. The girl guessed she was the Empress. The other newcomer was a dirty-looking man with the dark, lined skin of someone who has spent most of his life outdoors. His hair hung on his shoulders in matted strings. He wore a necklace made of animals' teeth and clothing made of poorly cured hides. The smell of him turned the girl's stomach. He had weapons and a length of chain hanging from his belt. He looked like a rough peasant, yet he sat facing the Emperor as if he were an honored guest, and the imperial ministers bowed to him.

Servants entered from the kitchen carrying silver trays on legs, set with gilt bowls and polished ivory chopsticks. With their heads bowed, they placed trays next to the Emperor and the Empress. The other trays were set among the ministers. The strange guest had a tray to himself just like the Emperor. More servants came in with bowls of steaming food and jars of wine. Everyone waited until the Emperor had finished eating the first course before they all began eating. The Emperor stuffed food into his mouth. They didn't have to wait long.

Three musicians shuffled into the room with their heads bowed respectfully. They knelt at a distance. One musician had a large stringed instrument, which the girl thought was a zither. He laid his instrument on the floor and started to play. The other musicians accompanied him with bells and drums. More and more food was brought from the kitchens. The attendants tried to stay one course behind their sovereign, but often had to leave food uneaten as the Emperor devoured each course at such a rate.

The girl's mouth watered as she breathed in the aroma of the food. She could smell fish and ginger and soya sauce and other delicious smells that she didn't recognize. She took a deep breath. It had been a long time since her midday meal of plain millet. The smells alone seemed to nourish her and brought a smile to her face. Her heartbeat slowed. Everything would be all right. She just had to stay hidden until the Emperor left. Then she could go back to where she belonged.

"Was His Majesty happy with the lions I delivered to Chang'an?" the unpleasant man asked.

The minister with the gold seal dangling from his waist shuffled forward on his knees, touching his forehead to the ground in front of the Emperor, who whispered a few quiet words to the back of the minister's lowered head.

"His Imperial Majesty was very pleased, Master Diao," the minister replied. "The lions provided great sport, though one mauled a minister to death before His Imperial Majesty was able to spear it."

The Emperor whispered something to the minister.

"His Imperial Majesty wishes to hear of your expedition in barbarian lands."

"I traveled to lands to the west in search of dragons." Behind the screen, the girl's smile faded.

"I didn't find any, unfortunately, but I killed a huge, gray beast with two white horns curling down on either side of a long snout. I have the horns, if the Emperor is interested."

The guest was silent while the Emperor ate three bowls of oxtail soup. Then he wiped his mouth on his sleeve and spoke to the minister again.

"Has the Emperor considered my proposal, Grand Counselor?"

Once again the minister shuffled forward to hear the Emperor's words. Then he turned and bowed to the guest.

"His Imperial Majesty has considered your proposal for several minutes, Diao." The Grand Counselor tried to smile at the unpleasant man, but only succeeded in producing a look of distaste. "His Imperial Majesty will accept no less than four thousand *jin* for each creature."

Diao sniffed and spat on the floor. "An excessive amount, Counselor Tian," he replied, "but I am a humble man, and the Emperor's will is the will of Heaven."

"Good," said the Grand Counselor. "We will be rid of the ugly beasts."

"His Majesty is not fond of dragons?" inquired Diao.

"His Imperial Majesty has no feelings about dragons," replied the minister sharply, without conferring with the Emperor. "But he believes they will be put to better use in your hands."

"Indeed." Diao's cruel face broke into a smile revealing three blackened teeth, a broken stump, and two large gaps. "Dragon brain cures nosebleeds and boils. The liver is good for dysentery, particularly if cut from the live animal. Dragon saliva is used to make perfume." Diao picked his teeth with a fish bone. "They are useful beasts."

"You are very knowledgeable on the subject of dragons, Diao," said Counselor Tian.

"I'm a dragon hunter. It's my job to know everything about them."

The girl couldn't believe what she was hearing. The Emperor was selling the imperial dragons to a hunter. What would he do when he discovered that only one beast was left?

"There can't be very many dragons left in the

world," the Empress remarked.

"There were never that many," replied Diao. "And there are very few now. Wild dragons are good at hiding from men."

"Try this, my lord," the Empress said to the Emperor. One of the smells that wafted toward the slave girl made her gasp with terrible recognition. It was a sharp, spicy smell she'd never forget as long as she lived. The dragon pickle. She watched horrified as the Emperor scraped the pickle onto his poached fish and picked up a morsel with his chopsticks. The girl didn't know what would happen, but she was sure it would be bad.

"It is the most unusual pickle I have ever tasted," the Empress continued. She turned to the Grand Counselor. "Tian Fen, find out what ingredient is responsible for its strange flavor."

The girl held her breath. This would be the moment that she would be struck down by Heaven and the palace would tremble and collapse. The Emperor chewed the fish, and shrugged his shoulders.

The girl took a breath. She was still alive. The palace was still standing. The Emperor picked up a bean with his chopsticks and ate it. She mouthed prayers of thanks and hugged Hua. The rat, startled from sleep, nipped her finger. She let out a sharp squeal. The room went quiet. The ministers looked around for a culprit. Their eyes fell on the servant who was taking a stack of dirty bowls to the kitchen. The frightened servant shook his head and pointed to the screen. The two guards marched over to it and folded back a leaf of the screen.

The slave girl felt every pair of eyes in the room on her—including the imperial eyes. The guards pointed their spears at her as if she were a dangerous criminal. The Empress stared with disgust at the grubby urchin girl who had materialized in the imperial dining room. Hua's nose peeped out, sniffing the fragrant air. The Empress screamed. The startled rat wriggled out of the girl's jacket and scurried across the floor. The guards forgot about the girl and chased the rat.

Hua disappeared into a hole near the bottom of the wall. The girl ran to the door, but the guards were close behind her. She felt their spears dig into her back. She held her hands up and turned. The spear tips glinted in the bands of weak sunlight that seeped through the hall windows. The guards grabbed hold of her arms. They glared as if they would spear her if she dared move. How stupid she'd been to think that Heaven would overlook her crimes. The immortal beings weren't favoring her. The Emperor was all-knowing, all-seeing—a god on Earth. He must have known about the death of the dragon all along.

She fell to her knees. "It wasn't my fault the dragon died," she pleaded. "I fed it and changed its straw. I know I helped turn it into pickle, but I had no choice.

If I didn't, Master Lan would have beaten me."

"Died?" queried the Grand Counselor.

"Pickle?" asked a minister.

"Tian Fen, bring Master Lan to me," demanded a deep voice she hadn't yet heard. It was the Emperor's.

The sound of the imperial voice struck fear into the girl. Somehow she found the strength to wriggle free from the guards' grasp. Somehow she managed to bolt to the door before they could grab her again. Somehow she found her way down the corridors without making a mistake. She didn't turn to see if anyone was pursuing her. She just ran.

CHAPTER FOUR

ESCAPE

As she ran, thoughts flashed through her mind—fear that she was about to die, plans for escape, concern that she hadn't washed her master's dishes from his midday meal. These thoughts, half finished, collided with each other, exploded, and popped out of existence. One thought was still and clear at the center of her confusion. She had to save the dragon. She ran to the animals' courtyard where the dragon was still tethered, enjoying the sunlight.

"Quick!" shouted the girl, undoing the rope with fumbling fingers. "You have to escape. There's a dragon hunter here at Huangling."

The dragon didn't move.

"Hurry! You're free now. The imperial guards will be here at any moment." She paused to catch her breath. "The dragon hunter will chop up your liver and cut out your heart." She tugged the rope that still hung from the dragon's thick neck. "You just have time to get to the gate and escape."

But the creature wouldn't budge. He obviously didn't understand a word she was saying.

"Move, you stupid beast!" she shouted, flicking him on the rump with the end of the rope.

The dragon was making anxious noises, like someone banging a gong as fast as he could.

"Stone." Words were forming unbidden in her mind. "Dragon stone."

Somehow the girl knew for certain that the dragon wanted the purple stone.

"Leave the stone," she shouted, trying to pull the awkward creature toward the gate. "Save yourself."

The girl couldn't bear the thought of another dead dragon, but the great beast refused to do as she said. He kept straining against the rope, pulling back toward the pit. There was nothing she could do to make him move. She had to think of her own safety. The guards would be coming in search of her. She had to find somewhere to hide—at least until the Emperor and his guards left the palace. She dropped the end of the rope and was making toward the gate, when she suddenly remembered Hua. She couldn't leave without him. He was just a rat, but he was her friend—her only friend. He was a clever rat. Whenever the Dragon Keeper caught sight of him and chased him with the fire poker, he would hide in the one place Lan never went—in the dragon pit.

The girl ran back to the pit and down the steps. It was the last place she wanted to be. The late afternoon light dimly lit a square underneath the grate, but no more. She didn't have a lamp. She felt her way into the darkness, arms outstretched, stumbling over the uneven floor. She called out to Hua. She could hear a faint squeaking far back in the depths of the pit. Her hands touched the pit wall. Her fingers rested on something cool and round. The dragon stone. Sharp claws dug into the thin fabric of her trousers, pricking her skin underneath. She smiled to herself as Hua burrowed into the folds of her jacket. Her hands were still on the cool stone. She picked it up and ran back to the light and up the steps two at a time.

She climbed out of the pit as six imperial guards, all in red tunics, ran into the courtyard and surrounded the dragon. Some had spears, others had swords. All the weapons were aimed at the dragon. The beast's gonging sounds rang out. The dragon hunter wasn't far behind the guards. When he saw the dragon, he stopped dead and stared at the creature. He moved slowly toward it and the girl could see the greed in his ugly face as he calculated its worth. He held a crossbow aimed at the dragon.

"No!" the girl cried. "Don't hurt him."

The dragon hunter laughed. It was a harsh, joyless sound. He walked toward the dragon, put down his crossbow, and pulled a length of iron chain from his belt.

Iron burns, thought the girl, though she knew for a fact this wasn't true.

Diao wrapped the chain around the dragon's forelegs to hobble him. The dragon's gonging sounds grew louder, faster, higher pitched, until they fused together in a screech like tearing metal. The sound echoed around the courtyard. The girl dropped the dragon stone and covered her ears in a useless attempt to block it out. But the screams that filled her mind were worse. She was dimly aware of the stone rolling in the dusty courtyard until it came to a stop against the water trough. The meaningless cries of pain in her mind started to form into words.

"Dragon stone. Save stone." The words were inside her mind, but she had the distinct impression that they were coming from the dragon.

The chains were chafing the dragon's scaly skin, which was raw and bleeding as if he had been chained for months, not minutes.

Diao saw the stone lying in the dust. He turned to the guards.

"Make fast the chains," he ordered.

The guards hesitated for a moment, unsure if they should take orders from the rough hunter.

"Do as I say," shouted Diao. "The Emperor's dragon must be secured."

The guards jumped to obey, their duty to the Emperor clear.

The dragon hunter went to pick up the dragon stone. His face had the triumphant look of a greedy man getting more than he deserved. The slave girl moved quicker. She ran toward the stone and picked it up with her left hand. The dragon reared up on his hind legs and flung aside the chain, which the guards were still struggling to fasten. He kicked the guards out of his way. Diao hesitated, looking from dragon to stone. For a moment it seemed he couldn't decide which was more important. He dived for his crossbow as the girl darted across the courtyard.

"Chain the dragon!" shouted Diao, and he ran after the girl.

The dragon hunter caught up with her in three strides. He had his crossbow in one hand. With his free hand he grabbed hold of her arm with a grip that threatened to break her bones. The dragon was making the angry rumbling sound the girl had heard him make in the pit when she had picked up the stone. The creature lumbered stiffly across the courtyard, trampling two guards, and appeared to be about to run into the wall of the ox shed. Then two leathery wings, like large bats' wings, opened out from the dragon's back. The guards stared in amazement as the dragon lifted himself into the air and flew above the stables. Now it was Diao's turn to cry out in anguish as he watched his prize escape.

The dragon banked in midair and swooped back. He

was diving toward the courtyard. Guards leaped out of his way, but the girl just stared in wonder. The wings had been so tightly folded, she hadn't even noticed them before. Diao let go of the girl and took aim with his crossbow. A crossbow bolt flashed toward the dragon and smacked into his shoulder. The dragon's arc faltered. He dropped lower, swooping over the girl's head. She thought he was going to crash into the court-yard, but she felt something sharp dig through the cloth of her jacket into her back. Then the ground disap-peared beneath her and her feet grazed the roof of the ox shed. She saw Master Lan outside his house, looking up and shaking his fist at her as imperial guards grabbed him. He mouthed words of rage which she couldn't hear. Lan and the guards shrank to the size of small statues. The stables became boxes. The black roofs of the palace were beneath her. They looked like the shells of shiny black beetles. The slave girl felt ill.

"Put me down, dragon," she yelled, still gripping the dragon stone tightly. "I want to be back on the ground."

The dragon made a sharp turn and the girl's heart lurched in her chest.

"I'm going to be sick," she shouted as they left the palace behind. The very peak of Huangling Mountain passed beneath them.

The dragon followed the ridge of the mountain. Then the mountain suddenly dipped and swayed as the dragon picked a spot to land. The girl screamed and closed her eyes.

"I'm going to die," she said to herself.

"No," said a voice in her mind.

The dragon started working his legs and landed at a run. He dropped the girl gently in a drift of snow. His legs were left behind as they hit the ground, and he fell forward and slid to a stop on his nose.

The girl felt the earth beneath her with relief. Her fingers, stiff with cold, were still clutching the dragon stone. Then she dropped the stone in the snow and grasped at her jacket as if she'd felt a sudden pain. Had she lost Hua during the flight? Had she squashed him to death when she landed? She pulled open the neck of her jacket. The rat was still there. He looked dazed, but otherwise all right. She looked over at the dragon, who was getting groggily to his feet.

"You could have killed me . . . and Hua!" she shouted.

With his right forepaw, the dragon grasped the crossbow bolt still protruding from his left shoulder and pulled it out. Then he set off with unsteady steps.

"Where are you going?" asked the girl.

The dragon made one of his strange metallic sounds. A word formed in her mind. "Cave."

Snow began to fall. The girl had no choice. She followed him. They trudged on for an hour or more. Finally the dragon found the cave he was looking for.

Once inside, the dragon collapsed from exhaustion. The girl's clothes were wet, and her teeth were chattering. She was shivering violently, and her head ached. She crawled up to the dragon. His scaly body was hard and rough. Close up he had a rather unpleasant smell, like a mixture of overripe plums and fish brine, but he did give off some warmth.

CHAPTER FIVE

FEAR OF FLYING

When the slave girl woke, she was lying in a nest of warm, dry moss. She struggled to her feet, surprised at how wobbly her legs felt. There was no sign of the dragon. Laid in a neat row on the cave floor were three dead thrushes, a bunch of cereal grasses, a few mushrooms, and a bundle of dry grass and twigs. She stepped over them and went to the mouth of the cave. The clouds had disappeared. The dragon was sitting in the sun examining his wings. They were undamaged. He turned toward the girl. His eyes had lost their yellow cast and were a warm brown. The metallic sounds rumbled from deep in his chest. As well as these sounds, which she heard with her ears, she also heard a voice inside her mind.

"Fire. Need fire."

The girl could hardly understand what had happened to her since the previous day, but making a fire and preparing food were familiar, reassuring

51

activities. She selected two sticks and some of the dry grass and knelt down to make a flame. She soon had the grass smoldering and built up a fire. While she waited for the smoke to die down and glowing coals to form, she plucked the birds. Then she skewered them with a sharp stick and cooked them over her fire. She picked the grains from their stalks and roasted them in the ashes with the mushrooms. She handed two of the birds to the dragon. They might not be at the palace, but it was still her job to feed the dragon.

"Thank you," said the voice in her mind.

They ate in silence and then quenched their thirst from a pool near the cave mouth where melting snow had collected in a small depression in the rock. She couldn't keep her thoughts on familiar activities though. They kept rushing back to the impossible events of the previous day.

"Since the night of the pickling, I've been hearing a voice in my head," the girl said. "Is that you?"

The dragon inclined his head. He was watching her carefully, assessing her reactions. How could she have been stupid enough to think he was an animal no more intelligent than an ox or a goat?

"Why didn't I ever hear you before?"

"Never spoke."

The girl watched as the creature carefully picked up one of the mushrooms. The inner talons on each paw could bend toward each other, just like a finger and thumb. He placed the mushroom in his mouth.

"Do you have a name, dragon?"

The creature made more metallic sounds. In her mind she heard the dragon's voice. "Everyone has name."

Hua scurried back from his search for food, attracted by the smell of cooking meat. He stopped dead when he saw the dragon staring down at him.

"Even rat has name."

"I don't," replied the girl.

"Do." The word echoed around inside her mind.

Hua scrabbled up her clothing and into her jacket.

She looked into the dragon's eyes. "How do you know?"

The creature reached out a paw and extended one of his talons toward her neck. The girl shrank back. Hua burrowed under her armpit. The talon was razor-sharp and could have cut her throat as easily as the Emperor's kitchen hands sliced beef.

"Do not be afraid," said the dragon voice.

The dragon's talon flicked out the bamboo square that hung around her neck. The girl looked down at the character that was carved into the bamboo. It was almost worn away.

"What does it say?" Her voice was just a whisper.

"Ping," the dragon voice said.

"Is that my name?"

The dragon inclined his head again.

"Ping," the slave girl repeated.

"Parents gave you this name," said the dragon.

Tears filled Ping's eyes as she said her name over and over again. Many people had two names. Some important people even had three. She was happy to finally have one.

"Thank you for giving me my name." She reached out and scratched the dragon in the soft spot under his chin.

"You didn't tell me your name, dragon," she said, wiping her eyes.

"Lived for long, long time," the dragon replied. "Had many names—Da Lu, which means Great Green; Dai Yu, Bringer of Rain; Lao Tang, Old Dignified One. Real name is Long Danzi—Courageous Dragon."

"I'll call you Danzi, then," said Ping. "You are very courageous."

She fingered the bamboo square with her name on it.

"What does my name mean?" she asked.

"Duckweed," replied the dragon.

"Oh," said Ping, but she was only disappointed for a second. It might not be an elegant name, but she had a name, a gift from her long-gone parents, and it was hers alone.

While Ping was lost in her thoughts, the dragon rolled the purple stone out of the cave into the light. He turned it over with one taloned paw, examining it carefully.

"Stone undamaged," he said.

Ping looked at the stone. "I'm not sure why you're so concerned about that stone," she said. "You were almost caught by the dragon hunter."

"Ping risked life for rat."

"Hua's my best friend," Ping replied. "I had to go back for him, but I don't see any sense in risking your life for a rock."

The voice in Ping's mind was silent.

"You've escaped, though," she said. "You're free at last. Now I have to get back to Huangling."

The dragon turned to look at her.

"Why return?"

Ping hadn't considered doing anything else. She had lived on Huangling for as long as she could remember. She couldn't imagine a life in any other place.

"Where else would I go?"

"Could find new place."

Ping shook her head. Just the thought of going out into the world terrified her.

"I have work to do at Huangling. I won't have you to look after anymore, but the oxen, the goat, the pigs, and the chickens still need feeding, and if the Emperor is going to visit Huangling from time to time, Lao Ma will need help keeping the palace clean," replied Ping.

Danzi's bright eyes narrowed. "Ping must not go back."

She smiled, pleased that the dragon was concerned about her safety.

"Master Lan has been arrested. Once the Emperor has gone back to Chang'an, it'll be safe for me to go back. I'll be punished, but then I can go back to work. You can stay here."

"Danzi not staying here," he said. "Going to Ocean."

"Ocean?" said Ping. "Ocean is just a place in stories, like the Kunlun Mountains and the Isle of the Blest. Lao Ma told me stories about them. They're pretend."

"All exist."

"Why would you want to go anywhere? This is a comfortable cave. You have everything you want here and the dragon hunter won't be able to find you. I'll come and visit you when I can."

"Danzi growing old. Waters of Ocean have magical powers, will renew strength."

Ping was beginning to wonder if being locked up for so many years had affected the dragon's mind.

"Ping must help Danzi," he said.

Ping stared at the dragon. "What do you mean?"

"Travel with Danzi to Ocean."

"I can't." Ping shivered at the thought of venturing out into the world, full of strange people and strange places. There were plenty of things that she didn't like about Huangling, but it was familiar.

The dragon bowed his head. "As you wish."

Ping sighed with relief. "Good. Now, how do I get back to the palace?"

"Danzi will transport Ping."

"You mean fly me back to the palace?"

"Yes."

"I didn't like flying."

Ping thought about the dragon's offer. They were only an hour or so away from Huangling as the dragon flew, but on foot she would have a longer journey. It would take a day or more to return.

"You can take me back," she said, "but not until the Emperor has left Huangling."

"Has already left."

"How do you know?"

"Dragons have excellent vision," Danzi replied proudly. "Can see for many *li*. Saw Emperor's party leave while on test flight this morning."

Ping peered into the distance, but could see nothing but snow and hills. "Are you sure?"

"Certain."

Ping wiggled her toes inside her soggy socks and thin straw shoes. It would be good to get back to Huangling. With a bit of luck she could have Master Lan's house for her own.

"Sit on back," said the dragon. "As willing passenger, Ping will be more comfortable."

Ping dreaded the thought of flying again, but now that she knew the Emperor and his guards had left, she wanted to get back to the palace. She wanted to go home.

"Doesn't Ping want to see the world?" asked the dragon.

"No." She gazed out at the endless white landscape. Mountain after mountain stretched in front of her. The world was far too big and frightening. Ping wanted to get back to the small part of the world that she knew.

She looked at the dragon. She'd never ridden on any sort of animal, let alone a dragon. Danzi's long scaly body looked slippery.

"I'll fall off," she said. "There's nothing to hold on to."

"Sit behind head. Hold on to horns," said Danzi.

Ping checked that Hua was tucked safely inside her jacket. Then she took hold of one of the dragon's horns to steady herself. The dragon held up a paw.

"Wait. Must get stone," he said.

"There's no one here to steal it, Danzi," said Ping impatiently. "It will be safe until you get back."

"Cannot leave stone," said Danzi.

Ping didn't want to waste time arguing with a difficult dragon. She looked up at the gray sky. A snow eagle circled slowly above them.

"Okay," she said, picking up the large stone and tucking it under her arm. She lifted her tunic and threw one leg over the dragon's back. Then she fitted her legs in front of the folded wings and held on to the dragon's horns. Her lap, her arms, and Danzi's neck formed a sort of basket in which the dragon stone fitted snugly.

"I'm ready," she said, though the catch in her voice betrayed her fear.

The dragon ran a few paces toward the edge of the mountain. He kept running as he opened his wings and strode right off the mountain and into the air around it. Ping screamed as the upward rush of air told her the dragon was falling. Danzi's leathery wings suddenly seemed as thin as silk gauze. The dragon plummeted down, unable to open them in the roaring wind. Then, inch by inch his wings opened, the rush of air slowed, and the dragon began to glide.

The dragon's scales had a rough surface that made it impossible to slip off, even though the dragon was listing slightly to one side. With her hands holding on tightly to his horns and her knees gripping Danzi's neck, Ping began to trust that she wasn't about to fall off. Below her, the sides of the mountain fell steeply away to a valley which was a long, long way beneath them. The rest of the featureless mountain range surrounded them on all sides. Ping felt her stomach lurch. She found it easier if she closed her eyes and pretended that they were only a few feet above the ground.

The sunlight was warm on her face. Her shoes and socks steamed as they began to dry out. She felt drowsy.

"We must be nearly there now, Danzi," Ping said, sometime later. She lifted her head, which had been resting on the dragon stone. Her neck was stiff. "Did I doze off?"

She looked around. The mountain had disappeared. Blue sky surrounded them.

"Danzi!" shouted Ping. "Where is Huangling Mountain?"

The dragon didn't reply. The wind carried the sound of his breathing. It was hoarse and strained, like an imperial messenger who had just run many li.

"Where are we?"

The dragon tilted his wings to allow him to turn. A mountain suddenly loomed in front of them. Ping searched the slopes for the palace, but couldn't see it. The mountain drew closer. Its slopes were patched like a moulting sheep where the snow was thawing and the dung-colored earth was showing through. She could make out rocks and a stream. A herd of wild goats scattered when they saw the dragon swooping down from the sky. There was still no sign of the palace. The dragon's breathing was getting more and more labored. His wings were straining. The ground raced toward them as the dragon lost control of his descent. He clipped the top of a rock with his tail and tipped sideways. His left wing scraped along a sharp ridge. He banked to the right and crashed into the earth. Ping was flung off the dragon's back. She saw Hua sail into the air, his legs spread wide. She hit the ground and tumbled head over heels until she collided with a large rock. The breath was knocked out of her. Her body was bruised and shaking. One of her sleeves was torn to the elbow. An outcrop of rocks lay less than an arm's length away, like a great row of gray teeth. If she'd landed there, she would have been killed.

Ping scrambled to her knees. The sudden movement made her dizzy. Hua lay in the snow, his eyes bright with terror. Ping gently picked him up and sighed with relief. The rat was stunned but unharmed. She crawled painfully toward the motionless dragon. His left wing lay open on the snow next to him, like a piece of discarded clothing. It had a large gash in it. The edges of the ragged tear rustled in the wind. She couldn't hear any words in her mind. She leaned close and was relieved to see the dragon's chest moving, though his breath was coming in raw rasps.

"Danzi," she whispered. "Look what you've done to yourself."

Ping found a stream and cupped icy water in her hands. She took it to the dragon, who lapped it up with his long red tongue. After a few minutes the dragon's breathing slowed.

"Stone," he said.

"I don't know where your stupid stone is," yelled Ping.

"Must find stone."

Ping looked around. "I can't see it. You should forget about the stone and take more care of yourself."

She scanned the mountaintop. She was reluctant to admit it, even to herself, but she was also anxious about the stone. It could easily have rolled down the mountain. It might have been smashed to pieces on a rock. The rim of the sun appeared beneath the clouds. Rays of orange light flashed out. She saw a glint in a shallow ravine. It was only a few steps away, but it took a while for Ping to make her bruised legs walk again. Ping lowered herself shakily into the ravine. The purple stone was resting on a bed of snow. She picked it up and clambered back to the dragon.

"Here it is," she said. Her legs crumpled beneath her.

The dragon let out a long sigh.

Ping turned the stone over. "It's still in one piece."

The sun's appearance was brief. It soon disappeared behind the mountains. The short winter day was almost over. Ping didn't want to spend another night on a mountain.

"Danzi, which way is the palace?" Somehow she would make her shaky legs walk the rest of the way.

"Huangling Palace over there," said the dragon.

Ping strained her eyes in the direction that Danzi's talon pointed. She was looking out over the valley, which had disappeared into the growing darkness. She was peering at another mountain, three peaks away, distant and snowcapped. It took her a few moments to comprehend.

"Is that Huangling?"

The dragon struggled to his feet and inclined his head wearily.

"You've taken me away from my home," she said, turning to him angrily. "Why are you doing this to me?"

"What was in front is now behind."

Ping's head was spinning at the thought of how many days it would take her to walk back to Huangling. A faint sound, which had been annoying her ever since they had landed, forced itself into her consciousness. It was a distant rhythmic thumping. It was getting louder.

"Are you making that noise?" the girl asked.

The dragon shook his head. "Cannot hear noise."

Ping faced the distant shape of Huangling and made a few unsteady steps toward it.

"Are you coming with me, Danzi?" she asked. She turned to see the dragon stumbling behind her, his damaged wing trailing on the ground. As they slowly descended, the sound grew. It had a relentless rhythm, not pleasing to the ear, a thudding beat like a bad headache.

The dragon pointed a talon into the dusk.

"We approach road to Huangling."

Ping peered into the half-light. She could just make out a stone marker on the path, no more than ten steps in front of them. There the path divided. One branch led west toward Huangling. The other led east. Ping hurried toward the fork in the road. She had no doubt which path she would take. She had almost reached it when she felt the dragon's talons encircling her arm, holding her back.

"Hear sound now," the dragon said, peering along the other branch of the path.

"I should think you can," the girl said. "It's as loud as someone pounding grain."

A clinking noise was added to the pounding and then a harsh voice shouting orders.

"Imperial guards!" said the dragon. "Hide!"

The dragon paw pulled her behind a rock that was just large enough to hide a girl and a crouching dragon.

"What do you—"

Guards in red tunics appeared on the path—many of them. The throbbing sound was the pounding of tramping feet. The clinking, the sound of swords and spears clashing together to make a marching beat. The rough voice shouted out a command. The tramping stopped. The feet came to a halt no more than an arm's length from where Ping and the dragon were hidden. Now Ping could hear the guards' heavy breathing. She could smell the sweat on their panting bodies.

"We'll rest for ten minutes," shouted the hoarse voice. "We've still got more than a day's march till we reach Huangling Palace."

The guards groaned.

"And I want two men to scout ahead," the commander added. "Remember what the messenger said. We have to keep a sharp lookout for the sorceress. She will appear to be a young girl, but she's very dangerous. The Emperor has ordered her to be executed on sight."

Ping's heart missed a beat.

"How will we know her?" said one of the guards.

"She wears a cunning disguise. She is dressed in rags and her hair is knotted like a vagabond's. But you'll easily recognize her. She's left-handed and she carries a rat in her clothing."

A murmur of fear passed through the guards.

"More important, she has a dragon with her—unless she's killed the beast. She's already slaughtered twelve of the imperial dragons and sold them. The Imperial Dragon Keeper was powerless against her sorcery."

The girl opened her mouth to protest, but was quickly stopped by a dragon paw.

The guards were complaining about their bleak surroundings.

"There are no trees, nothing to make a fire with," one said.

"I've seen no wild animals that we could spear for dinner," complained another. "There's not so much as a nut or a berry to stave off hunger."

"You'd better get used to it," replied the commander. "You're going to be garrisoned at Huangling from now on."

In a few minutes the grumbling guards were called to attention. Torches were lit and they continued on their weary way. The pounding started again. Ping didn't move until the sound faded.

"Lan has told them I'm a sorceress. He's blamed everything on me," she said. "I can't go back to Huangling."

Ping pulled Hua from her jacket and hugged him to her. Tears fell on the rat's fur.

"Ping's life not good at Huangling," the dragon said.

Ping pictured the warm fire in Master Lan's room and a pot of hot gruel.

"It was my home and I'd give anything to be back there now." Tears streamed down her face. She looked at the dragon. "This is all your fault."

"All answers lie beyond the gate of experience," he replied.

Ping was tired of the dragon's riddles. She shivered. The dragon cleared snow from a patch of earth with his tail and then coiled himself around her.

CHAPTER SIX

BEYOND THE GATE OF EXPERIENCE

Danzi picked delicately at the roots and herbs he had collected for their breakfast. Ping wasn't hungry.

"What will I do?" Ping whispered.

"Ping must help take stone to Ocean." The dragon's voice sounded soft and quiet in Ping's mind.

"I just want to go home."

"Ping no longer slave," said Danzi. "Free. Travel with Danzi to Ocean."

"There's no such place," said Ping. "It's just a place in stories."

Danzi shook his head. "Ocean real. Danzi has seen."

Ping turned to the dragon.

"Ocean is magical place. Much water. Very beautiful."

Ping was listening carefully, as she used to when Lao Ma told her stories. She imagined a country that looked like the scenes in the paintings at Huangling palace. Lovely flowers would be growing everywhere, and there would be rivers and lakes with pretty bridges to cross them.

"Drink water from Ocean and wishes come true," said the dragon. "What does Ping wish?"

"I wish I could go ho—"

The dragon interrupted before she could finish. "Waters of Ocean cannot turn back time."

Ping had never wished for anything more than a meaty bone to add to her gruel or an extra pair of hands to help her carry firewood.

"Wouldn't Ping like to live like princess? Wear fine silk gowns, embroidered slippers? Have servants to wait on her?"

"Can the waters of Ocean do this?"

The dragon nodded wisely.

"Would I have as much meat as I could eat?"

"Anything."

"Plums and mulberries?" Ping asked. "Peaches?"

"Peaches size of melons," replied Danzi.

"Can Hua come?"

The dragon's prominent brow creased. "There are no rats in Ocean."

"He'll be very good," Ping said.

The dragon reluctantly inclined his head.

"How long will it take you to fly there?" Ping asked.

The dragon inspected his damaged wing.

"Cannot fly until wing healed. Soon reach inhabited

lands anyway. Sight of flying dragon distresses simple people."

"You could fly at night," said Ping.

"In night sky, body collects moon's rays, becomes luminous. Even more disturbing to peasant folk."

"So how will you get there?"

"Walk," replied the dragon.

"Don't walking dragons disturb people?"

The dragon didn't answer.

Whether he walked or flew, Ping didn't think Danzi had the strength for a long journey. She didn't really believe his stories about Ocean, but she was a fugitive now. She had no choice but to follow the dragon on his foolish quest. With luck, she'd come across someone along the way who was in need of a good slave.

They scrambled down the mountainside. The slushy melting snow of the previous day had turned to treacherous ice overnight. The dragon's legs were still not healed where the dragon hunter's iron chains had rubbed them, but with four feet and great care, he negotiated the icy slopes slowly but safely. Ping, with only two feet and less patience, soon had a sore bottom from slipping over.

"Composure is the master of haste," the dragon said.

As they reached the lower slopes, the melting snow revealed soggy leaves that had lain hidden since autumn. Then green patches began to appear beneath their feet. At first nothing but sparse clumps of grass, but soon there was an endless covering of green, studded with small yellow and blue flowers. The soft cover of unbroken green beneath her feet reminded Ping of the carpets at the palace. No one but the Emperor was permitted to walk on them.

"Are you sure it's all right to walk on these plants?" she asked the dragon.

The sound of jingling bells told the girl that the dragon found this amusing.

The path stopped descending and turned to snake across the rocky lower slopes of the mountain. It was no longer slippery with ice, but Danzi still took great care where he placed his feet among the rocks. Ping wished he could manage a faster speed. As they walked, the dragon filled Ping's head with information about how to care for the dragon stone.

"Must be kept away from iron, five-colored thread, and the leaves of the chinaberry tree," he told her. "Dragon stone prefers an even temperature. Also benefits from occasional rub with arsenic. Ping must never lose sight of stone. Dragon stone has great value. Dishonest people, rich and poor, desire it."

Ping was only half listening. The dragon stone under her arm was awkward to carry. It was very beautiful, though. She traced the milky white swirls with a finger. She could understand why people would want to steal it.

"Tell no one we are traveling to Ocean," the dragon said, though Ping didn't know who he thought she'd tell, as they hadn't met anyone so far. "Keep destination secret."

As the days passed, the tiny flowers gave way to bushes and small pine trees until one day, Ping found herself in a wood for the first time.

"I've never seen so many trees," she said, staring in wonder at the pine trees surrounding them. "Why has no one chopped them down for firewood?"

"Some people value trees for beauty," Danzi replied. "Not many people here anyway," he added.

Hua poked his head out of Ping's jacket to look around. It was late in the afternoon and he was probably getting hungry. Danzi glared at the rat.

"Don't look at Hua like that," said Ping reproachfully. "You're making him nervous. He's worried he'll end up as a tasty dragon snack."

"Tasty!" the dragon rumbled. "Rat tastes foul."

Ping pushed Hua inside her jacket. She didn't want to ask how he knew. She changed the subject.

"What if we meet a tiger?" Ping asked.

"Danzi will fight."

Ping looked at the dragon's vicious talons and sharp teeth. He would be a match for a tiger.

"What about snakes?"

"Snakes are dragon friends."

"Is there nothing you're afraid of . . . apart from dragon hunters?"

"Dragon hunters are just men. It is iron weapons Danzi fears."

"So you don't fear any creatures?"

The dragon was silent for a moment.

"There is just one creature dragons fear," Danzi said.

"What's that?"

"Centipede."

"Centipedes?" Ping exclaimed. "Even I'm not afraid of centipedes."

"Centipedes crawl into ears. Find way to brain. Eat brain."

Ping had never heard of such a thing.

They had been walking for four days. The muscles in Ping's legs ached. The path, narrow and overgrown at first, had become broader. They passed occasional fields, most of which were bare and empty apart from straggly melon vines or a few rows of onions. After a while, they saw a man in one of the fields, a farmer wearing a bamboo hat, bent over some wilted cabbages. Ping remembered what Danzi had said about people being disturbed by the sight of dragons in their fields. She turned to the dragon who was lagging behind.

"Danzi, there's a—"

There was no sign of the dragon. Instead, on the path behind her, there was an old, old man shuffling along with the aid of a stick.

"Oh, good afternoon, sir," said Ping politely. "I was looking for my friend."

The old man ignored her and continued to shuffle along. Ping thought he might not hear well. He had a long white beard that grew down to his waist and a moustache that was almost as long and hung on either side of his mouth like strings.

"Keep walking," said the now-familiar dragon voice in her mind. Ping scanned the bushes on either side of the path. She thought the dragon must have hidden himself when he saw the old man approaching.

The farmer in the field straightened up slowly as if it were very painful. "Good afternoon to you. We don't often see travelers in these parts."

A young boy appeared from behind a low stone wall where he had been trying to turn over the half-frozen soil with a spade.

"Where are you heading?"

"To visit relatives," Ping replied. It was the first thing that came into her head. "In the next province." She hoped they didn't ask her the name of the province.

The boy came over to them.

"What news is there from the west?" he asked. "Imperial guards passed this way a few days ago."

"We have no news, I'm afraid," Ping said. "You're the first people we've seen since we left home."

"Perhaps you and your grandfather would like to eat with us," said the farmer.

Ping was about to explain that the old man wasn't her grandfather and politely decline the offer, when the dragon voice in her mind said, "Yes."

"Thank you," she said to the farmer.

"No need to thank us. The gods favor those who are kind to travelers."

Ping looked at the old man behind her. There was a strange green tinge to his skin as if he were recovering from a recent illness. He put his hand on Ping's arm for support. Just for a second, the stiff, wrinkled hand appeared to be a taloned paw. The peasant and his son didn't see this transformation. They picked up their tools and joined them on the path.

The peasant family's fields weren't rectangles, but irregular shapes. The fields lay anywhere there was a pocket of fertile soil among the rocky foothills. Low walls, made from stones that had been cleared from the fields, surrounded them. The path curved around the edges of the fields like a child's drawing in the sand. Behind a row of pine trees was a small house built from the same stones. The one-room house looked ancient. Its thatched roof needed repairing. Rain had washed away most of the mud cementing the stones together and one wall looked in danger of collapsing. Even the goat stall at Huangling was in better repair.

"You can spend the night with us if you wish," the farmer said. "If you don't mind sleeping in the barn."

"Yes," the dragon voice said again.

The farmer and his sons continued to walk toward their house. Ping realized that only she could hear the dragon's voice.

"We would like that," Ping said quickly.

Danzi leaned more heavily on her arm. As soon as they entered the barn, the air around the old man shimmered and twisted. The old man himself swirled and contorted. His skin turned green, his mouth and teeth grew larger. A long tail appeared behind him. Ping watched in amazement. The transformation made her stomach heave and she felt sick.

"Best not to watch shape changing," Danzi advised when he was back in his dragon shape.

It took a minute or two for Ping's nausea to pass.

"Why didn't you tell me you could change your shape?" Ping asked.

"Did. Ping wasn't listening," replied the dragon as he collapsed wearily. He looked exhausted. Ping suspected that the few minutes of shape changing had used up more energy than days of walking.

Inside, the house was full of warm air and the smell of goat stew. A woman was standing over a stove. She turned and bowed to Ping, refusing her offer of help. Ping sat and warmed her feet by the fire. It was the first time she had been in a family home. She liked the way they quietly went about their evening chores—the farmer mending a harness, the son carving a bowl from a lump of pine wood, the mother feeding the stove with wood chips.

The woman smiled at Ping. "Isn't your grandfather coming to join us?" she asked.

"He's very tired," Ping replied. "If you don't mind, he would prefer to eat in the barn."

"It's a long journey for such an old man," the farmer said.

"He's stronger than he looks."

Ping took a bowl of stew to the dragon. She picked out some morsels for Hua.

The dragon lapped the stew with his long tongue. "More turnip than meat," he said, "but tastes good."

Ping went back to the house and ate with the family. Afterward she helped the mother wash the bowls and spoons. She lingered by the stove.

"My parents would like to make you a gift," said the son. "They hope you will not take offense."

He was holding a gown and a pair of shoes. "These belonged to my sister. You are welcome to have them, unless you feel uneasy about wearing a dead girl's clothing."

"You have already given us food," said Ping. "And I have nothing to offer in return for your kindness."

"It would be a favor," replied the boy. "The sight of the clothes upsets my mother. She refuses to throw them away, but she's willing to give them to you. She made the gown. She thinks you need warmer clothing."

It was a simple gown made of hemp, but it looked thick and warm. The shoes were made of leather. Ping looked at her own thin jacket and ragged trousers, which were mended and patched all over and far too small for her. She stared at her worn straw shoes and was ashamed of her appearance.

"I would be grateful for the clothes," she said.

Ping said good night to the family and returned to the barn.

The meal had been the best they'd had since they left Huangling. Even Hua seemed satisfied. Most evenings he went off in search of more food. This evening he was content with the peasants' stew. He was lying against the dragon stone. Ping was sure there was a smile on his furry face.

The dragon looked content as well. He was curled up like a huge cat with his tail coiled around him.

"How do you change shape?" Ping asked.

"Do not really change. Is illusion. Make people think I am old man or snake, but am still myself. Requires much concentration of *qi*."

Ping looked puzzled. "What's *qi*?"

"Spiritual energy," Danzi replied. Though the explanation didn't make it any clearer to Ping.

Ping lay down. It was good to have a roof over her head. A high-pitched squeak and the deep rumbling of a very angry dragon stopped her gentle slide into sleep. Ping opened her eyes to see Hua hanging by his tail from the dragon's talons. Danzi was about to hurl the rat against the barn wall.

"Danzi!" Ping shouted. "What are you doing? You'll hurt him."

The dragon stopped mid-throw. "Ping is right. Do not want to hurt rat." Danzi put the stunned rodent on the ground. "Want to kill!"

He raised his foot, ready to squash Hua.

"No!" shouted Ping, snatching up Hua just before Danzi brought his foot down. "What's wrong with you?"

The dragon's eyes glowed red with rage. "Rat urinated on stone!"

Ping laughed out loud. She looked at Hua, who blinked up at her innocently.

"That was very naughty, Hua." She turned to the dragon. "But I don't think he deserves to die for it."

The dragon continued to rumble. "Rat must go."

"If Hua goes, so do I," replied Ping. "If we're going to Ocean together, you two had better learn how to get along."

Ping settled down in the straw again, Hua in the crook of her elbow.

The next morning they had an early breakfast and said good-bye to the peasant family.

"Thank you for your kindness," Ping said. She was wearing the first pair of leather shoes she'd ever owned, though she still had on her patched old jacket and trousers. "I hope the gods repay you with plentiful crops."

Ping watched the farmer and his son return to their work. Their stony soil gave them little reward for their labor, but they had each other. Ping envied them.

Danzi returned to his dragon shape as soon as the peasants were out of sight, but he remained sulkily silent. Ping kept Hua hidden. After an hour, the dragon finally spoke.

"Why not wear new gown?" he asked.

"It's too good," said Ping, who had never had a choice of what to wear before. "I'll wear it on special occasions."

The dragon was silent again.

Ping thought about the poor family who had given her, a complete stranger, more kindness in one night than the mean-spirited Dragon Keeper had in her whole life. She fingered the bamboo square around her neck.

"Master Lan must have known my name all along," she said.

The dragon nodded his head.

For the first time, Ping felt no regret about leaving Huangling. She turned to face the east and started to walk toward the rising sun, toward the distant Ocean. She heard a sound like tinkling wind chimes behind her. The dragon was happy.

"The journey of a thousand *li* begins with a single step," he said.

CHAPTER SEVEN

COMBING AND COUNTING

Ping finally summoned the courage to ask the dragon a question she'd been wondering about ever since they left Huangling.

"Danzi, why did the other dragon die?"

The dragon stopped walking, but didn't answer her. Ping could feel his aching grief, but this was something she had to know.

"Was it because I didn't feed her properly?"

"No, Ping," Danzi said sadly. "Lu Yu died of misery like others."

Ping had never known the other dragon's name.

"What others?" she whispered.

"Once there were two dozen imperial dragons. We lived in pleasure gardens outside city of Chang'an. Several died on journey to Huangling. Lan's father sold two to dragon hunters. Rest died of misery. Lan and his father not real Dragon Keepers."

"How do you know?"

"Dragon Keepers of old belonged to only two families, the Huan and the Yu. And then only one son each generation born to be true Dragon Keeper."

"How could they tell which son was the true Dragon Keeper?"

"There are signs."

"And Master Lan didn't have the signs?"

"Not one."

The memory of Lu Yu hung over them. They walked on for two or three hours in silence. Ping thought of her own family. She wondered if they were dead or alive and, if they were alive, if they ever thought of her. She had few memories of them—a smile, a baby's cry, the smell of wood shavings. She didn't know what these memories meant.

Breaks appeared in the clouds and sunlight poured through. When they stopped for food at midday, Ping put down the dragon stone and sat in the sun. Danzi inspected the stone.

Once he was satisfied it was okay, he also sought out a warm spot to rest in. Usually he sat on his haunches with his head up when he rested, ready to spring at any disturbance. Today he lay in the sun and closed his eyes. Ping felt Hua wriggle out of the folds of her jacket. He jumped down and found a rat-sized patch of sun that he could lie in out of the dragon's reach.

Ping closed her eyes, enjoying the warmth on her face.

A bird was singing in the branches above her. Danzi had been teaching her to recognize bird calls. She listened, trying to remember which sort of bird it was. A sudden roar drowned out the birdsong. It was the same disturbing sound that she had heard back at Huangling when the other dragon had died, the terrible sound of copper bowls clashing together. She leaped to her feet.

"What's wrong?"

"Centipede!" the dragon screamed.

"Is that all," said Ping, taking off her shoe, ready to squash the offending insect. "Where is it?"

"Crawled in ear!"

Through all their adventures, Danzi had always been calm. He'd never shown any sign of fear. Now he sounded petrified.

Hua sniffed the air and ran up Danzi's leg with amazing speed. He scurried up the dragon's neck, using his scales like rungs on a ladder. Then he plunged into the dragon's pointed ear until only his tail was visible. The dragon continued to roar.

"Hua!" Ping shouted. "What are you doing? Get out of there."

Ping grabbed hold of Hua's tail and pulled him out. He had the centipede in his mouth. Ping squealed and dropped the rat. He landed neatly on his feet and started chewing the squirming insect. Its many legs wriggled. Hua's sharp teeth pierced the centipede's casing. Yellow pus oozed out. The legs stopped wriggling.

Hua crunched the insect and swallowed it.

"That was disgusting, Hua." Ping felt the food she'd just eaten shift in her stomach.

She could hear the bird's song again. Danzi had stopped roaring.

"Thank you, honorable Hua," Danzi said, though Ping didn't think the rat could understand the dragon's wind-chime sounds.

The dragon bowed his head to the ground in front of the rat. Hua belched.

They walked on through a bamboo grove for an hour or more. Ping liked the tall swaying stems and the crisscross patterns their shadows made on the ground. Danzi suddenly broke the silence.

"Ping must cleanse," he announced.

Ping stopped while she tried to make sense of the dragon's words still echoing inside her mind.

"You mean confess my sins to Heaven?"

"No. Bathe."

"But I bathed three months ago!"

"Ping smells."

It was a ridiculous idea. Ping had no intention of bathing. Even Master Lan didn't bathe until spring was well established. Danzi turned off the track.

"Where are you going?" Ping asked.

The dragon didn't answer her question, instead he started to tell her how dragons and men had come to rely on each other. Ping followed the dragon into the trees.

"Long ago chiefs of tribes knew about dragons' love of jewels and precious metals," he explained, "so captured wild dragons to guard wealth."

It was discovered that some young men, when they were in the presence of dragons, developed a second sight. They were able to locate lost items and, when their skills developed, to read men's hearts. Those who developed a strong bond with a dragon could even glimpse the future. The tribal chiefs used these young men to help them make decisions.

The dragons were revered and treated well. They liked being cared for and developed a taste for the food of humans. The dragons became dependent on their keepers. The first Emperor had several dragons and they were kept in their own palace with beautiful gardens for them to roam in. The Emperor valued his dragons and ruled well, basing his decisions on the Dragon Keeper's ability to read the future. The sighting of a wild dragon was considered a sign of good luck. If a wild dragon were seen in the palace grounds, it was the best of omens for the ruling Emperor.

But as the ages passed, the Emperors stopped listening to the Dragon Keepers' advice. They forgot why they kept the dragons. A few dragons escaped, but most of them died, as they had forgotten how to look after themselves.

"Were you a wild dragon?" Ping asked.

"Yes," replied the dragon proudly. "Danzi was only

imperial dragon not born in captivity."

Ping tried to imagine the old dragon as a young beast, roaming the countryside with the wild deer and bears.

"Are you sure we're heading in the right direction?" Ping asked.

The path was taking them uphill again. A few flakes of snow drifted down.

The dragon made impatient gonging noises and kept walking. Ping continued to worry about her companion. Perhaps the dragon didn't know where he was going at all.

The light snow continued to fall. At least Danzi had stopped talking about bathing. She laughed to herself at the idea of washing at that time of year. Who had ever heard of such a thing when there was snow on the ground? She noticed smoke rising above the trees ahead of them. She couldn't smell it though. Danzi made tinkling sounds. Perhaps he knew there were peasants ahead who would give them food and shelter.

They came to a clearing and a small pond.

"Ping bathe," said the dragon.

Ping looked at the dusting of snow on the rocks around the pond. She was about to remind the dragon that no one in their right mind bathed until summer approached, when she felt his talons grasp the back of her jacket. Then she was lifted off the ground and dumped unceremoniously into the pond. Ping gasped.

She was up to her neck in water. She'd been expecting the pond to be icy. Instead it was warm as soup. The smoke that she had seen wasn't smoke at all but steam. Bubbles rose in front of her and Hua surfaced with a splutter. The rat clambered up her hair and sat on her head. Drops of water rained down as he shook himself.

"Hot spring," Danzi said and walked sedately into the pond himself.

Master Lan had made Ping bathe whenever he thought she had lice. She had only ever used cold water, just a basin or two to splash over her. Then she had had to rub on an awful-smelling ointment that made her skin sting. The water of the pond was deliciously warm.

Danzi sat on his haunches and opened his left wing so that it trailed in the water.

"Waters not only cleanse but also heal." He sighed deeply as the warm water soothed his damaged wing.

The warm water did feel soothing on the cuts and grazes that Ping had on her arms and legs.

"Are these magic waters?" Ping asked, trailing her hand through the snow at the pool's edge.

"Not magic," replied Danzi. "Hot water springs from deep in the earth."

"That sounds like magic to me," said Ping as she cupped water in her hands and poured it over her hair. She'd forgotten about Hua. He dived off her head into the water and swam to the shore, where he sat shivering miserably—but looking very clean.

When they had finished bathing, Danzi insisted that Ping wear the gown that the peasant had given her. Ping pulled on the gown and wrapped it around her, tying it at the back. There were flowers embroidered on the end of the ties.

Ping traced the flowers. "Is this what mothers do for their daughters?" she asked the dragon.

He didn't answer.

The gown was much thicker than her jacket. The fabric felt strange against her skin. It wasn't coarse like a new sack; it was soft. The sleeves were larger than the sleeves of her jacket. They were not so wide that they made it difficult to attend to a fire. Nothing like as wide as the Empress' sleeves. Not even as wide as the palace ministers' sleeves, but to Ping the simple gown felt as elegant as a silk robe.

She picked up Hua. "Look, Hua," she said. "There's plenty of room for you." She put the rat in one of the folds that fell around the gown's neck. "And you'll be much warmer."

As soon as the fire was burning strongly, Danzi dropped her old clothes into the flames, just to make certain she didn't put them back on.

"Now comb hair," the dragon said.

"I haven't got a comb, Danzi," said Ping. Bathing was one thing, putting on a new gown was another, but who had heard of a slave girl combing her hair?

"Has Danzi told Ping about scales?" asked the dragon.

"No." Ping normally got confused when he changed the subject suddenly, but this time she was happy to drop the topic of hair combing.

"Dragons have one hundred seventeen scales," Danzi told her. "Each has magical powers. Eighty-one can be used for good purposes and thirty-six for bad."

Such numbers had little meaning for Ping, but he certainly had many scales.

"Under chin there are five scales that lie in reverse."

Five was a number she could comprehend. Sure enough, on the dragon's chest there were five larger scales that grew up toward his head instead of down toward his tail like all the others.

"Do those scales have special magic powers?" Ping asked Danzi.

"No," replied the dragon. "But very useful for storing things." He inserted the talons of his left forepaw behind one of the reversed scales and pulled out a lovely comb. It was carved from ebony and had the finest teeth Ping had ever seen. The handle was inlaid with glittering mother-of-pearl.

"It's beautiful!" exclaimed Ping.

"Gift from grateful princess rescued by Danzi," said the dragon. Ping thought she sensed a hint of pride in the wind chime sounds he made. "Ping comb hair now."

Ping patiently explained to the dragon that only

wealthy women—such as princesses and ministers' wives—combed their hair. They did this to pass the hours of their long, idle days. Danzi was not about to take no for an answer. When Ping continued to refuse, Danzi held her down with one paw while he combed her hair with another.

"It hurts!" she cried. Danzi didn't worry about being gentle. He dragged the comb through the knots and snags in her hair. Ping could feel clumps being pulled out by the roots. Now she knew why hair combing was unpopular with ordinary people. Danzi paused to remove the knotted hairs from the comb and then continued his combing. The pile of tangled hair, as well as leaves, small twigs, and dead insects that Danzi combed from her head, grew steadily.

"I won't have any hair left if you continue much longer," Ping complained.

Danzi ignored her. After a while, the comb passed through more easily and he stopped. Ping reached up and felt her hair. There was still plenty of it left and it was smooth as corn silk.

"Now must cleanse dragon stone," Danzi said.

Ping sighed.

"Take to small pool."

The dragon pointed a talon to a smaller pool. Its waters were hot and milk-white.

"Small pool contains arsenic."

Ping vaguely remembered that the dragon had said

something about arsenic earlier.

"But isn't arsenic a poison?" asked Ping.

"Poisonous to humans," the dragon said cheerfully. "But beneficial to dragon stone."

It was also, it seemed, beneficial to dragons, as Danzi lowered his mouth to the surface and drank a little of the cloudy water.

Ping didn't have the energy to argue. She fetched the stone and dropped it into the pool. Using a bundle of twigs, she scrubbed the stone, careful not to get any of the milky water on her skin. Hua stayed well back from the pond's edge. He'd had enough of water.

"How long will it take us to get to Ocean, Danzi?" Ping asked when they were back on the eastward path.

The dragon didn't answer. Though he didn't like to admit it, Ping had come to realize that Danzi was a little hard of hearing. She repeated the question in a louder voice.

"Long time," the dragon replied.

"How many days?"

"Many days."

Now that her legs had gotten used to the walking, Ping had begun to enjoy traveling. The days settled into a familiar rhythm. Each morning, they rose early, walked until midmorning, and then rested for an hour or so as the traffic on the path increased. Then, when the weary farmers stopped to eat and rest in the afternoon, Ping and Danzi started out again.

Everything was new to her. The landscape was bursting into color. There were trees and plants Ping had never seen before. The sound of the birds singing was beautiful and unbelievably loud. Occasionally she glimpsed animals—deer, rabbits, pangolin. She was always asking questions. What is the name of that plant? What does that signpost say? Are there really such creatures as monkeys? The dragon was patient and always answered. Master Lan had taken great pleasure in telling her nothing. Whenever she'd asked him a question, he'd laughed at her ignorance or said, "If you don't know that by now, I'm not going to tell you."

Ping's memories of her life as a slave were starting to fade. She hadn't forgotten about her miserable years at Huangling, but they seemed more like a bad dream than something that had happened to her. Her days were filled with small freedoms. She might decide to stop and collect mushrooms or berries. She might decide to catch a fish. She chose what they would eat from their small store of food and where they would spend the night. Danzi was happy to let her take charge of these things, while he concentrated on instructing her and checking on the dragon stone.

"Ping must learn to focus *qi*," the dragon announced.

"What is *qi* again?"

"Spiritual energy."

"Do I have any?" Ping asked.

"All creatures have *qi*."

As they walked the dragon tried to get Ping to focus on the spiritual energy that she had inside her. She couldn't find any. Danzi explained that when she had learned this skill, it would be the only weapon she needed. Her *qi* would stream out of her fingertips with a force to block arrows and knock attackers to the ground. Ping didn't believe this for a minute.

They reached the crest of a small hill and, in the valley below, Ping saw her first village. She forgot about trying to focus her *qi*.

"Look, Danzi. There are so many houses."

"Twenty-seven," replied Danzi.

"I wish I could count beyond ten," said Ping sadly.

"If you can count to ten you can count to ten thousand," Danzi said.

Ping didn't believe him. As they descended toward the village, Danzi explained that adding one to ten would take her to ten plus one, adding another would take her to a dozen. Carrying on in this fashion would soon take her to twice ten and then three times ten. He then explained that ten times ten was a hundred and ten hundreds were a thousand, and before she knew it she was able to count to ten thousand.

"Master Lan told me that I was too stupid to learn how to count beyond ten," she said, her head dizzy with numbers.

"He was stupid one," replied Danzi. They had both suffered at the hands of the spiteful Dragon Keeper.

Ping turned to the dragon. "Can we—?"

Danzi had vanished.

"Now where have you gone?" she exclaimed.

"Someone approaches."

Ping looked around for the old man, but he wasn't there. All she could see was a snake slithering through the grass.

"I can't see you," she said.

A traveler came along the path. He looked suspiciously at the young girl talking to herself and hurried on. The snake stopped slithering. Its scales grew large and more greenish. It sprouted whiskers. Ping felt her stomach convulse and a wave of nausea made her giddy and unable to focus. Then the snake disappeared and the dragon was in front of her.

"Don't watch shape changing," the dragon reminded her.

Ping sat on a rock until the nausea passed.

"Can you change into anything, Danzi?" she asked.

"No."

Ping sighed. There were times when the dragon filled her head with too much knowledge, but other times, like this, when she wished he'd tell her more.

The dragon continued to walk along the path that passed the village. Ping looked at the cluster of little houses.

"Can't we stop at the village? Perhaps someone will invite us to stay the night."

"No," replied Danzi. "No more shape changing."

Ping reluctantly followed the dragon. She guessed he was too weary to change shape again.

Though the dragon instructed Ping about many things, he particularly liked to tell her about his own kind. He told her that dragons could live to an age of two thousand years or more. When they were born they had no horns or wings. It wasn't until they were five hundred years old that their horns were fully grown. They were close to a thousand before their wings first sprouted. He also told her that dragons were one of the four spiritual animals—the others were the giant tortoise, the red phoenix, and a strange animal with one horn called the *qilin*.

"I have never heard of any of these creatures," said Ping. "Apart from the dragon, of course."

"Nowadays *qilin* and red phoenix have left the earth," Danzi said. "There are few dragons. Only giant tortoise still seen in some numbers."

"What makes these creatures more spiritual than pigs and goats?"

"These four creatures are celestial. Their shapes can be seen in sky at night, marked out by stars. On earth they have more *shen* or soul substance than other animals. Dragons have most of all."

"What is soul substance?" asked Ping.

"Is what makes beings good and wise and humble," he replied. "Makes them see world as a whole with each insect, every blade of grass, as important as Emperor."

Ping remembered the day she had seen the Emperor. He had looked very important. Hua peeped out of her gown.

"Is Hua as important as the Emperor?"

"Indeed. We are each unique and therefore of great worth."

"Even me?"

"Even Ping."

Danzi spent the rest of the day telling her about the plants that were rich in *shen*—ginseng root, pine needles, and the leaves of a plant that Ping had never heard of called red cloud herb, which Danzi told her grew at the side of rivers after rainstorms. She yawned. Some of what the dragon told her was interesting, but there was only so much information she could take in at one time.

CHAPTER EIGHT

THE CITY OF
ETERNAL PEACE

"I can't do it," Ping said angrily.

The bleak mountain range was now behind them. Rain had been falling all morning. Wet, fertile country-side stretched ahead, divided into neat fields, some brown, some yellow, others dark green. They'd had a cold, damp meal at midday, sheltering under the dripping branches of a tree. The wet morning turned into a drizzly afternoon.

Danzi had been trying to teach her to focus her *qi* all day. He showed her how he could focus his *qi* on a rock and move it an arm's length without touching it. He asked Ping to throw a branch at him and he stopped it in midair. He'd suggested she start with a leaf. So far the leaf had stubbornly stayed still.

"Ping try again."

Ping's gown was soaked. At least the dragon's scales seemed to be waterproof. She felt very silly pointing her fingers at the sodden leaf as Danzi asked her for the hundredth time to concentrate.

"I'm sick of trying. I haven't got any *qi* to focus! I wish you'd stop trying to make me do it."

The leaf fluttered to the ground.

"Was that the wind?" Ping asked.

"There is no wind."

"I did it!"

"Anger focuses *qi*," the dragon remarked. "But better if use more positive emotion."

Ping was pleased with herself, though she couldn't see that the ability to move leaves would be very useful. She walked ahead. She'd had enough dragon instruction for one day.

After an hour or so of walking in silence, she turned to ask Danzi if they could shelter from the rain, and found a young man walking along the path behind her. He was dressed in sturdy traveling boots and had a hemp cloak over his shoulders. On his head was the sort of bamboo hat she had seen peasants in the fields wear to keep off the sun. There was no sun, but the hat was doing an excellent job of keeping the man's head dry.

"I wish you'd stay as one thing or another," Ping complained. "Just when I get used to traveling with an old man, I turn round and you're a young man."

Ping was expecting to hear the low rumbling noises that the dragon made when he was angry. Instead the young man spoke to her in a clear voice.

"I beg your pardon," he said, backing away from her as if she might be dangerous.

"Oh," said Ping, glancing in the trees on either side of the path for the missing dragon. "I thought you were someone else."

Danzi was nowhere to be seen. All she could see was a bronze hoe with a tarnished green handle leaning against a tree. The young man peered at Ping and decided that she wasn't dangerous after all.

"Are you going to the capital?" he asked.

"No." Ping remembered Danzi's warning not to tell people where they were going. "Not that far."

He was a young man of about twice ten and two, who was happy to have someone to talk to as he walked. Ping fell into step alongside him. She glanced back just in time to see the bronze hoe grow scales and a tail. The air around it started to shimmer and twist. Ping looked away as her stomach started to turn. It was the first time she had seen Danzi transform into something that wasn't living. She wondered if this was a sign of the dragon's weariness. It was now her job to hold the young man's attention so that Danzi could resume his dragon shape and walk at a safe distance behind them.

Some travelers, she'd discovered, were wary and would exchange nothing more than a nod in greeting. This man, however, seemed to have been storing up

conversation for days. As soon as Ping showed an interest in his journey, words poured out of him like grain
from a split sack.

"I have been waiting for this for many years," he said
excitedly. "I am on my way to the imperial capital to
become a scholar."

Ping was thinking of a polite question to ask, but she
didn't have a chance to speak before he continued.

"I am honored to be the only person from my village
ever to go to the imperial school in Chang'an," he said.
"The village elder had his eye on me from a very young
age. He thought he saw potential in me, though I don't
know why."

Ping had only to nod from time to time to keep the
man talking.

"I came into possession of a copy of a page from the
Book of Rites—one of the Five Classics. I have studied
this page for six years. It is my hope that if I study hard
and pass the examinations, I will be able to work with
the Scholar of Great Knowledge who is the expert on
the *Book of Rites* and . . . " He drew a deep breath so that
his excitement didn't overcome him entirely. " . . . if
the great man will permit it, I will study the whole
book and be privileged to gaze on the original copies
found hidden in the walls of the house of Confucius
himself."

By this time the scholar was hopping from one foot
to the other like an excited child. "Can you imagine?"

he asked Ping. "The bamboo books that were actually in the hands of such an illustrious man."

Ping had never heard of a man called Confucius, but she was enjoying the story.

"Why did he hide the books in a wall?" asked Ping.

"To save them from the great burning, of course." He looked at Ping as if he could hardly believe she was so ignorant. "A hundred years ago the First Emperor was so concerned about ordinary people having more knowledge than himself that he ordered all the books in the empire to be burned. Some scholars memorized entire volumes. Other brave souls risked death and hid books. Thanks to their courage, we still have copies of the great books today."

The man strode ahead as if inspired by the brave scholars. Ping had to hurry to keep up with him.

"I am very fortunate. There will be many illustrious scholars in the capital at this time."

"This time?" asked Ping.

"Haven't you heard?" The scholar stopped dead and turned to Ping in astonishment. Ping was relieved to see that the dragon was back in his hoe shape.

The scholar tried to change his smile into a look of sadness, though it wasn't convincing. "The Emperor has died, Heaven protect his souls."

"The Emperor is dead? What happened to him?"

"I believe it was something he ate," replied the scholar.

Ping turned pale, but the scholar didn't notice.

"Important people are gathering to ensure that the new Emperor's reign will be auspicious. Great scholars, astrologers, and shamans are coming from all corners of the empire. Ordinary citizens will be flocking to the capital to celebrate the beginning of the new Emperor's reign."

The scholar glanced at the sky. "In fact, it's getting late. If you'll excuse me, I must hurry on my way. I have to reach the next village before it gets dark."

He bowed politely to Ping and ran off along the path.

The dragon re-emerged from his hoe shape.

"Did you hear that?" Ping asked.

Danzi nodded.

"It must have been the pickle." Ping leaned against a tree for support. "I'm responsible for the death of the Emperor."

"The way of Heaven is to diminish excess."

Ping supposed that was meant to make her feel better, but, since she had no idea what the words meant, it didn't.

Their evening meal was very small. The dragon was too tired to hunt for birds and there were no streams nearby where Ping could trap fish. They ate raw mushrooms and nuts. Hua, who wasn't fond of mushrooms or nuts, went off to find his own dinner. Ping thought the dragon didn't eat enough for a creature his size.

As they sat in the growing darkness, sipping water heated over a fire, Ping finished the basket she had been weaving from dried reeds. She was tired of carrying the dragon stone under her arm. It was an awkward size, too heavy to hold with one hand, far too big to fit in her pouch. She was glad when they stopped in the evening and she could put the thing down. She had other things to carry as well—a melon gourd for heating water, a stick that she'd carved into a spoon, a stone on which to sharpen her blade. She hoped a basket would make her job easier.

"The only reason you want my company on this journey is to carry the stone for you," Ping grumbled. "A donkey would have done the job as well."

Danzi was examining the stone as he did every evening, turning it over, being careful not to scratch it with his talons. As he did, he repeated the instructions about the stone's care, which Ping had heard on at least three times ten occasions already. *Don't leave it in a draft. Don't wrap it in fabric made from five-colored thread.* Danzi stopped halfway through telling her not to put the stone anywhere near the leaves of the chinaberry tree.

"Something is wrong with stone," he said.

Ping went over to look at the stone. It had lost its luster. The milky white swirls had turned gray. The purple had faded.

"Ping must be doing something wrong." Danzi was making anxious gonging sounds.

She sat down on a rock with a weary sigh. "What makes you think it's my fault?" There was a clink as the blade in her pouch struck the rock.

"What was that?" Danzi asked sharply.

"It's my blade," said Ping, pulling it from the pouch.

The dragon was at her side in two strides. He grabbed the blade between two talons and hurled it into the bushes as if it were burning hot.

"Blade is made of iron!" He made a deep, loud rumbling sound.

"I know that."

"Which arm do you use to carry dragon stone?"

"My right, so that my left is free to do other things."

"Stupid Ping! That's why stone is unhealthy. It rubs against blade. Stone cannot be near iron. Not ever!"

Ping glared at the dragon. "If you don't like the way I carry it, carry it yourself!"

Danzi stroked the stone.

"Must go to Chang'an," he announced.

"But Danzi, we've been avoiding people ever since we started traveling. Why do you suddenly want to go to the busiest place in the world?"

"For stone," the dragon replied.

"I don't want to go to Chang'an," said Ping.

"Danzi decides."

Ping had a strange feeling, a foreboding that something bad would happen if they went into the capital. She tried to explain it to the dragon, but he wouldn't listen.

"Those filled with life need not be afraid of tigers," he said.

She ignored the dragon. She was tired and soon went to sleep despite her fears, but she woke when it was still dark from a dream about being trapped in the dragon pit, with Lan laughing down at her. After that she lay awake until a gray dawn softened the darkness.

Ping didn't know what to expect of Chang'an. Master Lan and Lao Ma had both talked about the capital from time to time, but she couldn't picture it.

Over the next days, the path turned into a well-used track and then into a wide road. It was the first road Ping had ever seen. It was divided into three sections. In the middle was a smooth stone path that was almost empty. This was the part of the road on which only the Emperor, his ministers, and messengers could travel. On either side was a pebble path crowded with carts, horses, and people on foot.

Danzi spent entire days in his old-man shape. At night he fell into a deep exhausted sleep. Ping was relieved when the walls of the capital finally came into view. As the city loomed closer, her relief turned to anxiety. The mud brick city walls were the highest that she had seen. The gateway was higher still. It had towers four stories high on either side.

"Chang'an has eight gates," Danzi's weary voice whispered in her mind. "This is southern gate, known as Gate of Luminous Virtue."

Ping gazed up at the wooden towers, which were painted blue and red and green. Statues of snarling dogs crouched below the eaves. There were balconies at each level from which imperial guards armed with crossbows glared down at the crowds.

By the time the road reached the gate it was almost five times ten *chang* wide. Many wagons could have traveled side by side along it. Hordes of people pressed around them, pushing and shoving, all trying to get through the city gate. Ping wanted to get away, but she couldn't. She was carried forward by the crowd.

The city was overwhelming. Ping had never imagined that so many people could be in the same place at one time. In fact, she thought the entire populations of the Han empire and foreign lands must be in the city that afternoon. The main street, the Street of the Vermilion Sparrow, stretched north in a straight line. The buildings towered high on either side of the road. They were beautiful, but too big. The middle of the street was full of officials and messengers. The sides were packed with people and wagons and carriages. She felt Hua wriggling in her gown. He hadn't been able to come out all day. She held the neck of her gown shut so he couldn't get out. The air was stale, as if many other people had already breathed it in. It was also laden with smells—perfume, horse dung, roasted meat, and sweat—all mixed together.

Ping thought that she would suffocate. She grabbed hold of the old man's arm to steady herself. Instead of feeling the fabric of the sleeve that she could see, she felt the dragon's scaly skin. The strange sensation made her feel sick.

On one side of the street, high walls surrounded houses. Polished wooden gates hid the houses, but their steep tiled roofs, glazed with blue and green, were visible over the walls. There were towers four and five stories high, all with beautifully carved eaves and roof decorations—twisting carp, prowling tigers, magnificent birds. On the eastern side of the street were the walls of the Emperor's main residence, Changle Palace. It stretched on for many *chang* and must have taken up a quarter of the entire city. The walls were decorated at intervals with glazed terra-cotta roundels, some with green and blue coiling dragons, others with red phoenixes.

Every few steps brought something new for Ping to marvel at. Outside the main palace gate was an avenue of ten plus two enormous bronze statues of men and horses towering above the walls. Ping had to lean back so far to see their heads she thought she would fall over backward. The huge gates opened and a two-wheeled carriage pulled by a prancing horse came out. Through the gate Ping glimpsed a beautiful building with a black-tiled roof supported by pillars painted gold and inlaid with jade. It made the palace at Huangling look like a peasant's barn. The gates closed and the vision was gone.

Even the street beneath her feet was a wonder. It was paved with perfectly flat stone slabs. On each side of the street were gullies made of curved terra-cotta tiles. Ping couldn't work out what they were for, until she saw someone throw a bucket of dirty water out of a doorway. The gully carried the water away. Ping imagined that when it rained the gullies would stop the street from flooding.

The people coming and going along the street amazed Ping as much as the buildings. They wore gowns of patterned silk and fur-trimmed coats. Gold and jade jewelry hung around their necks. The women wore ornaments in their hair, delicate birds and flowers that fluttered in the breeze.

"I didn't realize city people were so rich," Ping said.

The noise of the city was like nothing Ping had ever experienced. As well as the many people shouting at each other to be heard over the noise of other people shouting. Entertainers were performing by the roadside. There were dancers twirling to the sound of drums and bells, sword jugglers, and acrobats balancing one on top of another. Each of these performances attracted a crowd of applauding spectators. Ping would have liked to stop and watch, but Danzi hardly seemed to notice the entertainment. He kept walking, focusing on some purpose unknown to Ping.

They entered a different area of the city where the houses were smaller and simpler, though still well built. They were freshly painted. Neat potted plants sat on either side of the front doors. They passed through a marketplace with stalls offering everything imaginable for sale. Fruit and vegetables were displayed in piles like jewels. There were some that Ping had never seen before. Cooked-meat stalls made Ping's stomach grumble. Fish and turtles swam in shallow dishes. There were bowls full of snails, some trying to make a slow escape from their fate as someone's dinner. Other stalls sold beautiful black and red lacquered bowls and cups, or jewelry, or bolts of colored silk. For the first time in her life, Ping wished she had money to spend.

It was growing dark. The stallholders began packing up their wares. Lanterns were lit and hung in the streets. Although he had said nothing, Ping sensed that Danzi's ability to hold his old-man shape was nearly exhausted.

"Where are we going to spend the night?" asked Ping.

She knew that there were inns where travelers could sleep, but she also knew they cost money—and they had none. Danzi didn't reply but turned in to a narrow alley. This part of the city didn't have an air of festivity like the other streets. The houses were low, narrow and patched. Chickens and the occasional pig grubbed in the dry earth lanes. The people were dirty and ragged and glared at Ping and Danzi. Their faces, lit by lamps and candles, cast sharp shadows and looked harsh. The foreboding she had felt before entering the city became stronger. She was sure something bad was going to happen. Ping longed to be out in the countryside again, where there was nothing to fear but tigers and snakes.

She glanced at Danzi. His old man's skin was turning green, his arms were becoming scaly, his hands were turning into paws. He staggered, and Ping caught his arm. It turned into a dragon leg and paw, and rested heavily on her own arm. It was dark now but there were still plenty of people in the alley. Some were cooking on open stoves, others were sitting on steps eating their evening meal. Lamplight spilled out onto the street from open doorways. Ping was envious. She longed for a roof over her head, a pile of dry straw beneath her, and a lamp to light the darkness. Danzi still hadn't told her why they'd come to the city.

They turned in to an even narrower alley. There were fewer people, less lamplight. They passed a man who had a scarred face. Ping was certain she saw a blade glint in his hand. The dilapidated houses seemed to close around them. Ahead, the end of the alley disappeared into darkness. Ping glanced behind them. The scarred man was watching them. Two others joined him. They moved closer. Ping had nothing of value that would interest thieves. Her heart started to thud—nothing but the dragon stone in the basket slung over her shoulder. She held on to it tightly.

Danzi pointed a taloned finger at a small house. There was a sign outside, cracked and with paint peeling off it. Even if Ping had been able to read, she couldn't have made out what it said in the darkness.

She knew that at any moment she would have a green dragon leaning on her arm. What these people would make of that, and what they would do to her and Danzi, she didn't care to know.

She did not know who lived in the house, but she was sure she'd rather face one person's reaction to an old man transforming into a dragon than that of a whole street of people. She banged on the door. The old man now had two taloned paws instead of hands, and his gown was melting into the darkness, revealing scaly green legs. His teeth were growing long and sharp. His hair was disappearing and horns were growing on his head. Ping looked away to stop herself feeling sick. A small child saw the dragon face and started to cry. Ping hammered on the door again. It opened a crack. Ping had no time for polite explanations. She pushed the dragon through the doorway and into a courtyard.

A man wearing a gown with wide sleeves and his hair tied in a tight knot on top of his head stared in amazement as Danzi completely materialized in his dragon form. The dim light from the man's lamp threw shadows of sharp horns and talons. Ping had never realized how frightening Danzi looked. The man's face suddenly broke into a smile.

"Long Danzi!" he said. "It has been many, many years."

OLD FRIENDS

The man's smile faded as Danzi collapsed. With Ping's help, the man half carried, half dragged the exhausted dragon into a room off the courtyard. A fire was burning in a hearth. A pot of something that smelled very good was bubbling on the fire. The house, which had appeared to be dark and threatening just a few minutes earlier, had transformed into a warm and welcoming place.

The man helped Ping bring the dragon closer to the fire. He wasn't a young man, but he wasn't old, either. His hair was graying at the temples and receding a little from his forehead. He introduced himself to Ping with a formal bow. His name was Wang Cao. He seemed at ease with a dragon in his house. His face showed his concern for Danzi, but there was also a calmness about him. Though she didn't know who he was, Ping trusted him. It was a relief to hand over responsibility for the dragon to someone else. Danzi started to make low metallic sounds, but the man held up his hand to stop him.

"Food," he said. "You need nourishment."

Ping sat down on a carpet next to the dragon. Wang Cao filled bowls with gruel and then brought roast chicken and vegetables. Ping couldn't remember a better tasting meal. Danzi was too weak to feed himself. Ping picked out pieces of chicken and lotus root with chopsticks, and fed him.

"I am an old friend of Long Danzi's," Wang Cao explained.

Ping wondered how this man had become a dragon's friend. Had Danzi plucked him from a mountainside as well? She kept her questions to herself, though.

"Let's find out what ails our friend," Wang Cao said, after they had finished eating.

"Stone," said Danzi feebly. "Show stone."

Wang Cao looked at the dragon. "What stone?"

Ping realized that he could hear the dragon's voice in his mind just as she could.

"Your health is more important than the stone, Danzi," said Ping.

The dragon shook his head. "Bring stone."

Ping pulled the dragon stone from her basket. Wang Cao's eyes widened in surprise. He gently lifted the stone from Ping as if it were made from the finest porcelain and turned it over in his hands.

"This is a rare thing indeed," he said. "But what

happened to make it so dull and colorless?"

"I was carrying it close to my iron blade," Ping confessed.

Wang Cao shook his head gravely. "Another day or two and it would have been beyond my help."

He put the stone down and carried a lamp to the other side of the room. The wall was lined with small wooden drawers. Another wall had shelves holding jars, lumps of mineral rock, and mother-of-pearl shells. Wang Cao pulled down one of the jars.

"This is red cloud herb ointment," Wang explained to Danzi. "It should restore the dragon stone to its former health. Your assistant can take care of that."

Ping was wondering who Danzi's assistant was. She was surprised when Wang Cao put the jar in her hands.

"Rub this into the dragon stone," he told her. "I will attend to our friend."

Ping scooped out a handful of sticky ointment and smeared it onto the stone. It was the color of dried blood. She smiled at Wang Cao. It was kind of him to humor the old dragon and pretend that the stone was sick.

Wang Cao turned his attention to the dragon. "Now, Long Danzi, let me see your tongue."

The dragon poked out his long tongue. Instead of its usual bright red, it was the dark color of old meat and coated with a yellow film. Wang peered at it closely, muttering words that Ping didn't understand. Then he felt Danzi's pulse at all four ankles and asked questions about his bowel movements. He inspected the sores on his legs.

"His wing is torn," Ping said. "He can't fly."

Wang pulled out the damaged wing as if he were opening a fan. The gash in the central membrane was starting to heal, but it looked inflamed.

"A crossbow bolt struck him in his left shoulder as well," Ping added.

Wang gently prodded the wound. Green liquid seeped out of it.

"I can see you have not had an easy journey," Wang Cao said.

Ping told him about their escape from the dragon hunter.

"It isn't every day I treat a dragon," the man said. "I will need to consult a book."

Ping had never seen a book before. It was made of thin strips of bamboo about the length of a chopstick and not much wider. About twice ten of these strips were bound together at the top and bottom to make a mat. Small characters were written in black ink down the length of the bamboo strips. Wang put down the book and went over and opened several of the drawers. Each one was full of a particular type of dried leaf or root or else stuffed with seeds or crushed flowers. He scooped out a little from each of the open drawers and weighed out precise amounts on a small set of scales.

"I am an herbalist," he explained as he opened one more drawer and scooped out what looked to Ping like dried earthworms. "I make my living by prescribing herbal medicines to the inhabitants of Chang'an."

After he had finished weighing the herbs, Wang consulted the bamboo book again and then took down a lump of rock from a shelf. He banged it with a bronze hammer until some chunks split off. He ground the chunks to a powder and weighed this as well. Then he mixed all the ingredients with water in a ceramic pot and set it on the fire. The room was soon full of a pungent smell that reminded Ping of Master Lan's dirty socks.

"A female assistant?" Wang asked the dragon.

Danzi moved his head from side to side. The herbalist was watching Ping rub ointment into the stone.

"She uses the left hand," he remarked to Danzi, raising an eyebrow.

Ping put the jar of ointment down, not wishing to draw attention to the fact that she was left-handed.

"And she hears your voice."

The dragon said nothing.

Wang took the jar and carefully applied some of the ointment to Danzi's damaged wing, his shoulder wound, and the sores on his legs.

Ping collected up the bowls and spoons, trying hard to use her right hand, and took them outside to wash them. The house wasn't as small as it seemed from the street. The courtyard was quite large and there were other rooms leading off it. There was a flourishing garden. It was hard to tell by the lamplight, but Ping guessed it was a herb garden. She finally let Hua out of the confines of her gown and gave him a morsel that she had saved from her meal.

As she returned with the clean dishes, Ping stopped outside the door. The herbalist was still asking questions about her.

"Are you sure of her?" Wang asked.

The dragon didn't answer.

"It has never been a female before. You could be mistaken."

The dragon still didn't answer.

"She is young and inexperienced," the herbalist said.

The dragon finally spoke. "It is because of its emptiness that the cup is useful."

Ping entered the room and the herbalist got up to stir the bubbling pot of herbs. Ping noticed that the herbalist was left-handed, just as she was. They sat in silence until Wang decided the herbal brew was ready. He poured the thick, brown liquid into a bowl and gave it to the dragon. If it tasted as bad as it smelled, Danzi gave no indication. He lapped it up like a cat drinking milk. Soon the dragon was asleep.

"Is he going to be all right?" Ping asked.

"If he takes a day or two to regain his strength, he will recover." Wang smiled at the sleeping dragon. "But it will be some time before he can fly again."

"How do you know him?" Ping asked. "Did you work at the imperial palace?"

The herbalist shook his head. He stared into the glowing coals of the fire. Ping thought that that was the only answer she would get, but after a long while Wang Cao spoke.

"Long Danzi was not an imperial dragon when I first met him," he explained. "He was a wild dragon."

Ping looked at the herbalist's face. He must have been much older than he appeared.

"When I was a young man, I was an assistant to an herbalist in a small town. One of my tasks was to roam around the countryside looking for plants. It was on one of these journeys that I came across Long Danzi." Wang Cao was still staring into the coals as if he could see images of his past within them. "We were both searching for red cloud herb after a thunderstorm. I slipped on the muddy riverbank and fell into the rain-swollen river. You can imagine my astonishment at seeing a dragon appear out of the mist to pluck me from the river."

"Were you afraid?" asked Ping.

"I was pleased that I wasn't about to drown, but I was convinced I was about to become a dragon's breakfast." Wang Cao smiled at the memory.

The dragon hadn't eaten the young man, of course, and Wang told no one about his encounter.

Wang discovered that he could understand the strange sounds that the dragon made and over a period of time, the two became friends.

"When Long Danzi asked me to accompany him on a journey, I left my home without a second thought," Wang Cao continued. "I happily wandered throughout the empire at the dragon's side for many years."

The herbalist's smile disappeared.

"We had many adventures together, but that all came to an end when an imperial hunting party captured Long Danzi. I didn't know it, but they had been tracking us for some days. There were six of them." Wang Cao's voice turned bitter. "We didn't have a chance. They were after the dragon of course, not me, so I was easily able to escape." Wang Cao shook his head unhappily. "I was unable to rescue him. I came to live in Chang'an hoping to free him, but the dragons were moved to Huangling before I had a chance."

The herbalist suddenly stood up. "You must be tired," he said.

He showed Ping to one of the rooms off the courtyard. On the floor there was a mattress stuffed with straw and covered with a sheepskin. It was soft and warm. Ping was asleep in seconds.

When Ping returned to the main room of the house the next morning, Danzi was still asleep. Wang Cao was already up and preparing breakfast. The herbalist asked her many questions. Not about the dragon as she was expecting, but about herself. He wanted to know how old she was, where she was born, who her parents were. The answers for all his questions were the same, "I don't know," but the herbalist sat and pondered this as if she had given him a great deal of information to consider.

Just as breakfast was ready, Danzi awoke. His scales were a lustrous blue-green again. His eyes were bright and brown. He flicked his tail as if he were ready to face whatever challenges came his way. They ate a pleasant breakfast of dumplings filled with sweet bean paste. Wang Cao fetched a jar of dried leaves from the shelves. He threw some of the leaves into a pot of boiling water.

Ping wrinkled up her nose. "Are you making more herbal medicine?"

"No, no. Just a special drink."

Danzi made sounds like wind chimes in a low breeze. After a few minutes Wang poured some of the flavored water into cups.

"Do you know what this is, Ping?" he asked.

Ping shook her head.

"It is tea," the herbalist replied. "People in the south drink it. I bought a box of it for a good price."

Ping sipped at the steaming drink. It had a pleasant taste. She sat quietly in the corner while the herbalist and the dragon conversed. It was strange to hear the man speak in a normal voice and the dragon respond with his metallic sounds.

Wang Cao then turned his attention to Ping. "You have a long journey ahead of you," he said. "I had better check your health as well."

She poked out her tongue. Wang studied it silently. Then he took her right wrist and felt her pulse.

"You seem to have a strange palpitation in your chest," said the herbalist as he reached for her other wrist.

Ping smiled. "That's just Hua," she said.

Wang Cao jerked back his hand as Ping pulled the rat out of the folds of her gown.

The herbalist glanced at the dragon as the sound of bells filled the room.

"Our other companion," said the dragon. "The honorable Hua. He has been of great assistance."

Ping put Hua on the floor and the rat scampered off. The herbalist recovered his composure and finished examining Ping.

"You are a healthy young woman," said Wang when he had finished his examination. "Strong, but with a tendency to wind in the liver."

Ping was glad that Wang didn't think she needed an herbal draft, but he gave her a small packet of pills for the next time she had digestive problems.

"I have something for you, old friend," said Wang Cao.

Wang went over to one of the drawers in his herbal cabinet.

"I vowed that if ever I saw you again, I would make up for my failure to protect you," Wang said. His eyes were sparkling and he held his mouth tight.

"You did what you could," replied Danzi.

Instead of pulling out a handful of dried leaves or berries, he pulled out several pieces of gold, a string of copper coins with square holes in the middle, and a jade pendant in the shape of a fat child. "I have put aside some cash for you."

Ping thought the dragon would refuse the gift, but he thanked Wang Cao and placed the gold pieces in one of the reversed scales below his chin. The jade and the copper cash he handed to Ping.

"You must look after these," Wang said.

"I can't," stammered Ping, who had never touched anything valuable before. "I'm not used to money. I might lose it."

"Recognizing one's limitations is wisdom," said Danzi.

Wang Cao nodded in agreement.

With trembling fingers, Ping took the money and jade from the dragon.

"I will also give you herbs to take with you on your journey, so that you can prepare herbal drafts for Long Danzi should he need strengthening. You must go to the market and buy a small ceramic pot and some bowls.

You will need a bronze knife to replace your iron blade."

"I don't know how to buy things," said Ping. "Couldn't you do it, Wang Cao?"

"I have sick people to attend to."

Ping argued, but Wang Cao was determined that she would go to the market.

"It is a great honor to be a dragon's companion," he said sharply. "You should do your duties without question or complaint."

Ping didn't think she had any duties. She was just traveling with the dragon as a favor, but neither the herbalist nor the dragon seemed to see it that way.

"If there is anything you require, Ping," said Danzi, "you should purchase that as well."

The street outside Wang Cao's house didn't seem so frightening in the daylight. The people waiting at the door to see the herbalist bowed politely to her. Ping's sense of unease about Chang'an was still with her, though. She held on tightly to the pouch hanging from her waist. Wang Cao had told her that there were thieves in the capital and she must always be alert. She had taken only ten of the copper cash—a fraction of the money that she would be responsible for when they left Chang'an—but she felt as if she had a fortune hanging from her belt.

It was still early in the morning, but the market was already crowded with people. Stallholders shouted out the prices and qualities of their wares, trying to make their goods sound more appealing than those of the next stall. A wagon full of ducks made its way slowly through the shoppers. Musicians entertained the crowds. The music mixed with the noise of people shouting, ducks quacking, and pigs grunting unhappily in their pens. Ping had never heard such a racket.

She decided to start with a small purchase and bought a pair of wooden chopsticks. When she handed the stallholder one of her copper coins and he gave back five smaller coins, Ping was confused. The man looked at her as if he couldn't believe anyone could be so stupid, but explained that the smaller coins were of less value. Ping then bought a ceramic cooking pot with some of the smaller coins. Her next purchase was two bamboo bowls. It wasn't until after she had tucked them in her basket that she realized that the man had overcharged her. She noticed that other people never paid the amount the stallholder first asked. They argued about the cost until they came to a price they agreed on. Dealing with any number greater than ten still made Ping's head spin. Shopping was harder work than anything she'd been required to do at Huangling.

After she had bought all the things Wang Cao had told her to buy, Ping still had four cash and a number of smaller copper coins left. She thought about what she would buy for herself. She looked at the stalls of sparkling hair ornaments, at colorful silk belts, and polished bronze mirrors. None of these things were suitable to take on a long journey on foot, and she knew she didn't deserve such luxuries. Instead Ping bought herself a pair of thick warm socks. She managed to bargain the price of the socks down from five small copper coins to four and was pleased with herself. As the socks cost very little, Ping decided she would buy herself a small cake as well. She was standing at the stall, trying to decide between a cake sweetened with honey or with jujube jelly, when she felt a sharp tug at her waist. The cord around her waist broke. Someone had stolen her pouch.

She saw a figure dart away into the crowd. "Stop that thief!" she shouted.

One or two people turned to her with mild interest, but then returned to their business. When Ping realized that no one was going to help her, she hitched up her gown and raced after the thief. He was wearing a fur cap and he could run fast. Ping wasn't used to running. She was carrying the things she had bought at the market and the hem of her gown threatened to trip her up. She wasn't going to let the thief get away, though. She shouted angrily at people to get out of her way. She leaped over a pig that wandered into her path, never taking her eyes off the fur hat bobbing ahead of her in the crowd. She chased the thief out of the market and into the back alleys of the city. The fur hat turned down an alley-way. Ping followed, her chest heaving. She found herself in an empty street. On either side were ramshackle houses. They hardly deserved to be called houses—they were huts made out of things that other people had thrown away. There was no sign of the fur hat.

Ping was furious. The dragon and the herbalist had entrusted the money to her. She'd lost it in less than an hour. The owner of the fur hat had made her fail. She felt her anger as a point of power in her mind—a small hard speck. Her anger fed the point and it grew. She closed her eyes and pictured the fur hat. Her feet started walking, though she'd made no decision to move. It was as if an invisible thread, fragile as a strand of spider's web, were connecting her mind to the fur hat. If she lost her focus, she knew the strand would break and float away, out of her grasp forever. She concentrated hard, focusing her whole being on that one thought. Her feet turned to the right, her eyes were shut tight, but she was confident she wouldn't bump into anything. She made several more turns and stopped. Ping opened her eyes.

She was standing in front of a lopsided hut made of bamboo poles leaning at different angles and covered with worn reed matting. She pulled aside a piece of the matting. Inside the one-room hovel was an old woman, two small children, and the owner of the fur hat. They all huddled in the corner of the room, terrified by the angry figure standing in their doorway. Ping looked closer. The woman wasn't as old as she'd thought, just thin and worn. The cowering children had hollow cheeks and snotty noses. The thief with the fur hat was a young boy probably a year or two younger than Ping. He held out her pouch and muttered something in a dialect she didn't understand. Ping looked around the room. It was empty except for a pile of rags that must have been the family's bed. Her anger disappeared. She took back the pouch and opened it. She took out two cash and some of the smaller copper coins and gave them to the boy. She knew what it was like to be hungry enough to steal.

As she walked back to the herbalist's house, Ping's hands trembled. She didn't understand where the power that she had felt had come from. It had frightened her, but at the same time she was relieved. She had known something bad would happen in Chang'an. Now that it was over, she could relax. She also had a new feeling in her chest, as if her heart had grown a little bigger. It was pride. She'd found the thief herself, without anybody's help.

Ping showed her purchases to Danzi and Wang Cao, but they weren't very interested. The two friends were engrossed by the herbalist's favorite pastime. When he wasn't dispensing herbs to the inhabitants of Chang'an, Wang liked to dabble in alchemy. Like all alchemists, his goal was to create gold from plentiful metals such as lead or copper. He believed the red mineral cinnabar could be the key to success. Wang was demonstrating one of his experiments to Danzi. Ping didn't tell them about her experience in the market. Instead she settled down to sew a pocket onto the inside of her gown, so that she had a safe place to keep the cash.

"Watch," Wang said as he mixed together some cinnabar, powdered charcoal, and a white crystal. He lit a taper and threw it into the mixture, which burst into flames with a loud bang. Ping leaped up from her place on the floor. The dragon found this most amusing and made Wang repeat the demonstration.

When she had finished her sewing, Ping rubbed more ointment into the stone. It was already looking brighter.

"You should stay for a few days," Wang Cao said. "The new Emperor will be enthroned the day after tomorrow. It would be a pity to miss the celebrations."

Danzi said he would like to stay.

The herbalist made another herbal draft for the dragon. He taught Ping to recognize certain herbs that she would be able to find growing in the countryside which would help keep Danzi strong.

The following day, Ping left the two friends chuckling over Wang Cao's experiments like children with a new toy. She had to face the market again to buy food for their journey. This time she was more wary. She kept her money in the pocket sewn inside her gown, carefully calculated the amount of change she should receive, and checked it twice to make sure she wasn't being cheated. She bought millet, dried lentils, and ground ginger. Her socks would need mending on the long journey ahead, so she also bought a fine bone needle and a length of silk. A functional brown thread would have been more sensible, but she couldn't resist buying a length that was a rich shade of red. She managed to buy everything without being robbed or cheated.

Nearby, three musicians were playing clay instruments shaped like chickens' eggs and pierced with several holes. They played these instruments by blowing in one of the holes and covering the others in turn with their fingers. Ping stopped to listen. The notes were high and sweet, but the tunes they played had a sadness to them. A woman began to sing. The song wasn't sad at all. In fact it was an amusing tale of a young girl who fell in love with a donkey. Ping laughed along with the crowd.

Suddenly her happiness turned to fear. One minute she'd been chuckling about the girl and the donkey, the next a wave of terror passed through her body and drowned her pleasure. Someone was arguing. Ping found the source of the argument at the cooked-meat stall behind the musicians. A man was quibbling over the price of a few slices of beef. He wore clothes made from animal hides, which Ping could smell even from that distance. From his belt hung an ax, a short sword, and a length of iron chain. The man stopped bargaining and turned around, as if he sensed someone was watching him. It was Diao, the dragon hunter. Ping forgot about the song. She turned and ran.

CHAPTER TEN

MAGIC AT MIDNIGHT

Ping breathed in the clean country air and listened to the birdsong.

"Ping didn't like Chang'an," said Danzi.

She shook her head. "No. I knew something bad awaited us there."

The dragon turned to her. He studied her face but said nothing.

It had been two days since they'd left Chang'an. As soon as he'd heard that Diao was in the capital, the dragon had wanted to leave immediately. Ping, and Danzi in his old-man shape, had been the only ones leaving the city, outnumbered a thousandfold by fresh crowds pouring in. Ping had fought her way toward the city's eastern gate against this tide of people. She was sure that the dragon hunter hadn't seen her in the market. Almost sure. At every second step she'd glanced over her shoulder, half expecting to see Diao behind them.

"If there are so few dragons in the world," Ping asked, "why would anyone want to be a dragon hunter?"

"Dragon hunting not profitable business," Danzi replied. "But once hunter has killed dragon, craves more dragon kills. Often goes many years between kills."

"So how does a dragon hunter live until he catches the next dragon?"

"Hunts other animals and sells them at markets. But is always craving for dragon kill."

Ping remembered the horrible dragon hunter and shivered.

"When he does kill dragon, rewards are great. Blood and organs of dragon now rare, worth fortune to those who know their virtues."

Ping looked over her shoulder again and quickened her step.

By the first afternoon they had gotten clear of the houses clustering around the capital. The wide road soon dwindled to a path snaking through fields being prepared for spring planting. Then they reached wooded land. The dark branches of the trees were speckled with new leaves. The leaves sprang from the branches in tufts, each one shaped like a tiny fan. The green of the new leaves was so bright, Ping couldn't believe it was natural. Danzi told her the trees were called ginkgo.

"An infusion of the leaves helps relieve a cough," the dragon explained.

Ping wasn't interested in their medicinal value, she was just enjoying their beauty.

"Are you sure a painter hasn't colored them all?" she asked.

Danzi shook his head.

They hadn't passed anyone for hours, so Danzi was in his dragon shape. He looked stronger than he had when they'd entered Chang'an. He walked with a light step and his head held up. Ping had enjoyed their time at Wang Cao's house, but she was glad to be away from the capital. She wasn't sorry they'd missed the new Emperor's celebrations. She'd seen enough wonders in Chang'an as it was. As they'd said farewell to Wang Cao, he had given Ping a small packet of tea leaves, some of the dark red ointment for the stone, and a goatskin bag for carrying water. At the dragon's request, he had also given them a little of the explosive mixture.

Ping tried to get Danzi to talk about his years with Wang Cao, but the dragon wasn't in the mood to talk about himself.

"Nature dislikes unnecessary chatter," he said, and that was all she could get out of him.

It didn't spoil Ping's good humor. Yellow and orange spring flowers, strongly perfumed, were pushing their way out of the cold earth. The weather was improving. The clouds thinned and the sun broke through, warming Ping's face. She was glad to be moving again. Now that she was sure Diao wasn't following them, she didn't feel afraid. In the country, there were wild animals and bad weather, but the few people they met were kind and friendly or kept to themselves. There had been some friendly people in Chang'an, but there were unpleasant people as well. The capital was too big and it confused her. Before, she had thought that there were two types of people in the world—good and bad. Now she had learned that she wasn't the only one who got too hungry to be good.

On the afternoon of the fourth day after leaving Chang'an, they reached the top of a hill. Below them a small village clung to the hillside. All Ping could see was a cluster of wooden roofs huddled together like sleeping dogs. The houses seemed to grow out of the hillside. They were made of old, dark wood and built up on stilts or piles of stones to level them. Flights of stone steps led up to the front doors. Verandahs were hung with washing. As they got closer, dogs started to bark. Ping counted the number of houses in the village as they approached. There were ten and five. This was the sort of village she liked, small enough that everyone would know each other. If she ever got to choose where she lived, it would be in a small village like this one.

Farmers with hoes over their shoulders were climbing back to the village from their fields in the valley below. The murmur of their conversation drifted up to

Ping and the dragon as they walked down the hill toward the village. Cooking smells also reached them. The air around the dragon started to shimmer, and Ping looked away as he transformed himself into his old-man shape. A group of young women carrying baskets of melon gourds sang as they walked. Children playing a game with a goatskin ball by the side of the path laughed and waved as the travelers approached.

"Welcome to Fengjing," shouted one of the men.

"What news do you have?" shouted another.

A family invited them to stay the night and share a meal of pork and roast vegetables. Ping looked at Danzi. He nodded. Ping smiled. It was just as she'd hoped.

Ping chatted to the villagers, enjoying this simple communication with other people. Then the smile drained from her face. She didn't know what had changed her mood. One minute her mouth was watering at the thought of a hot meal, the next she felt a terrible dread in the pit of her stomach, as if food that refused to be digested was slowly decaying inside her.

"Danzi," she whispered to the dragon, "I don't want to stay here."

"Why?" said the voice in her mind.

"I don't like it."

"Only one night," the dragon replied as a farmer came up to walk alongside them.

A few minutes ago all Ping had wanted was to climb

the stone steps to one of the houses in the village, to sit down to a hot meal, to get off the endless road and rest. Now she would rather have been anywhere else.

"Please come up!" shouted the farmer's wife from her verandah.

"We haven't had visitors in our village since last autumn," the farmer was saying. "And suddenly we have three travelers passing through in one day."

Ping was about to put her foot on the bottom step of the flight of stone stairs that led to the villager's house. She felt the back of her neck prickle.

A harsh voice rang out, drowning out the soft sounds of evening. "Find me somewhere to put my cart. It might rain."

Ping's foot never reached the step. She spun round. Standing next to a cart full of sharp metal blades and ugly cages was a dark, dirty man dressed in stained animal hides. Weapons hung from his belt. The dragon beside her suddenly groaned and clutched at her arm.

Ping, with a clean face, combed hair and a new gown, no longer looked like a grubby slave girl, but as Diao glared at her, his unpleasant face twisted into a half-smile. She knew he had recognized her. He looked at the old man with the greenish face and the long side whiskers. His half-smile became whole.

"That girl is an evil sorceress," Diao shouted. "The old man is a shape-changing demon."

The villagers stared at him in surprise.

"Don't just stand there. Seize them!"

The entire population of the village left their chores to see what the fuss was about.

"I've come across them before," Diao continued.

The villagers looked from the young girl and her frail grandfather to the grimy man with the unpleasant voice. They gathered protectively around Ping and Danzi, blocking any chance of escape.

"Don't trust them because they look innocent."

Hua chose that moment to reposition himself in the folds of Ping's gown.

"See for yourselves," said Diao. "The girl has creatures living in her gown."

The villagers' eyes widened as they did indeed see something moving beneath the girl's clothing. They took a step away from Ping and toward Diao.

"And the old man can't stand the touch of iron," said the dragon hunter.

One of the villagers picked up an iron scythe and held it up against the old man's arm. Danzi groaned with pain. The villagers backed farther away.

"I know their ways," said Diao. "I will protect you from these evil demons."

The dragon hunter lunged forward and struck Danzi with his sword. Danzi screamed and fell to his knees. His cry was like a screech of tearing metal.

Diao strode over and grabbed Ping. The villagers shouted encouragement to the foul-smelling man.

"We'll give you all our money if you get rid of the demons," they promised.

Diao was trying not to look too pleased. His mouth had returned to its usual sneer, but his eyes glittered with pleasure.

Instead of the comfortable house in which Ping had imagined they would spend the night, the villagers pushed them into a pigsty. It was a small round bamboo construction on stilts with a thatched roof. It was already crowded with four pigs. Diao came in himself to chain one of Danzi's legs to a bamboo pole. Danzi cried out when the iron chain came into contact with his leg. Diao laughed. Ping wanted to launch at him and scratch his ugly, smiling face, but she didn't. She'd only end up in chains herself.

Compared to Diao the pigs were welcome companions. Ping had nothing against pigs. She knew that they were clean animals if given the chance, but people were in the habit of feeding them rubbish. She squatted ankle-deep in rotten vegetables and spoiled grain. The smell in the sty was unbearable. Danzi had returned to his dragon shape. His foreleg, where the chain was rubbing against it, looked as if it had been scalded with boiling water. Ping could have easily broken out of the flimsy pigsty, but Diao had set three villagers outside to guard them.

"You have to reveal yourself to them, Danzi," said Ping. "You said peasants are frightened of dragons."

Danzi was crouched awkwardly between two pigs. He shook his head. "Iron saps strength. Ping must think of way to escape."

"We need weapons to fight our way out," Ping said, even though she had never used a weapon in her life.

"Sharp weapons are not the tools of the sage," replied the dragon.

Ping sighed, wishing the dragon had more to offer than riddles.

"Can't you use your *qi* to disarm the guards?" Ping asked.

"Cannot focus *qi* near iron," the dragon replied. "Ping try."

"I've only ever moved a leaf, Danzi. It's not even worth trying."

She could hear Diao outside telling the villagers to put Danzi in one of the iron cages on his cart in the morning.

"Why doesn't he kill you right away?" asked Ping.

"Too far from Wucheng," replied the dragon.

"Wucheng?"

"Town where sorcerers and necromancers gather. Many people interested in purchasing pieces of dragon flesh for its magical properties."

Ping shuddered at the idea of such gruesome people.

"Diao wants Danzi alive. When reaches Wucheng, will sell parts fresh."

Images of that terrible night on Huangling returned

to her—Master Lan's blood-splattered face, the ax in the firelight, the congealed dragon blood in the snow. Danzi, despite the danger and discomfort, was so weary he was soon asleep.

Ping squatted with the pigs until the village was in darkness and the guards outside had stopped talking among themselves. Through the slats of her prison, she watched the moon rise above the mountain like a slice of bright melon. She knew it must be nearly midnight. Ping was wide awake. The cold and discomfort had sharpened her wits. She remembered the dragon hunter's smug expression—half-smile, half-scowl—as the villagers had pushed them into the pigsty. She had to think of a way to escape from him.

She took stock of her situation. It did not take long. She had nothing. The guards had taken her pouch and her basket. Unless she could think of a way of fashioning rotten vegetables and chicken bones into a weapon, she had nothing to work with. She felt Hua stir. Since they'd left Chang'an, he had taken to sleeping in the pocket she'd sewn inside her gown. Hua crawled out and set to work enthusiastically on the pigs' scraps. The rat had a way of turning a bad situation to his advantage. Ping had to do the same. She took stock again. She had two things to work with—a rat and a dragon. She took out the contents of her secret pocket. She had copper cash, a jade pendant in the shape of a child, and a small amount of the explosive powder Wang Cao had given her. She had a needle and red silk thread. Her legs were aching from squatting. She stood up, and sat on a snoring pig. How could she make use of what she had?

The moon was high in the night sky when Ping prodded the sleeping dragon.

"Wake up, Danzi," she said. "I've got a plan."

The dragon groaned. His leg, which had only just healed from the chains at Huangling, was raw and bleeding again.

Ping pulled out her bone needle and poked it into the lock holding the ends of the chain together. Picking locks was a skill she'd learned at Huangling. Master Lan had had a habit of locking away food he didn't want her to get her teeth into. It didn't take long. The dragon groaned with relief as the chain fell away. Ping kicked it as far away from the dragon as possible.

"What is Ping's plan?" asked the dragon.

Before Ping could answer, the door opened a chink. A terrified face appeared.

"Don't think you can escape!" said a timid voice. "There are three guards with knives outside ready to attack you if you do anything unnatural to me."

The face and the voice belonged to the boy who fed the pigs. He inched in holding a bucket of food scraps in front of him like a shield. He emptied the bucket and was about to run out when Ping grabbed his wrist. The boy made a terrified squeak and closed his eyes, waiting to be turned into a frog or disappear in a puff of smoke. He opened his eyes again and seemed surprised to find himself still in his usual form.

"Would you like to earn a copper coin?" Ping whispered, holding out one of her coins to him.

The boy shook his head.

"I'm not a sorceress," Ping reassured him, pressing the coin into his hand. "I'm just a child like you."

He wouldn't look at Ping. Instead he peered into the darkness behind her and started at the black shape he saw hulking there.

"My grandfather is asleep," she said, trying to convince the boy that all he saw was a harmless old man.

The boy relaxed his grip on the bucket.

"I'm afraid of the dark, and the moon has disappeared behind a cloud. Could you do one small thing for me?" Ping pleaded. "Could you put a lamp outside the pigsty, in a place where the guards won't see it? You can leave it out of my reach. Just close enough so that a little light seeps through."

The boy chanced a nervous look at Ping. She smiled. Ping placed another coin in his hand.

"Are you all right in there, boy?" one of the guards shouted from a safe distance.

The boy opened his mouth as if he meant to cry out. Ping's smile faded. She twisted his wrist tighter.

"Okay. Do you see this?" Ping held out the jade pendant. The small figure was just visible in the faint moonlight. "This was the last person who refused to obey me."

The boy stared at the small green figure in the palm of Ping's hand.

"If you don't do as I say, I'll turn you into a piece of jade."

She let go of his wrist and the boy ran out, hurriedly latching the door behind him.

"I'm all right," she heard him tell the guards in a trembling voice.

The guards settled down around their fire again. A few minutes later, Ping saw a lamp approach. The boy carried it round behind the pigsty and placed it more than an arm's length away from the wall. His frightened eyes looked at Ping for a moment, and then he disappeared.

An hour or two later the guards' fire had died down and the murmur of their conversation had stopped. Ping crept over to the door. She threaded a length of the silk thread through the jade pendant and tied the ends as if she meant to wear it around her neck. Then she pushed the pendant through a gap in the bamboo just above the door latch. She fed out the silk thread, letting the weight of the pendant pull it down. When the loop of thread was below the latch, she hooked it under the latch and gently pulled the thread. The latch lifted. She pushed the door open just a crack.

"Are you ready for the last part of my plan?" Ping asked the dragon.

The dragon nodded slowly. She placed a small pile of Wang's explosive powder in each of three melon rinds that she'd retrieved from the pigs' dinner and set them on the floor. Then she climbed on the back of one of the sleeping pigs and pulled down a stalk of straw from the thatched roof. She pushed it through a gap in the bamboo wall. With her arm outstretched she could just reach the lamp outside with the end of the length of straw. The straw started to burn, but the lamp spluttered and went out. If this didn't work, she would have no second chance. She crouched behind one of the pigs and set the flaming straw to the first melon rind.

Outside, the dozing guards leaped to their feet, awoken by a loud blast like bamboo exploding in a fire, an unearthly roaring like copper pans being clashed together, and a flash of blinding light that briefly lit up the night. The startled guards looked around for the source of the commotion. There was another flash, another explosion, more roaring. It was all coming from the pigsty.

Ping hid behind the largest pig and with her foot kicked open the unlatched bamboo door. The three terrified guards gaped as a third explosion sounded and a flash of light revealed the occupants of the pigsty. The four pigs were there, squealing in terror, but instead of the old man and the young girl they had locked away, in the doorway there was a long green snake and a large rat.

"I am an evil sorceress," Ping said from her hiding place in the pigsty. "Those who stand in our way will be sent to the worst regions of Hell."

The three guards, simple farmers armed with nothing more than a rusty scythe and two sharpened sticks, screamed and ran. Ping collected Hua as she jumped down from the pigsty. Danzi slithered after her. Villagers stumbled sleepily from their houses, but stopped dead when they held up their lamps and saw a snake transform into a dragon. They fell to their knees, some of them shouting prayers of forgiveness, others feeling sick from watching the transformation. Ping ran to find her basket and pouch near the fire where the guards had searched through them. Diao appeared on one of the verandahs. He ran down the steps toward them. In his hurry, he stumbled. Ping would have liked to watch him fall, but she didn't have the time. The girl and the dragon disappeared into the darkness.

The pair didn't stop running for half an hour. Ping rested her hands on her knees as she tried to get her breath back. Danzi was gulping air in ragged gasps.

"Stone is safe?" he asked.

Ping felt inside her basket. She looked at the dragon. "The dragon stone is gone," she said. "Diao must have taken it."

CHAPTER ELEVEN

OFFERINGS

Usually Ping was forever asking when they could stop for a rest or a drink of water or a meal. Danzi's most common contribution to their conversation was "Not yet." Since they had run off into the darkness, Ping had strode ahead of Danzi, not stopping for anything, just turning every now and then to hurry the straggling dragon. Every time she slowed her pace, she felt the hairs on the back of her neck prickle as if the dragon hunter were right behind them.

It was midmorning before Ping dared stop to rest by a small stream. Its noisy chattering, as the water rushed over the stony bed, did nothing to ease her agitation. Once Danzi had caught his breath, the rumbling sound of his anger welled up and drowned out the bubbling stream. Ping had never heard the dragon so angry.

"Ping has failed," he said over and over again. "Ping responsible for stone. Dragon stone comes first. Even before own safety."

They were deep in a wood of slender trees. Ping knew, by their leathery leaves and the faint spicy smell whenever her sleeve brushed the bark, that they were cassias. If she concentrated on something else, like counting the number of withered berries still clinging to the tree branches, Ping could shut out the dragon's words in her mind, hearing only his crashing rumblings. He didn't have the strength to keep it up for long.

Ping was angry with herself—angry that she had lost the stone to Diao. She imagined the dragon hunter's rough hands touching the smooth surface of the stone or holding it up against the stinking hide of his clothing. The stone served no purpose, but it was beautiful. It was valuable, too. It had to be if Diao was so keen to possess it. They could have sold it if the dragon's gold ran out.

"Must return for stone," the dragon said.

His rumble had changed to a sad, flat note, regularly repeated, like the tolling of a bell.

"We can't go back for the stone. It's too dangerous."

"Journey pointless without stone," the dragon said.

"What do you mean?" Ping asked.

The dragon didn't answer, but Ping thought she understood what he meant.

"Diao will track us," she said. "He wants you more than the stone. If we're going to keep walking with no sleep, we must eat."

Danzi wouldn't let her light a fire. They ate nuts and

dried persimmons. Ping was still hungry, though the dragon had eaten less than she had.

"You aren't eating enough, Danzi," Ping said. "You're getting thin."

The dragon examined his wing. The edges of the tear in the membrane had rejoined and, though it looked sore and puffy, it was healing. Ping searched through her basket. The jar of red cloud ointment was still there.

"Let me rub some of Wang Cao's ointment into your wing," she said. "There's no point in letting it go to waste."

Danzi didn't object, so Ping dipped her fingers into the dark red ointment and smeared it onto the healing wound. The wing felt leathery and the scar lumpy. She was used to rubbing it onto the cool, smooth surface of the stone. She missed its deep purple and milky swirls that had seemed to change from day to day. She shook her head, trying to dispel such silly emotions. How could the loss of a stone have such an effect on her?

"How close are we to Ocean?" she asked Danzi, to take her mind off the stone.

The dragon was silent.

"We've been walking for weeks," she persisted. "We must be getting near."

"Not yet halfway."

Ping's legs suddenly felt heavy and tired. She didn't feel like she had the strength to lift them to cross the stream, let alone walk hundreds more *li*. It seemed as if they were in a dream where the more they struggled to reach the Ocean, the farther away it became.

"Must go back for stone first."

Ping sighed. She thought she'd convinced him that they couldn't go back.

Danzi flexed his wing. "Wing almost healed," he said. "Will be able to fly in seven days. Then soon reach Ocean."

Ping didn't like flying, but she would be glad to get the journey to Ocean over and done with. Danzi took a long drink from the stream. Ping was refilling their goatskin water bag, when she heard the crack of a twig breaking among the trees.

"Did you hear that?"

"Heard nothing. Saw flash of metal. Hide!"

The dragon had taken on the shape of a hoe and concealed himself behind a tree. The trees were too slender to hide Ping. She slung the basket and goatskin over her shoulder and clambered up one of the trees, climbing as high as she dared among its slim branches. There was another crack and two men broke out of the trees. Ping recognized them. They were from Fengjing. She could smell the cinnamon fragrance released from the bark as she'd scrambled up the tree. One man, wearing a battered sun hat, sniffed the air as if he could smell it too. She was only a few feet above him. The foliage was not dense. All he had to do was glance up and Ping would be in clear view. The other man kicked over the pile of nut shells and persimmon stalks that she hadn't had time to hide.

"They've been here." He examined the flattened grass where Ping and Danzi had been sitting. "And not that long ago either."

"Which way do you think they went?" asked the man with the hat.

Daylight and the promise of gold had given them courage.

"Hard to say." The other man searched the undergrowth. "Look what I've found! It's a hoe."

"It's a bit old," said his companion.

"I could clean it up," he said.

Ping didn't know what to do. If the man touched Danzi, he wouldn't feel a metal implement but a scaly dragon. The man reached out to pick up the hoe.

"Hey! I've found something better," the man with the hat said. "A footprint. It's the sorceress' by the look of it."

The other man drew back his hand from the hoe and went over to inspect the footprint his friend had found in the soft sand at the stream's edge.

"There are no footprints leading away from this spot," said the first man.

Ping held her breath. They were going to work out where she was hiding.

"The sorceress has disappeared into thin air," said the man with the hat.

"No," said the other man. "They've crossed the stream. Come on. If we find them, we'll get the reward."

The two men splashed over the stream and disappeared into the trees again. When she was sure that they weren't returning, Ping slid down the tree.

"Cannot travel on road any longer," Danzi said before he'd even returned to his dragon form. "Not safe."

"So we're going to keep going?" Ping asked. "We're not going back for the dragon stone?"

The dragon shook his head sadly. Then he set off into the trees at right angles to the path. Ping followed him.

The weather was getting warmer. Every day seemed to bring flowers or trees that Ping had never seen before. She asked the dragon their names to try and take his mind off the lost dragon stone, but he didn't answer. Animals occasionally appeared among the bushes or on the branches of trees, looked startled at the strange creatures hurrying through their forest, and scurried off. Normally the sight of a squirrel or a deer would have delighted Ping, but coming across two small red bears tumbling in the grass gave her no pleasure.

When they stopped for the night, Danzi still wouldn't allow Ping to light a fire. She soaked millet and they ate it raw with wild mushrooms and birds' eggs. When they left their camp, the dragon swept the area with his tail to erase their footprints.

"The skillful traveler leaves no trace," he said.

They walked through a thick cypress forest for three days without catching sight of another person. The ground neither rose nor fell, and with the tall trees crowding against them, it was impossible to get a view of the sky or the land that they were walking through. As they traveled, the ground beneath them grew drier. The grass became sparser and more yellow. Buds on the trees withered before they had a chance to open.

Danzi said nothing more about the dragon stone. Ping was surprised that he had so easily agreed to leave it behind.

Eventually the trees thinned and they found themselves surrounded by fields again. The peasants that they met seemed strangely idle. Despite the warm spring weather, no one was plowing or sowing seeds. No one invited them to sleep in their stable or barn. They didn't ask for news from abroad either, but nodded curtly as the travelers passed without meeting their eyes. When Ping asked if she could buy vegetables from an old woman, she shook her head and held her turnips and onions close to her as if they were precious stones.

Late in the afternoon they came across a crowd of people gathered around a small lake. Dried mud rings around its banks indicated that the level had fallen several feet. It had once been a lake almost half a *li* wide. It was now little more than a pond. A small shrine stood back on what had previously been the lake's edge. It was a simple wooden structure, not much taller than Ping, with a wooden roof newly painted green. Ping glimpsed a primitive painting of a dragon inside. Below the painting was a neat pile of four oranges, a rock shaped like a lizard, and a cone of smoking incense. The fragrance of the incense mingled with the smell of cooking meat coming from a three-legged bronze cauldron with a fire smouldering beneath. A village elder, wearing a tattered gown with green embroidery, was muttering prayers to the spirit of the lake.

"Accept our humble offerings, Father Dragon," he was saying. "Awake and bring us rain."

The people threw things into the lake—old iron bowls, rusty farm tools, a broken sword.

Ping was watching from behind a tree. "What are they doing?" she asked.

"People believe dragon lives in lake and has not awoken from winter sleep to bring spring rains. Know dragons hate iron, so throw iron in lake to drive him out."

"Is there a dragon in the lake?" Ping asked.

"Perhaps centuries ago, but no longer."

Some of the people were looking up at a trace of wispy cloud in the sky.

"Look," said one of them. "Do you see that cloud? It is shaped something like a dragon. That's a good omen."

Danzi changed into his old-man shape, and he and Ping walked past the lake. The people watched them suspiciously, but no one spoke to them.

It was getting dark and the wind was strengthening. Ping headed for a small hill and found a rocky outcrop where they could stop for the night sheltered from the wind and hidden from the peasants by an overhang of rock.

Ping risked a small fire and cooked a simple meal of lentils and wild melon. It was the first hot meal they had had for a week. It filled their stomachs, but it was tasteless. Danzi was weary as he was every evening, but more so as he had spent time in his old-man shape for the first time in days.

"Have some more lentils, Danzi." As usual the dragon had eaten less than Ping.

"No more food," the dragon replied. "But would like tea."

The goatskin bag was almost empty.

"I'll go and get some water."

Danzi was already nodding off.

The moon hadn't yet risen. The wind had blown away the few wisps of cloud and the sky was studded with a multitude of stars like salt grains spilled on a dark cloth. Ping carefully picked her way through the undergrowth, hoping that she'd be able to find her way back to Danzi in the dark. Voices drifted toward her on the wind. They were loud and angry voices. As she got closer to the lake, she could see torches blazing and realized that the peasants were still gathered there. The gusty wind was only carrying snatches of what they were saying.

Other voices joined in the argument, shouting all at once and getting more and more agitated. A child started screaming. In the flickering torchlight, Ping could see that one of the men was holding a struggling girl. A woman tried to take the child from him, but others came to hold her back.

Fragments of their shouted conversation reached Ping on the wind.

". . . just a girl."

"Only Heaven . . . take life away."

The woman was crying. Ping edged closer, trying to make out what it was they were talking about.

". . . a single life will be lost . . ."

"If the rains don't . . . many people . . . die of hunger."

Hands reached out from the darkness and grabbed Ping from behind. She called out to Danzi to warn him, but the wind carried her words in the wrong direction. The old dragon, partially deaf, would never hear her. Her first thought was that it was Diao, but neither of the men holding her had the awful dead-animal smell of the dragon hunter. Ping tried to wriggle out of their grasp but they tightened their grip and dragged her to the edge of the lake.

When they reached the crowd by the lake, Ping could see the peasants' faces in the torchlight. They were unsmiling, creased with weariness and worry. In the middle of the group was a girl about two years younger than Ping. Her face was frozen in a mask of fear. Her hands were bound in front of her, her wrists bleeding where she'd tried to twist out of her bonds. She wore a short shift made of hemp with a crude green dragon painted on the front. It wasn't a cold night, but the girl's body shook uncontrollably from head to foot. A woman was on her knees in front of the elder, weeping and grabbing at his robes. Whoever had hold of Ping dragged her to the elder.

"Look what we found hiding in the bushes," said a voice behind her.

Ping saw the faces of her captors for the first time. They were hardly men at all, just young boys with fierce faces.

The woman looked at Ping. Her grimy face streaked by the flow of tears suddenly brightened.

"We can use her instead of Wei Wei," the woman said.

Ping didn't know what they were talking about. The elder nodded. The man who was holding the young girl let her go and the child ran to her mother. The boys holding Ping tightened their grip. Another woman took the shift off the girl and wrapped her trembling body in a blanket. She turned to Ping, undid the sash around her waist, and pulled off her gown. She dragged the shift over Ping's head, roughly pushing her arms through the short sleeves. She then held Ping's arms in front of her and tied her wrists with a leather thong.

"You must have mistaken me for someone else," Ping said. "I'm a stranger in this region."

The fierce faces broke into mean smiles. "We know."

The peasants knelt by the edge of the lake, chanting prayers to the dragon god they believed lived in its depths. The boys made Ping kneel with them.

"Accept this sacrifice, oh Great Dragon," the elder said. "Forgive us for whatever wrong we have done to you. Bring us rain, and we will worship you always."

Everything suddenly became clear to Ping. They were going to sacrifice her to the dragon god of the lake. They were going to throw her into the water and leave her to drown.

She tried to squirm out of their grasp. "Danzi! Help me!" she shouted, even though she knew there was no chance that the dragon could hear her from this distance.

The moon appeared above a distant hill. The peasants gathered around the lake as if they were eager to watch her drown. The boys led her down the steep bank to a bamboo raft. When she resisted, they tied her feet as well. She tried to twist out of their grasp, but it was useless. She wasn't strong enough. They threw her onto the raft. One of the boys held her down, while the other rowed to the center of the lake. Ping thought that there would be more chanting, other offerings, that she would have some time to devise a way to escape, but she was wrong.

There was an urgency about the ceremony. They wanted to get the sacrifice over with as soon as possible, so that the dragon would be appeased. They rolled Ping to the edge of the boat as if she were a sack of grain. She could see the reflection of the moon rippling on the surface of the lake like molten silver. Then she felt the sharp, cold slap of the water as the men threw her in headfirst.

She opened her mouth to cry out and swallowed a mouthful of water. She needed air. She breathed again but found there was nothing to fill her lungs with but water. She'd always taken for granted the air around her, never realizing how precious it was. She pulled up her legs and tried to reach the thong around her ankles with her bound fingers. Her body tumbled forward in a slow-motion somersault. Then she saw a face wavering in the water. A dragon face. There is a dragon living in the water, she thought. At least I won't be lonely at the bottom of the lake.

The dragon face came closer and then a dragon paw with four sharp talons reached toward her and grabbed hold of the shift she was wearing. Then she was out of the water, but she still couldn't get any air into her lungs. A deafening rumble filled the night air. It sounded as if ten men were beating copper drums with wooden mallets. Ping was in the air herself, high above the peasants who had all fallen to the ground covering their ears to block out the terrible sound.

Her lungs felt as if they would burst. There was a glowing light above her. It wasn't the moon; she could see that in front of her. It was something else. She twisted her head and for a moment she saw a pale dragon. It looked as if it were made of moonbeams. Her vision blurred and a loud buzzing in her ears replaced the rumbling.

Ping felt an intermittent pressure as if something heavy were pressing on her chest. The water in her stomach and lungs rushed out through her mouth and nose so fast that it burned. She breathed in. This time she sucked in a lungful of air. She breathed again, deeply this time. The air had no taste or smell, but somehow it seemed like honey and wine. It was the most wonderful thing she had experienced in her life. The heavy weight pressed on her chest again. She opened her eyes. It was a dragon paw.

"That hurts," she complained when the paw was lifted.

Danzi was looking down at her. Dragons don't exactly smile, but she noticed a softening around his lips and heard the sound like wind chimes.

"I saw the dragon in the lake," Ping said, still drinking in air as if it were nectar.

"Saw me," replied Danzi. "Ping confused. Danzi above surface of lake, not below it."

Ping frowned as she tried to understand this.

"How did you know I was in trouble?" asked Ping. "I didn't think you'd hear me crying for help."

"Didn't hear. Saw. Dragons are hard of hearing but can see a mustard seed at a distance of hundred *li*, even at night. I told you this as we walked. Ping doesn't listen."

"I'll listen closely to everything you say from now on. I promise."

A DARK CLOUD

Danzi had rekindled the fire and a pot of water was steaming over it. "Thought Ping would like tea," he said. "Have caught cicada for honorable Hua." The dragon held out a dead insect.

"Isn't he here?" Ping dropped her bowl and snatched up her gown which was drying by the fire. The copper coins and the jade pendant were still inside the pocket, so were the remaining crumbs of Wang Cao's explosive powder. But there was no sign of Hua.

"Where could he be?" Ping looked around frantically, hoping to see the rat warming himself by the fire or nibbling at their food supplies.

"Have not seen rat," said the dragon.

Ping called his name, but he didn't come. She slumped back down by the fire.

"He must have run away when they took off my gown," she said.

"Rat is loyal beast. He will return."

"Why would he want to stay with me? All I ever do is get him into dangerous situations. He'd be much happier living wild with all the other animals."

The next morning, Hua still hadn't returned. Ping searched for him near the lake. She couldn't find him. She slipped back to their hiding place when the peasants gathered near the water's edge again.

The dragon sighed. "Should be working in fields."

"Now they're convinced there's a dragon in the lake," said Ping. "They won't stop praying until it brings them rain."

"If bring rain, peasants will believe it is because they sacrificed young girl. Every time they want rain, they will do the same."

"Can you make it rain, Danzi?"

The dragon moved his head from side to side in a way that meant neither yes nor no.

"News of a dragon sighting will spread like spilled milk," Ping said. "It won't be long before Diao picks up our trail again. We have to get away from this place quickly, Danzi."

Danzi continued to stare at the peasants around the lake. "Wait a little while." Ping imagined Diao moving closer and closer as they delayed.

"I'll explain that the dragon doesn't want sacrifices."

"Won't listen. Want rain."

"Why do the people think you can make it rain?"

"Long ago, when there were many dragons, each dragon was responsible for certain rivers, ponds, and streams. Kept them in order. Peasants started to worship dragons, believing they brought spring rains."

Ping straightened her gown and smoothed her hair.

"I can try and make them understand," she said.

She walked over to the lake, trying to look important. A hushed silence fell over the group of peasants.

"I am the princess of the pond," she said. "The great dragon is angry with you."

The peasants moaned.

"Tell the dragon we're sorry we've offended him. We'll make another sacrifice to him."

"He doesn't want you to sacrifice people to him."

"What will we do?"

"It is spring. You must plant your seeds."

"But without rain our crops will die. There's no point in planting."

Ping tried to argue that if the seeds weren't planted, they wouldn't grow even if it did rain, but the peasants didn't seem to understand.

"We have offended the great dragon," wailed the elder. "All is lost."

They bowed their heads down and threw dirt in their hair. Ping could see she was only making matters worse.

"The dragon will bring rain," said Ping. "But only if you make a solemn promise."

The people stopped wailing, looked up, and said they would promise anything.

"You must start planting your fields immediately," Ping told them in the stern voice she'd used to get the animals back into their enclosures at Huangling. "And you have to promise never to sacrifice people to him again."

"Not even girls?" asked one man.

"No," said Ping firmly. "He prefers offerings of roasted swallow."

The people brushed the dirt from their hair. "If we make these promises, the dragon will bring the spring rains?"

"Yes," Ping said, thinking it was better to tell one small lie than let a whole village go hungry.

The elder ordered his people to get the plow and hoes. He selected three young men to go hunting for swallows. The peasants ran off to do the dragon's bidding.

Ping went back to the dragon.

"Peasants are working," Danzi said. "Well done. What did Ping tell them?"

Ping was silent. The dragon's prominent brows furrowed as he turned to Ping.

"What did Ping say?" repeated the dragon.

"I told them that if they promised to go back to their fields and never sacrifice people that you would . . . make it rain."

The dragon made deep rumbling noises.

"I didn't know what else to say," Ping said. "They need rain."

"Heaven decides if spring rains will come."

Ping looked at the dragon. "Can't you just try?"

"Dragons can encourage rain from clouds. Don't know if damaged wing is healed enough for such a flight," the dragon said.

Danzi unfurled his left wing. The scar across the thin membrane of the wing had pulled apart at one end.

"You must have damaged it when you flew to save me last night," said Ping guiltily.

The dragon folded his wing away again.

"I didn't realize you'd have to fly to make rain," Ping said. "I thought you'd recite a spell or make one of your sounds."

"Will have to fly up above clouds," Danzi said.

Ping looked up at the sky. There were only wispy gray clouds that reminded Ping of the fluff in the corners of halls at Huangling Palace. They looked a long way away.

"Then what do you do?"

"Spit on them," the dragon replied.

"Spit?"

The dragon nodded as if this was nothing unusual. "Dragon saliva has many uses."

"But you can't fly up to the clouds with a tear in your wing," Ping said, wishing she'd never made the promise to the peasants. "I'll go and tell them."

Ping ran back to the lakeside. She explained to the peasants about the damaged wing.

"Why doesn't the dragon come to us himself?" asked the elder.

"He's angry with us," said one of the boys who had captured her the night before. "He wants another offering."

"No, he doesn't," said Ping.

The peasants started to surround her. Their faces had turned fierce again. Ping got ready to defend herself.

Then she realized they weren't listening to her. The peasants were looking over her shoulder. Ping turned around. The surrounding countryside was flat, except for the hill where she and Danzi had made their camp. The peasants were pointing excitedly at a small figure laboring up its slopes. It was Danzi.

Getting off the ground was the most difficult part of flying for a dragon. It took a lot of energy. Ping guessed it had been pure terror that got Danzi airborne at Huangling when the dragon hunter was after him. Their second takeoff from the mountaintop had been assisted by a strong updraft. Ping didn't know how he'd gotten into the air to save her the night before, but she was sure that the muscles in his wings would be sore after the unfamiliar exercise. She stared anxiously at the distant dragon. He looked small and frail. With tired muscles and a torn wing, she was afraid he wouldn't be able to fly as high as the clouds.

Ping held her breath as Danzi started to run down the hillside. It seemed odd that he was running downhill in order to fly, but Ping knew he was trying to get up enough speed. He was three-quarters of the way down the hill and still showing no signs of taking off. What would the peasants do if the dragon crashed in a heap? Then, as his legs collapsed beneath him, the dragon opened his wings and soared into the air. The peasants cheered. Ping breathed again but kept her eyes fixed anxiously on the dragon as he ascended slowly into the sky. From that distance his wings looked as fragile as a butterfly's.

One of the fluffy clouds was grayer and heavier than the other two. Danzi's wings labored. Slowly he spiraled up toward it.

It took him almost half an hour to reach the clouds. He looked no bigger than a sparrow. Then he disappeared through the cloud. Ping wanted to believe that the dragon could make it rain, but it seemed impossible. The peasants' upturned faces were all smiling as they chanted prayers to the dragon-god of the lake. They had no doubt that the dragon would bring them rain. More long minutes passed as the cloud drifted slowly, stubbornly refusing to release any water. There were more clouds now. Ping started to mutter her own prayers. Danzi had damaged his wing trying to save her and it was she who'd made him take this flight. He shouldn't have to die because of her stupidity. She was the one who should be punished. She gazed up at the gray clouds, powerless to help.

The peasants' smiles began to fade. Their cries of praise faded away. Where was the rain? They muttered darkly to one another. Their hopes had been raised. They had imagined their lake full again. They had cast aside their cares and worries, but it had all been false hope. They grabbed Ping.

"You won't get away from us again," shouted the elder, pulling his rusty sword from its scabbard.

Ping didn't argue with them. Perhaps this was the gods' will. If the peasants killed her, Danzi might be spared. Then there was a flash of light in the sky and a deep rumble of thunder. Ping looked up. The clouds were darker and heavier. More clouds were approaching from the west. There was another flash, another growling rumble. It sounded like Danzi when he got angry. A fat drop of water splashed on Ping's cheek, then another. The peasants' mutterings stopped as raindrops fell on their upturned faces. They let go of Ping and started to laugh and shout. Soon there was steady rain. The peasants danced in the puddles.

Ping kept her eyes on the sky. Where was Danzi? Suddenly he broke through the clouds. His wings were beating rapidly. They looked small and delicate, too fragile to keep his heavy body aloft. He beat them faster, but he was falling. His feeble wings couldn't beat against the updraft. They stopped flapping and streamed behind him uselessly like a flimsy gauze cloak. Danzi continued to fall. Ping couldn't bear to watch, but she had to. She had to know where he landed. The dragon was fighting to control his fall, trying to get his wings outstretched again. He couldn't. Then he pulled his flailing legs in along his sides and pointed his head down. He curved his body so that the path of his descent turned back toward the lake. Instead of falling to his death on the earth, Danzi plummeted headfirst into the lake. A fountain of water, higher than the highest building in Chang'an, shot out of the lake. The water was shallow, though. Ping felt a jarring impact through the soles of her shoes.

"The dragon has returned to his home at the bottom of the lake," said the elder. "Now we must celebrate his gift of rain."

Forgetting about Ping, the peasants left the lake and went back to their homes, singing and dancing in the rain.

Ping stood by the side of the lake, peering desperately into the dark water, hoping for some sign of movement. Nothing disturbed the surface of the lake except the raindrops. The rain was falling heavily. The clouds were black. It was more like night than day. There was no point in her jumping into the water to look for the dragon. She couldn't swim. She walked around the edge of the lake, peering into its depths, but she could see nothing. She sat down in the mud, shivering violently. What would she do without the dragon? Where would she go?

Ping had always been alone. The only people she could remember being in her life were Lao Ma and the horrible Lan. They weren't friends, though. Master Lan had never shown her a moment of warmth, and though Lao Ma had been kind enough to her, she had only ever thought of her as a slave. At Huangling she had often wished for one thing even more than she had wished for a bigger dinner, a warmer jacket, or fewer things thrown in her direction. She had wished that she had a real friend to talk to. She had never imagined a friend would arrive in the shape of a dragon. At Huangling she had been friendless but not lonely. Now she had experienced friendship and lost it; she felt lonely for the first time in her life. Her only friends had been a dragon and a rat and now they were both gone. Tears welled and mingled with the rain already running down her face.

Ping sat by the lake's edge all day, watching the water level slowly rise. Behind her the sounds of celebration drifted from the village—singing and shouting, cheering and laughter. Her gown was soaked, her hair hung in wet strings. The sky was so dark, Ping hardly noticed that night had fallen. She finally got up and made her way back around the lake in the direction of the rock shelter. She trudged through the sticky mud in the growing darkness. She stumbled and fell headlong. She thought she had fallen over a log, but though it seemed to be covered in scaly gray bark, it was softer than wood. What she first thought were branches, she realized were horns. It wasn't a log at all. It was the body of a dragon.

A STITCH IN TIME

Ping knelt down in the water at the edge of the lake and felt for the beat of a heart in Danzi's scaly chest. She couldn't find one. Her own heart was pounding as if it were trying to keep both herself and the dragon alive. She felt around his neck until she found the soft unscaly patch where he liked to be scratched just above the reversed scales. She dug her fingers in. There was a pulse. It was slow and shallow, but Danzi was still alive.

The rising water was already lapping over Danzi's tail and back paws. Ping had to move him. She had to get him back to the overhang of rock where she could warm him and give him food and herbs. She thought about asking the peasants to help her, but she didn't want them to see the dragon in such a pathetic state. She had to drag him there herself.

Ping had walked hundreds of *li* since she'd been with the dragon, but she knew the next half *li* would be the hardest. The earth was soft and muddy from the rain. Using a branch, she smoothed a path leading to their camp, removing stones and pulling up grass. Then, using the same branch, she levered the dragon onto his back. Even that left her short of breath. She held the dragon under his forelegs and pulled. His body had settled into the mud. She couldn't shift him. She pushed and pulled, tugged and strained, falling over in the slippery mud. Heavy rain continued to fall. The level of the lake was rising at an alarming rate. It was now covering half his body. Ping closed her eyes and thought of Master Lan, of the years of harsh words and bruises from flying objects colliding with her flesh. If it weren't for Danzi, that would still be her life.

She concentrated hard to summon every *shu* of energy from every part of her body. She grasped the dragon and heaved again. There was a sucking sound as his body dislodged from the mold it had settled into.

Ping had shifted the dragon no more than a couple of inches, but it gave her heart. If she could move him two inches, she could move him two more. She pulled him again. His body slid up the steep slope from the water's edge. He was a heavy load and she couldn't stop to rest for fear he would slip back and all her effort would be wasted. After half an hour of straining, Ping's arms ached and she was dizzy from exertion. After an hour, the ache had turned to a piercing pain, but she continued. Finally she reached the top of the incline.

She pulled the dragon onto level ground and rested. The next part of her path was flatter. The rain had made it treacherously slippery and Ping was able to push the dragon more easily. Finally she reached their shelter and dragged the unconscious dragon out of the rain.

Although she just wanted to collapse, Ping knew she couldn't. She rekindled the fire and settled the dragon close to it. All the wood she had collected the day before was wet. The fire smoked and gave off little heat for some time. As she waited for it to burn properly, she constructed a screen of branches on one side of the overhang to stop the driving rain from slanting into their shelter. She stacked more wood close to the fire to dry and made the dragon as comfortable as she could on the hard earth. The fire finally stopped smoking and started to flame. She made an herbal draft for Danzi with the last of the dried herbs that Wang Cao had given her. She set the pot on the fire. Danzi would need food. Their supplies were running low. In any case, Ping thought the dragon would need more than millet and wild vegetables.

She made the slippery journey back to the lake. The meat offering was still in the cauldron in the shrine. Ping felt no qualms about taking the meat. It was an offering to the dragon of the lake. Danzi had done what the peasants wanted, risking his own life. If he wasn't entitled to the meat, no one was. Ping took the four oranges as well.

As soon as it was ready, Ping forced some of the dark brown herbal liquid between the dragon's teeth. He showed no sign of reviving. She ate a little of the meat and one of the oranges, then banked the fire and lay down beside it.

Ping slept longer than she had meant to. It was well past dawn when she woke. She looked anxiously at the dragon. His eyelids flickered. Relief washed over her like hot spring water. He was still alive. The fire had gone out but she was able to revive it by blowing on the ashes and adding dry wood. The front of her gown was dry where she'd lain facing the fire, but it was still damp at the back. The heavy rain had slackened to drizzle. Ping reheated the herbal liquid and managed to get the dragon to swallow a few mouthfuls. She ate more food and made herself some tea. It revived her.

She heard a faint metallic chiming. "Ping has done well." It was the most beautiful music she'd ever heard.

"It's good to hear your voice again, Danzi," Ping said, smiling at the dragon.

Another faint noise came to her ears. Not metallic dragon sounds, but small squeaks and scratchings. She looked down and saw a bedraggled rat struggling to climb up the folds of her gown.

"Hua!"

The warmth from the fire made the rat steam. Ping laughed out loud. Danzi made the sound like jingling bells. Her arms ached, her gown was damp, but at that moment Ping had everything she wanted.

Her happiness faltered when the dragon held out his wing and she saw the damage he had done by flying up to the clouds. The thin stuff of his wing hung in tatters.

"Danzi," she cried. "Look at your wing. Perhaps I can bandage it with some strips of cloth. I'll get the red cloud ointment."

"No!" said the dragon as Ping reached for her bag. "Must save ointment for stone."

"The stone's gone. Don't you remember?"

"Of course," said the dragon.

"You're not thinking about going back for it again, are you?"

"No."

Ping wasn't sure she believed him. "We have to do something to your wing or you'll never be able to fly again. Please let me put some ointment on."

The dragon shook his head firmly. He contemplated his ruined wing. "Too damaged," he said. "Ointment will not heal. Ping must sew."

"Sew?" said Ping.

"If shreds are sewn together, wing will heal in time."

Ping had never imagined when she bought the needle and thread that she would be using them for such a purpose. She threaded up the red silk and started to sew together the ragged tatters of Danzi's wing.

"Doesn't it hurt?" she asked, wincing as she pulled the thread through the membrane.

"No pain."

When Ping had finished, Danzi held out his wing again. Ping couldn't help smiling. "It looks like a patched blanket," she said.

"You really made it rain, Danzi," Ping said.

The rain continued to fall. Ping sat with the rat and the dragon in the rock overhang, sipping tea and looking out at the wet landscape and the rapidly filling lake, enjoying the simple pleasures of being warm, dry, and well fed.

CHAPTER FOURTEEN

SWIFT PASSAGE

After two days the clouds cleared and the rain stopped. Danzi got to his feet and walked to a spot from where he could see the peasants busy in their fields. One was pulling a plow, others were bent double as they planted seeds. Ping heard the dragon's melodic wind chime sounds.

"Time to resume journey," he announced.

Danzi didn't mention the dragon stone. He seemed to have forgotten about it. Ping was sad that she would never see it again, but at least they were moving toward Ocean again.

A few hours after they set out, Ping was surprised when Danzi suddenly turned from their eastward path and started to head north.

"Isn't this the wrong way?" asked Ping. "Ocean is in the east."

"The straight path must sometimes be crooked," replied the dragon.

The dragon walked slowly, as if each step needed careful concentration. He spoke even less than usual. His last disastrous flight and his contact with iron had weakened him. Ping had to wait until they stopped for their midday meal before Danzi explained the change of direction.

"Must go to Yellow River," he told Ping. "Travel by boat."

This was an even greater surprise. The dragon had previously been reluctant to spend any of the money that Wang Cao had given them. Ping had had to argue for hours just to spend a single copper coin on food.

"Cannot fly for many weeks," Danzi explained. "Must reach Ocean before summer ends."

The dragon had never mentioned that their time was limited before, but though Ping questioned him, he wouldn't tell her why. Her feet were callused from so much walking. If river travel meant that she didn't have to walk, she was happy to go along with Danzi's new plan.

When they reached the Yellow River, Ping could only stand and stare. They had passed streams on their travels. They had walked beside canals. They had crossed over a rush of water that Danzi had called a river, but it was a mere trickle compared to this seething river. The Yellow River was so wide that Ping had to strain her eyes to see the other side. It raced along at such a speed that she didn't know how the boatmen stopped their boats from being overturned. The other startling thing about the river was that it really was yellow, or at least a sandy brown color.

"Yellow earth from distant land washes into river," Danzi explained. "Travels all the way to Ocean."

They were on the outskirts of a busy town that seemed to have the sole purpose of providing a harbor where boats could tie up to collect or deliver large amounts of cargo. As they approached the crowded wharves, Danzi explained to Ping what she must do. She had to find a small boat that was traveling, not just to the next town, but as far eastward as possible. Then she had to offer the boatman a reasonable sum of money (not so much that he would become suspicious) to give up his living quarters for the journey. Ping was to tell him it was because her old grandfather was ill, but in fact it was so Danzi could stay undercover and not have to spend too much time in his old-man shape.

The wharf was a solid construction of stone where many men were loading and unloading cargo. Piles of sacks and crates of chickens were stacked everywhere. Carts, packhorses, and sedan chairs made it difficult to find a path through. Steps led down to the water's edge, where at least four times ten boats were tied up. Some were large boats crowded with passengers. Smaller boats were piled high with sacks of grain, mounds of vegetables, or bolts of silk fabric.

The boats, whether large or small, were all built the same way. They were made of thick wooden planks and had a deck that sloped up slightly at either end so that both prow and stern were raised out of the water. The decks of the larger boats were roofed to protect the passengers from wind and rain. The cargo boats had small cabins where the boatmen lived, but the rest of the deck was cleared for cargo.

Teams of rowers manned the larger craft, but the smaller boats were each managed by just two men. There were also fragile craft—nothing more than large bowls made of leather bound on to bent bamboo—carrying baskets of grain and dried fish. These flimsy craft, poled by fishermen or farmers on their way to market, looked in danger of sinking.

Ping left Danzi behind a stack of grain sacks where he could rest in his dragon shape unseen by the people on the wharf. A large ginger cat with one eye came and sat next to Danzi.

"There," said Ping. "You've got a companion while I go and find a boat."

She spent several hours going from boat to boat, trying to find one with room for passengers. The boatmen were suspicious of her and unwilling to give up their quarters. They all told her to go to the passenger boats. Ping didn't like the river. It was too fast-flowing, too dangerous. She didn't like the unfriendly people who worked on it, either.

She returned to where she had left the dragon.

"I wish we were back on the road," she said. "I don't care about blisters and aching legs. Can't we continue walking?"

"What is Ping afraid of?" the dragon asked.

"Drowning."

"Boatmen very skilled. Few people drown in river."

Ping didn't care if only a few people drowned. She didn't want to be one of them.

"There's only one boat I haven't tried, and that's the one right at the end."

She pointed to a boat that was moored at a distance from the other boats. The deck had fewer sacks and crates piled on it.

"It looks like it's got plenty of space."

"Boatman must be dishonest or unfriendly," said Danzi. "Possibly unskilled."

Ping liked the look of the boat, though. It was well kept. The sacks of onions and melons were neatly stacked and the ropes, sails, and poles were carefully secured on deck. There was something about the boatman she liked as well. While the other boatmen were lounging around in noisy groups telling stories of their travels, this one was busy sweeping the deck. She ignored the faint sounds of Danzi's anxiety and went up to the boat.

"I'd like to inquire about passage east," Ping said.

The boatman turned and came over to Ping. She

suddenly realized why she'd felt drawn to this particular boatman. It wasn't a man at all, but a woman. She wore her hair uncovered and tied back in a rough plait. Her face was darkened and lined from many years on the river.

"I don't take passengers," the boatwoman said.

"We wouldn't get in your way," Ping replied.

The boatwoman was dressed in hemp trousers and a wraparound jacket like the men. She wore heavy waterproof boots. Her palms were callused from constant rowing and poling her boat in the strong current. The one-eyed ginger cat strolled up the gangplank and rubbed itself up against the boatwoman's legs.

"All right," she said. "I wouldn't mind some company."

"Is this your cat?" Ping asked.

The woman nodded. Her stern expression disappeared as Ping stroked the cat. Ping struck a deal with the boatwoman and went back to bring Danzi on board.

"For a few extra cash, the boatwoman will cook meals for us," Ping told the dragon.

Now that her journey was going to be profitable despite her small load of cargo, the boatwoman was eager to set sail.

"Couldn't we wait till morning?" asked Ping, who wasn't as eager to venture onto the river.

"There are still four hours of daylight left," the boatwoman said. "And if we leave now, that's one night's mooring fees I won't have to pay."

There was nothing more to delay them. Ping led Danzi to the cabin. The boatwoman untied the boat and pushed it away from the wharf. She poled out of the sheltered harbor until the fast current grabbed the boat and pulled it out into the river. Ping held on tight. The boatwoman's eyes sparkled and then disappeared in folds of cheerful wrinkles as she laughed at Ping's discomfort.

"I can see you haven't sailed before," she said. "Don't you worry, I've never lost so much as an onion to the river."

The boat skimmed through the water at an alarming speed. It had seemed sturdy enough tied up to the wharf, but now it was being tossed about like a toy. The banks on either side of the wide river rose up in steep cliffs, but they seemed a long way away. Pinnacles of rock reared out of the water, and Ping was afraid the boat would crash into them. The boatwoman, steering the boat alone, had to work hard, but she confidently guided the craft around the pinnacles. Two large islands appeared in front of them, dividing the great river into three narrow channels.

"The Three Gates," said the boatwoman. "The right channel is the Gate of Men, the middle channel is the Gate of the Gods, and the left one is the Dragon Gate. Which one will we go through?"

Ping was flustered. "I don't know anything about sailing. Can't you choose?" Why did everyone expect her to make decisions?

"I don't often have traveling companions. I'd like you to decide."

Ping looked at the three channels. "The Dragon Gate."

"A good choice," said the boatwoman. "It is the longer channel, as it curves around the largest island, but the current is slower there, so it is easier to steer through."

"What are the other two like?"

"The Gate of Men has the slowest current. It seems to be an easy path, but it has hidden dangers as there are many half-submerged rocks to negotiate. The Gate of the Gods is the shortest and the straightest route, but the current is treacherous. You chose well."

The boatwoman steered the boat toward the left channel. The wind dropped. The current slackened, the boat slowed. Steep cliffs shut out the afternoon sun. Ping felt more secure with the banks closer. She noticed holes carved into the cliffs, which the boatwoman said were the cave homes of poor people. Some of the caves' inhabitants were walking along precarious paths cut in the side of the cliffs. They waved as the boat passed. In the sheltered curve of the channel the cliffs were replaced with grass-covered hills and a bamboo thicket. Then the cliffs reared up again. The boat passed around the northern shore of the island, and they were pulled back into the angry current of the river. The boat picked up speed again. Ping felt sick.

The boatwoman's name was Jiang Bing. Her boat was about twice ten paces long and the deck sloped up at both ends just like the other boats. At the stern was a large rudder which the boatwoman used to steer the boat. In the middle of the deck was the boatwoman's cabin. This was nothing more than a wooden hut with a roof of woven bamboo. Inside was a straw mattress. It was simple, but it provided the privacy for Danzi to spend whole days in his dragon shape. The sides of the boat were only a foot higher than the deck. Ping was convinced that she was going to fall into the river. There was only a short length of railing, outside the cabin. This was where Ping sat, clinging to the rail.

The boatwoman didn't have to row. The current was very fast and she only had to stand at the stern and steer with the rudder. The boat dipped and rose in the turbulent river waters. It needed all her strength to keep the boat on course. Ping tried to imagine the backbreaking work that Jiang Bing would have to do to row back against the current.

It didn't seem possible that the boatwoman, not much bigger than Ping, could do this by herself, but she must have done it many times.

Danzi had told Ping that in one day on the boat, they would travel the same distance as they could walk in four days. Ping was pleased that they were making such speedy progress, but it also made her uneasy. It seemed unnatural to be moving so quickly while doing nothing more than sitting on a sack of onions. Ping stared down at the swirling yellow water. Its force frightened her. She had felt the power of water when she had been thrown into the still waters of the lake. If she fell into the Yellow River, it would suck her into its muddy depths and not even Danzi would be able to save her. Ping watched Jiang Bing sitting at the stern, firmly gripping the rudder and scanning the river ahead. She felt confident that they were in good hands.

The cat sat on a basket, staring at Ping with its one yellow eye. Where the other eye should have been was a crooked scar. The cat didn't ever seem to blink. It made Ping uncomfortable.

"He isn't usually so interested in people," the boat-woman said. "I don't know what he finds so fascinating about you."

"I do," said Ping. She carefully pulled Hua from her gown.

The cat crouched, ready to pounce. Hua looked at the cat and frantically tried to wriggle away. Ping quickly stuffed him back into the folds of her gown.

The boatwoman laughed. "Now I understand."

When the sun had disappeared below the horizon, the boatwoman steered the boat toward the bank and found a narrow inlet where the current wasn't so strong. She dropped a small anchor overboard and then started to make their evening meal. Ping lit a charcoal fire in a metal dish on legs, which Jiang Bing used to cook on. The boatwoman scaled the fish she'd caught earlier to make fish stew.

After the meal, Ping washed the bowls and chopsticks in the shallows. Then when she had made sure that Danzi was comfortable, she made a bed for herself between sacks of cabbages and crates of melons. The deck rocked as the boat pulled against the anchor, as if it were eager to be moving again. The black, starspeckled sky stretched above them. She could see the constellation of the Azure Dragon that Danzi had taught her to locate. Each night the moon traveled across the sky from the dragon's horn to its tail. It had just reached the horn, but she was so tired she knew she'd be asleep before it got as far as its neck.

The next morning, not long after dawn, they were coursing down the river again. Ping was still troubled by the force of the water that bore the boat along as if it were no more than a floating twig. She tried not to look at the swirling water, but the distant bleak cliffs that bordered the river provided little distraction.

Since there was nothing to look at, Ping decided she would talk to Jiang Bing to take her mind off the rushing river. She cautiously negotiated her way to the stern of the boat, clinging to crates and boxes as she went, then wedged herself between some sacks.

Ping asked the boatwoman about herself. Jiang Bing

said she was from a part of the empire even farther away than Huangling.

"I was married to a man much older than me," she told Ping. "My parents chose him because he had ten *mou* of good land and paid a sizeable dowry."

"Was he unkind to you?" Ping asked.

"No. He was a good man, but he died soon after our marriage. Our land went to his brother, and I was supposed to spend the rest of my life serving my mother-in-law."

"What did you do?"

"I was only sixteen. I ran away instead."

"How did you manage all by yourself?" Ping asked.

"It was hard at first," the boatwoman replied. "I worked wherever I could. After many years I saved enough money to buy this boat. The boatmen are unfriendly. The merchants are wary of a woman who has no family and whose only companion is a ginger cat. They prefer to send their goods on boats operated by men, so I still barely make a living, but I am happy."

Ping knew that she should be sitting with Danzi, but she was enjoying Jiang Bing's company too much.

"What about you?" asked the boatwoman. "What causes you to be traveling with your grandfather?"

Ping had known that her questions would inevitably mean that questions would be asked of her. Danzi had warned her to keep to herself, but she didn't want to lie to Jiang Bing.

"He isn't my grandfather," she replied softly so that the dragon couldn't hear her.

"My family sold me as a slave when I was a child," she said. "I worked for a cruel master until quite recently. The old man helped me escape. In return I agreed to accompany him on this journey."

Jiang Bing nodded and smiled a sad smile. Ping felt that no one had ever understood her life more.

"Where are you and the old man going?"

"To Ocean," Ping replied. "He wants to see Ocean before he dies."

Ping looked to see what the boatwoman's reaction was.

"It is said that this river flows all the way there," she said.

Ping relaxed a little, beginning to trust Jiang Bing's skill. It was warm enough to take off her shoes and socks. Perhaps the worst of the journey was behind her now. Perhaps she wouldn't have to struggle all the way to Ocean on foot. Perhaps, instead, she could just sit on the boat for a week or two and Ocean would come to her.

CHAPTER FIFTEEN

IN THE SHADOW
OF THE FIRE MOUNTAIN

After five days afloat, Ping got used to the movement of the boat as it pitched and tossed on the river. She no longer worried about falling overboard, and moved around the boat confidently, doing whatever she could to help the boatwoman. She had quickly grown to love life on the river. It had a soothing rhythm. There was work to be done, fish to be caught, but she still had hours each day to do nothing but enjoy the changing view.

The stark cliffs gradually softened to hills, which in turn became flat fertile land. Villages and fields slipped by. Scenes of rural life—farmers plowing fields, women washing clothes at the river's edge, a young boy minding a wallowing water buffalo—appeared and disappeared as if she were looking at a series of paintings rather than real events. Mulberry orchards crowded to the water's edge.

Jiang Bing knew everything there was to know about the river and its banks.

"Mulberry trees aren't grown just for the sweet berries," she told Ping. "They're also grown for the leaves, which are the favorite food of silkworms. In exchange for all the mulberry leaves they can eat, the little creatures spin silk thread."

"The world is full of wonders," Ping said.

They passed terraced hills that looked like they had been carved into enormous steps, as if a passing giant with his giant knife had cut steps into the hillside to make it easier to climb. Jiang Bing laughed when Ping said this.

"They haven't been cut by a giant," she said. "Farmers dug out these flat areas with simple spades so that they could grow vegetables and grain on the hillsides."

At noon the boatwoman tied up the boat, as she did each day, while they ate their midday meal. It was always the same—fish and onions flavored with a little ginger and an herb that was a favorite of Jiang Bing's.

The only thing that Ping didn't like about the river journey was the ginger cat. It watched her all the time, staring with its one unblinking yellow eye. Poor Hua only got to come out of the folds of her gown for a few minutes each day and slink around the deck while Ping watched over him.

It was hard to tell how old Jiang Bing was, but Ping thought that she would be about the right age to be her mother. She imagined what it would be like to live and work on the river with this woman as a companion. She thought it would be a good life. Perhaps after Danzi had reached Ocean, she could come back. The sound of hissing and spitting roused Ping from her daydreams. Hua ran across the deck followed by the boatwoman's cat. The rat clawed his way up Ping's gown, scratching her in his hurry. Hua wouldn't be so keen to stay on the river. The cat glared at Ping. Ping liked all the four-footed creatures she had known—the oxen and the goat back at Huangling, the pigs she'd been imprisoned with, Hua, and the dragon, of course—but she disliked the boatwoman's ginger cat.

Danzi was content to doze in his cabin for most of the day. Ping was glad he had given up all thought of finding the dragon stone. She knew she should spend more time with the old dragon, but she preferred to stay on deck listening to Jiang Bing's stories of life on the Yellow River. It was good for Danzi to get lots of quiet rest, she told herself. It would mean all his *qi* could go to healing his wing.

They had just eaten their midday meal. Ping was making some tea for Jiang Bing, boiling water over the charcoal fire. There were only a few of Wang Cao's tea leaves left, but Ping was happy to share them with the boatwoman.

"We'll tie up at the next town," Jiang Bing said, sipping her tea.

Ping looked downriver. On the horizon she could see a dark smudge. She shivered despite the warmth of the spring sun.

"Is that the town?" Ping asked. She strained her eyes but couldn't make out any detail.

Jiang Bing nodded.

"What's it called?" asked Ping, though she had a sudden feeling she didn't want to know.

"Wucheng."

Ping's vision of sailing all the way to Ocean disappeared like bubbles in soup. She shivered as she remembered what Danzi had said about Wucheng—where sorcerers in search of dragon heart gathered.

"Must we stop there?" she asked.

"I have cargo to deliver," Jiang Bing replied.

"If you sail past it, we'll pay more to make up for the money you lose by not delivering your cargo," Ping insisted.

Jiang Bing seemed puzzled by Ping's concern. "It'll only take an hour or so to unload."

Danzi appeared beside Ping in his old-man shape. It was the first time he'd been on deck for days.

"Danzi," said Ping. "It's Wucheng!"

The old man stared ahead without any sign of being surprised.

"You knew we were coming here?"

Danzi nodded. Ping wanted to question him, but she couldn't with Jiang Bing within hearing.

As the river carried them closer, the black smudge took on the shape of a dark mountain, but still looked blurred. A plume of smoke was curling from its peak. The smoke didn't rise, though; it slowly sank and wreathed the mountain slopes in a gray haze.

"It's a fire mountain," Jiang explained. "There's a hole at the top that leads down to fires deep underground."

Ping watched the mountain grow as they drew closer. Its slopes were covered with small gray stones like cinders, except for what looked like a stream of dark liquid which had frozen as it flowed down one side of the mountain.

"It's so hot inside a fire mountain that rocks melt," Jiang Bing told her. "Long ago the molten rock spewed out of the mountain, so they say. It was fiery red and poured down the hillside, engulfing half the town. Then it cooled, turned back into rock, and the rest of the town was spared."

Wucheng was the ugliest place Ping had ever seen. Nothing at all grew anywhere on the mountain. Even on bleak Huangling there had been a few straggling melon vines and some thistles. On the fire mountain there was nothing. Not a single blade of green.

The town was surrounded by a high wall made of broken pieces quarried from the wave of rock. Wucheng looked like a town with secrets to hide. It crouched in the shadow of the wave of solidified rock as if it were trying to avoid the sun.

The boat rocked from side to side as Jiang Bing steered it across the current and toward the shore. Ping led the dragon to where the boatwoman couldn't hear them. She shooed the cat from its position on a sack of onions so that she and Danzi could sit down and hold on to the rail.

"Why do you want to go to this awful place?" Ping asked.

"To find dragon stone," the dragon replied.

"I thought you'd forgotten about it."

"No. This is where Diao would bring stone. Sell it for much gold."

"You think Diao is here?"

The old man moved his head from side to side in the annoying way that meant neither yes nor no.

"I don't want to go there," Ping said, but she felt no sense of terrible foreboding about going to Wucheng. The cat nudged her arm, wanting to be stroked. In her heart Ping wanted to go to the town if there were even the smallest chance of finding the stone.

"Sometimes advancing seems like going backward," the dragon said.

The boat bumped against the wharf, and Jiang Bing tied it up. Instead of steps, there were just rickety ladders leading up to the rotting timbers of the wharf.

The old man–shaped dragon bowed to the boatwoman and walked across to the ladder. "Pay boatwoman, Ping," said the dragon's voice in Ping's mind.

Ping took out some coins from her inner pocket and handed them to Jiang Bing.

"I wish I could travel farther with you," she said.

The boatwoman took Ping's hand in hers and held it for a moment.

"Perhaps another time," the boatwoman said sadly. Then she went back to her work.

Ping followed the dragon to the wharf with a sinking heart.

As soon as she was back on land, she felt dizzy. Her legs wobbled as she walked. She was so used to the movement of the boat, the solid earth seemed to rock beneath her feet. She hadn't felt sick on the river, but now that she was back on land her stomach felt upset.

The dark gray stone that made up the town's wall was blistered and pockmarked. On the top of the wall the jagged points of rock were sharp enough to pierce skin if anyone tried to climb over. But the gates in the walls were open and unguarded. If Ping and the dragon were foolish enough to enter the gray town, no one was going to stop them.

Three streets of equal width fanned out from the gateway into the town.

"Which way?" asked the dragon. He already sounded weary.

"How would I know?" Ping asked irritably.

"Ping decides which way," the dragon said.

Ping didn't know why Danzi wanted her to make

the decisions, but she knew that arguing with the dragon was a waste of time. She pointed to the middle street and the dragon set off down it.

Wucheng was drab and shabby. The streets were made of trampled cinders. The houses were old and tumbledown. Some were made of ancient wood, others were made of the same ugly rock as the town walls. The shingle roofs were covered in a layer of gray ash. There were no palaces, no beautiful halls, no statues. There were no people either. It was like a ghost town, empty and quiet. The only living things Ping could see were two great black crows perched on a ridge beam. Flakes of fine ash drifted down from the mountain and settled on Ping's sleeves. The smoky air stung her eyes and smelled like rotten eggs.

"You can't be sure Diao would come here," whispered Ping.

The metallic sounds of the dragon echoed in the dismal streets. "Danzi knows the ways of dragon hunters."

"How can we find it?"

"Ping must find it."

"I don't know where it is!"

"Ping can find stone. Search with mind."

Ping looked at Danzi. There was no one to see him, but he was in his old-man shape. "You must be crazy if you think I can do such a thing," replied Ping.

"Ping has sensed things before."

Ping remembered the sense of dread she'd felt, once

in the market at Chang'an, and again as they'd approached the village of Fengjing. She shivered at the memory. Both times Diao had been near. Her stomach was unsettled, but it wasn't the same feeling of dread she'd felt before. They walked along each of the three streets without seeing anyone. Once or twice, Ping imagined she glimpsed eyes in a window or thought she saw a figure in a doorway out of the corner of her eye; but when she looked back, there was no one there. Their only companions were the two crows that flapped lazily from rooftop to rooftop. The only sound was the birds' slow, mournful caw trailing into silence.

When they had walked down each of the three streets, Ping stopped. She didn't like Wucheng, but she had no sense of dread.

"Diao isn't here," she said.

"Good," said the dragon.

"Let's leave then," Ping said, turning back toward the gate. "If we hurry we might get back to the wharf before Jiang Bing casts off."

Danzi shook his head wearily. "Must find inn."

"What for? You're not thinking of spending the night here, are you?"

She had never seen the dragon look so tired.

"It's such an unnatural place and we haven't seen a soul the whole time we've been here. I'd rather sleep on a raft in the river."

As the half-light gave way to darkness, lights started

to appear in windows. Danzi led Ping toward one of the gray stone buildings. Ping cried out in surprise and fear when she saw a dark animal shape standing by the door.

"Innkeeper," Danzi said.

Ping looked closer. What she had at first taken to be some sort of strange beast, she realized was just a man. His hair hung down to his shoulders. He had no teeth, and a scar ran from the corner of his left eye to his chin. He wore a tunic over his gown that looked as if it were made from wolf hide. He glared at them suspiciously, but though he looked sour he didn't seem evil. Ping gave the man some copper coins, and he led them to a room.

Ping wasn't hungry, but Danzi insisted that she ask the man to bring them food. Sometime later the innkeeper brought them a covered clay pot. Ping opened it and steam rose from a stew thick with chicken pieces. It smelled good, with a hint of the herb that Jiang Bing used. Danzi ate a bowl of the stew. Ping didn't trust anything that was made in Wucheng. She dipped a spoon into the stew and sipped a little of it. It tasted quite good, but her stomach was churning, and she could only swallow a few mouthfuls.

With the strange town of Wucheng on the other side of a bolted door, Ping began to relax. All they had to do was wait out the night, then in the morning they could go back to the river. She found clean mattresses and blankets in a chest and laid them out on the floor. Danzi, back in his dragon shape, ignored his mattress and sat on the floor with his tail curled around him like a great lizard. Ping lay back on her mattress and was thinking about how strange it was to be sharing a room in an inn with a dragon, when Danzi stood up.

"Time to go outside," he said.

Ping groaned. "What do you want to go outside for? It could be dangerous."

"Must look for dragon stone."

"But we already walked all around the town. I couldn't feel Diao anywhere."

"This time not looking for Diao. Looking for dragon stone."

Ping turned her head away quickly as the dragon began to transform into the old man. She heard him unbolt the door and followed him out into the night.

Wucheng was very different at night. The streets were now busy with strange people going about their business. There were hooded figures whose faces were hidden. There were men wearing gowns painted with strange shapes. There was a woman whose hair was pure white.

"Alchemists, astrologers, and sorcerers not bad people," the dragon told her. "No need for Ping to fear them . . . only necromancers."

"What are necromancers?" Ping asked.

"Sorcerers who raise the dead to find out future."

Ping didn't know how to tell a necromancer from an alchemist, so she decided to be wary of everyone.

Many of the blank buildings Ping had seen during the day had opened up and become shops or food stalls. People were eating bowls of hot stew and plates of roasted meat. It almost looked like a normal town, except that in a normal town people would have been sleeping at that time of night, not shopping and eating as if it were the middle of the day.

Ping didn't have much experience with towns, but Wucheng was unlike any she had seen. The items for sale were different from the goods at the market in Chang'an. One stall sold dead insects—centipedes, spiders, beetles—all neatly pinned onto pieces of bamboo leaf in rows of ten or twice ten. Another sold rocks, some with glittering specks of silver and gold, or veins of red and green, others that were shaped like living things—a turtle, a pear, a fist. Other rocks looked like any that you could pick up off the ground, but the stallholder was calling out their magical properties.

On another stall there were bowls of organs bathed in blood—kidneys, hearts, lengths of gut. There were snakeskins, bears' ears, and jars containing teeth, claws, and eyes. The woman who was selling these things mistook Ping's wide-eyed, open-mouthed stare for interest in her wares.

"Tiger liver and bats' blood," she called out. "Fresh today."

The woman was a foreigner. Her hair was the same

color as the foxtails she was selling. Her skin was pale and her clothes glittered with spangles.

A man wearing wide trousers gathered at the ankles bought a few *shu* of monkey brain, then started bargaining with the stall keeper over some lumps of dried organs that Ping couldn't identify.

"It's the first dragon heart I've had for five years," the stallholder argued. "I couldn't possibly let you have it for less than five *jin*." She held out a piece of the shriveled flesh.

Ping felt the dragon next to her stiffen. No doubt his thoughts were the same as hers. Was it a piece of Lu Yu, Danzi's mate, hacked from her dead body by Lan? Had it found its way to Wucheng?

She moved on quickly, only to be confronted by a stallholder who sold live animals. He had a snake wound around his neck. In cages there were toads, a sad-eyed monkey, and a yellow bird with three legs. The man wore a purple gown painted with strange symbols.

"You're too young to be an alchemist or a sorceress," he said. He was looking at a spot on the ground, but Ping knew he was talking to her. "You must be a seer. Every seer needs an animal companion."

Ping tried to walk away, but he stepped in front of her. He had a dark, almost black face, white eyes, and wore a bamboo hat even though it was night. Ping realized he was blind.

"I have just the thing for you—light to carry, easy to

train, nonvenomous." He held up a mewing kitten by the scruff of its neck.

"I already have a pet," Ping said, pulling Hua from the folds of her gown.

The man felt the rat's sleek fur and let her pass.

Ping was aware that someone was watching from the shadows. She could see a face with a short, thick beard and a dark birthmark on one cheek. Ornaments hung from his ears. He was wearing a cloak, but beneath it she glimpsed another garment which shimmered. Whether he was staring at her or Hua or the blind man, she wasn't sure.

Ping quickly stuffed the rat back into her gown.

A faint whimpering sound, almost beyond the range of her hearing, was troubling her. She'd been hearing it ever since they'd entered the town. There was no point in asking the dragon. He wouldn't be able to hear it. She walked back to the man who was selling rocks.

"I'm looking for a large purple stone," she said. "Shaped like a melon and with a smooth surface. Have you seen such a stone?"

The man tilted his head to one side as if he were listening to something in the distance. His eyes were glassy. Then he shook his head as if trying to dislodge a fly from the end of his nose.

"I might have seen it, but if I had I wouldn't tell you," he laughed as if he'd heard an extremely funny joke.

"This is a pretty stone," he added, showing Ping a greenish crystalline rock. "When ground up and drunk with deer's milk, it enables you to last without sleep for a week."

Ping told him she wasn't interested and walked away.

"It's a waste of time, Danzi," Ping said. "I don't know where the stone is."

"Ping must search heart to find stone."

"I don't know how to do that," replied Ping wearily.

"Will be hidden. Must really want something, then will find. Has Ping never experienced this?"

"No," snapped Ping. "I don't know why you think I have. I'm a slave, not a sorceress."

The whimpering sound was getting louder. It set her teeth on edge. She wanted to get off the streets of Wucheng.

The dragon sighed. "Return to inn then."

Ping couldn't believe the dragon had given up so quickly, but she didn't argue. A stomachache that had been troubling her all day had become a sharp pain.

The innkeeper was outside the inn when they returned. He was chasing away a cat the same ginger color as the boatwoman's, shouting at it and waving a broom. Ping wished she were back on the boat, but since she couldn't be, at least she could be behind a locked door.

Ping could hear the regular hum and buzz of the

sleeping dragon's breathing before she'd had a chance to lie down. Though she was exhausted, she couldn't sleep. Her mind was whirling with the things she had seen that night and wouldn't allow sleep to empty it. Her stomach ached and the sound she'd been hearing all night was still there. It became a sharp and shrill keening that hurt her ears. She was still awake when gray light slowly defined the shape of the sleeping dragon. She heard others return to their rooms in the inn and then all was quiet. Her mouth was dry. She'd had nothing to drink since she'd eaten the salty stew. She tiptoed out of the room, barefoot and wearing nothing but the sacrificial shift with the green dragon painted on it, which she had kept as a nightdress.

Outside in the courtyard the air was still foul smelling and hazy with smoke, but the sky was brightening. It would soon be daylight and they would be able to leave Wucheng.

Ping hadn't admitted it to herself, but she had clung to half a hope that they would find the dragon stone. She was angry at the dragon for getting her hopes up, only to leave her disappointed. Why had he relied on her to reach out and find the dragon stone? Why hadn't he done something himself? He was the dragon. He was the one with the mystical powers, not her. It had all been a wild goose chase. They could have stayed on the boat with Jiang Bing.

The inn's courtyard was reassuringly normal. A

stove made of mud bricks was still warm to the touch. There was a well. A clay pot and the dishes from their meal had been washed and were upended to dry. Ping drew up a bucketful of water from the well. A ladle with a curved handle hung from a hook. She took it down, dipped it into the water, and drank thirstily. She couldn't relax, though. There was a nagging voice at the back of her mind. Not the dragon's voice, but the voice of her conscience.

She hadn't been truthful with the dragon. She recalled the other sensation she'd had in Chang'an. The one she hadn't told Danzi about. When the boy in the fur hat had stolen their coins, she had been furious. Somehow her anger had given her the power to reach out. She had been able to locate the boy among the thousands of people in the capital. Something inside her had drawn her to him. She hadn't told the dragon about the keening sound either.

Ping pictured the dragon stone, its beautiful purple depths, its milky swirls. She recalled its smooth, rounded shape and how she liked to feel it bumping against her hip as she walked. The memory of it filled her with sorrow. She missed the stone. She remembered the greedy pleasure in Diao's eyes when he first saw it back at Huangling. She imagined his dirty hands pawing its cool surface, the greasy hide of his clothing fouling its colors. A point of anger formed inside her, small at first but steadily growing. She was angry with

Diao for stealing her stone, for defiling its beauty. But she was angrier still with herself. She was the one who had let it go. She hadn't resisted when the guards at Fengjing took it from her.

The dragon stone didn't deserve to be in the hands of the dragon hunter or anyone who was evil enough to live in Wucheng. Ping had done nothing to try and get it back. She had allowed herself to be seduced by the rhythms of the river and the warmth of friendship.

The anger grew to the size of a taro root. Ping could feel the shape of it inside her. She didn't try to stop it: she let it grow until it filled her. The strength of it made her shake. She reached out with her mind, searching for the dragon stone the way she had searched for the fur hat. She wasn't expecting to feel anything. The dragon stone could have been anywhere in the empire. She was hoping at best for a faint whisper of knowledge, a vague shimmer that would give her a direction in which to search. What she felt was so strong it knocked her off her feet. It was a wave of emotion—fear, anger, and loneliness mixed together. The dragon stone was close, very close. The sound she'd been hearing all day was louder, shriller. It filled her mind. It seemed unbelievable, but she was sure now. The dragon stone was calling to her.

She got up, closed her eyes and turned in a circle until she felt a force draw her forward. She opened one eye just to make sure it wasn't the dragon pulling her back to the room by the front of her shift. There was no one there. It was as if strong cords were drawing her somewhere, pulling her. She held on to her anger. It led her out of the inn and into the deserted street. Wherever it was taking her she wanted to go.

Ping opened her eyes. A door had stopped her progress. She was outside one of the houses built of the pitted rock of the fire mountain. The cry of the dragon stone calling her was more urgent. The door wasn't locked. It creaked on its hinges as Ping slowly opened it. She held her breath as she entered the house, half expecting to find Diao inside. There was a sleeping figure curled up on a mattress. It wasn't Diao; it was the man Ping had seen earlier watching her from the shadows.

CHAPTER SIXTEEN

LOST AND FOUND

Ping could see horrible things scattered around the room—a tiger's tail, the skull of a dog or wolf, a dried liver. There were plants that had been roughly uprooted, piles of bleached bones. A dead baby goat was spread on the floor, its stomach cut open and its entrails pulled out. Movement startled her. In a cage there was a large bird that had lost most of its feathers. A rancid, sickening smell came from a cauldron on the hearth. On the wall were charts of the constellations and a circular bronze mirror. Ping thought she saw the face of an old wrinkled woman in it, then realized it was her own reflection.

The man was sleeping soundly, the memory of a smile on his lips. Ping saw that what she had thought was a birthmark on his cheek was in fact a tattoo. It was in the shape of a fantastic creature with a striped tail, a mane that was made up of flowers and open jaws full of sharp teeth. The man had a patch over one eye and his head was completely bald. His thick beard wasn't black but an orangey color. Unlike Master Lan's beard, which was a straggly bunch of long, black hairs, this beard was made up of short, stiff hairs, more like the pig bristle in the brush Lao Ma used for scrubbing. The ornaments that hung from the sleeping man's ears were birds carved from turquoise. A wooden staff lay beside the mattress, alongside an old cloak. He was wearing a tunic made of a fabric that shimmered even though there was little light in the room. Around his waist was a cord made up of five different colored threads braided together. In sleep, he didn't look evil, but the dragon stone's cry was filling her mind. It was a desperate cry of fear and pain. She knew that he was no harmless sorcerer.

A goblet lay on its side by the mattress. A dark stain spread out from it. She would have turned and tiptoed out of the room, if she was relying on her eyes alone. But she wasn't. The inner vision that had brought her to this terrible place told her to stay. The cry she could hear had become a shriek. She looked closer. In the half-light she could see that the man was clutching something to his chest. His fingernails were black and several inches long. She knew exactly what he was holding even though she couldn't see it clearly, even though it was wrapped in a piece of cloth.

In her mind Ping could see smooth curves, purple crystalline depths, beautiful milky streaks. She had found the stone. All she had to do was get it out of the grasp of the strange man. But how? The power suddenly dropped out of her like yolk from a broken eggshell. The cry faded to a faint whimper again. Ping had no experience in the world. Now, it seemed, she was required to come up with plans and plots on a daily basis. She had to make decisions and locate powers within her which she would rather leave hidden. She squatted on her haunches, feeling weary and stupid. The inner vision was gone and she'd run out of ideas. She was an ignorant slave girl again.

The smell of spilled wine drifted toward her. It was a familiar smell that reminded her of Master Lan's house. Ping suddenly realized that she'd had a lot of experience with situations like this. Master Lan had often fallen into a drunken sleep holding on to something—a dirty cup, a ripe peach, a chicken leg.

She had an idea.

The ladle from the well was still in her hand. She went over to the bird's cage and picked up one of the feathers that lay beneath it. The bird ruffled its few remaining feathers, but didn't make a sound. She had all the tools she needed.

When she had felt the vision within her, she had been fearless. Now she was terrified. She knelt down at the edge of the sorcerer's mattress and, with a trembling hand, reached out with the feather. She tickled the end of his nose. Just as she had hoped, the sorcerer, still asleep, reached up to swat away whatever it was that was disturbing his rest. His hand then flopped down beside his head. He now held the stone with only one hand. Ping gave him a moment to settle back into sleep. Up close, his tattoo was even more sinister. The creature's mane wasn't made of flowers, but skulls. She took up the ladle and grasped hold of the spoon end. With it she reached toward the stone. She hooked the curved handle into the loose weave of the cloth that it was wrapped in. With the tiniest of movements she gently pulled it toward her. The man's fingers, relaxed in sleep, allowed the stone to be pulled away. When it was almost out of his grasp, the bird in the cage let out a miserable squawk. The man's long, black fingernails dug into the cloth. His one eye opened. It was staring right at Ping. She didn't move.

The man's eye was an unnatural color, dull yellow, like urine, but glazed and unfocused. Ping was so close she could smell his foul breath. She could see the ginger pig-bristles of his beard, the holes pierced in his ears. She realized that the ornaments hanging from his ears weren't birds, but bats. The pale dawn light seemed too bright for him. He muttered an animal sound like an angry goat, and flung his arm across his face. Ping waited, not daring to move a muscle, until the sorcerer's breathing became regular, with a faint snore at every intake of air. Then once again she pulled gently at the dragon stone. His fingers uncurled. The cloth came free from his grasp. Ping pulled it toward her until it was close enough for her to pick up. She held the stone in her arms for a moment. It made her heart sing with happiness.

Ping's weariness disappeared. She was filled with strength, enough to run all the way to Ocean, but she made herself creep slowly out of the room. She ran down the street to the inn and returned to the room where the dragon was still sleeping. She could barely stop herself from shouting out loud. Couldn't he feel the stone's presence? Couldn't he hear the stone singing like she could?

"Danzi," she said. "I've got it! I've found the dragon stone."

She unwrapped the stone and her smile faded. The dragon stone was dark and dull and covered with brown blotches. The swirls weren't milky white, but gray and crisscrossed with bloodred veins. It took a while for Danzi to awake. He didn't seem to know where he was. Then he saw the stone.

"Who had stone?" he asked.

Ping described the sorcerer's tattooed face.

"Necromancer," the dragon said.

"We have to get it away from this place."

"Now even more important to get stone to Ocean."

Ping didn't care where they went as long as it was away from Wucheng. She was halfway out the door.

"Ping should dress." The dragon's voice was calm in her mind.

Ping looked down at herself. She was still barefoot and wearing the sacrificial shift. She quickly pulled on her gown, her socks and shoes, packed up their few belongings, and put the dragon stone in the reed basket. The dragon lumbered creakily to his feet. Ping didn't wait for him.

Outside, the street was empty. The inhabitants of Wucheng had all disappeared with the darkness. Ping ran toward the gates. Six people were standing across the street, barring her way. She stopped. They were strange, thin figures with fluttering gray robes and long straggly hair that blew about their heads even though there was no wind. They had blank staring faces. There was something else about them. They were floating just above the ground.

"Sentry spirits," the dragon said. "They will warn the necromancer."

Ping felt the back of her neck prickle. The necromancer was behind her, his face like a thundercloud. He held a staff in his hand. Ping clutched the dragon stone close to her, closed her eyes, and ran. She felt an icy chill, but she kept running through the eerie people—straight through them, as if their bodies were made of mist.

When she reached the gates, she found they were shut. They looked as heavy as lead. She could never have opened them—even if they hadn't been locked. Something sharp and shiny skimmed past her ear and dug into the dark wood of the gate. It was a disc, made of bright metal with three barbs radiating from it, curved and sharp like cats' claws. She turned. The necromancer was standing in the middle of the street, hurling more of the barbed discs at her. Ping ducked out of the way of the first and the second, only to find a third spinning straight toward her. It missed her body by less than an inch, but pinned her gown to the gate. The necromancer pointed his staff at the dragon. The force from it threw Danzi against the wall, winding him.

"Ping must stop him," the dragon gasped.

"I'm not strong enough," Ping replied.

"Nothing under Heaven is softer than water," Danzi said. "Yet it can overcome the hard and the strong."

The necromancer was walking toward her, his eyes fixed on the dragon stone. She hugged the stone close to her with one hand. It was shrieking with fear again. She held up her free hand as if to stop him. He laughed at her, sneering and scornful. He had no doubt he could take the dragon stone from her as easily as taking a jujube from a baby.

He raised his staff. Ping felt the anger grow within her again. Her body tingled from head to foot. She felt her *qi* focus in a rush that filled her within seconds. It coursed down her arm and burst out through her fingertips. The necromancer was thrown to the ground by its invisible force. He scrambled to his knees and pointed his staff at her. Ping was still pinned to the gate. Before the necromancer had a chance to summon his own power, Danzi appeared at her side and swiped at the necromancer with his talons. The man looked down as blood oozed through his shimmering tunic.

"Can you fly over the wall?" Ping asked.

"Cannot," he replied "Need height to take off. Must climb over."

Ping looked at the sharp rocks that made up the wall. "Those rocks will cut me to shreds."

"Cut human flesh," the dragon said. "Not dragon scales."

The necromancer was on his feet again. This time the force from Ping's fingertips only made him stagger. She slung the reed basket over her shoulder and leaped onto the dragon's back, clinging to his horns and clamping her knees around his neck. The jagged rocks provided plenty of footholds and the dragon laboriously climbed the wall, hauling himself and Ping up over the vicious rocks. They reached the top of the wall. The river, on the other side, was no more than a *li* away. Behind her, the necromancer was holding his chest, summoning the power to break the lock.

Ping felt flapping around her head. The two crows they'd seen when they first arrived at Wucheng were pecking at her. She held up her arms to protect her eyes from the stabbing black beaks. One punctured her arm, piercing deep into her flesh. She cried out in pain, but the angry rumbling roar of the dragon drowned her cry. The birds flapped away, and Danzi opened his wings. Ping's red stitches were still holding the shreds of the left wing in place. The crows returned, ignoring the dragon's roaring this time.

Danzi swiped a forepaw in the direction of the birds. Blood dripped from a wound ripped open in one crow's chest by his talons. The bird fell to the ground. The other crow pecked at the red thread, out of reach of Danzi's talons. Roused by the smell of blood, Hua emerged from Ping's gown and ran along the dragon's outstretched wing to where the crow was pulling apart Ping's needlework. The bird saw the rat coming, flapped its wings and took off. Hua launched himself at the crow and clamped his teeth around the bird's foot as it lifted into the air. The crow flapped off with the rat hanging on to its foot.

Ping lost sight of Hua as Danzi leaped off the wall. The ground came up fast to meet them as he glided down on the other side. The dragon landed clumsily but safely. Ping looked up and saw the crow flapping higher in the air with Hua still dangling beneath it. The crow let out an agonized squawk and Hua was suddenly plummeting to the ground. Ping ran to catch him. She tripped on the hem of her gown. Hua was plunging toward the earth and Ping couldn't get to her feet. A dragon paw reached out and caught Hua no more than two inches from the ground. Ping and the dragon ran toward the river.

When they reached the wharf, Ping was delighted to see Jiang Bing's boat still tied up. The boatwoman looked up, surprised to see Ping running toward her with a dragon at her side.

"We must leave now," said Ping as she scrambled aboard the boat. "There's a necromancer after us. I'll explain later."

The dragon labored down the ladder and collapsed exhausted on the deck. Ping glanced toward the town walls, but could see no sign of the necromancer.

"I was just about to leave anyway," said Jiang Bing calmly.

She looked around the wharf. She didn't call or whistle, but the ginger cat appeared from behind some sacks of grain and leaped aboard.

Jiang Bing untied the boat. Ping helped her push it away from the wharf. The boatwoman poled the boat until the current grabbed it, sucking them into the middle of the river. Wucheng began to shrink and Ping breathed in the air rushing past them with relief. Hua, who still had the crow's foot in his mouth, scrambled out of Danzi's grasp. The cat was between him and the safety of Ping's gown. He ran up the dragon's leg and disappeared behind one of the reversed scales beneath his chin.

"It's wonderful to be back on the river," Ping said.

She was still clutching the reed basket to her. She turned to Jiang Bing with a smile.

The boatwoman's face was grim. She was looking at the dragon.

"I'll give you gold if you tell no one about this," Ping said.

"I don't want gold," said the boatwoman in a harsh voice that Ping didn't recognize.

"What do you want?" asked Ping.

"I want the dragon stone. It belongs to my master."

Ping couldn't believe what she was hearing.

The ginger cat strolled over to Jiang Bing. Ping noticed there was blood dripping from a wound in its belly. The air around the cat shimmered and flickered. The animal twisted and contorted. Its fur transformed into flesh and cloth. Ping was mesmerized by the horrible transformation even though it made her feel sick. Before her eyes, the cat became a man. He was dressed in a dark cloak, but something beneath it caught the morning sun. He had a patch over one eye, a tattoo on one cheek, and a ginger beard. It was the necromancer. Jiang Bing moved to stand next to him. She looked at him with admiration and then at Ping with scorn. Ping staggered to the side of the boat and vomited over the side.

"Give me the dragon stone," said the necromancer as he moved toward Ping.

"Danzi!" Ping called out, clutching the stone to her. "Help me!"

The dragon staggered to his feet. He tried to summon his *qi* power, but he couldn't. He was too weak.

The necromancer's fingers reached out to the dragon stone. His long, black fingernails hooked into the weave of the reed basket. He pulled it from Ping's grasp. She let the basket go but held on to the stone. The black fingernails reached out again and scratched the surface of the stone with a sound that set Ping's teeth on edge. The necromancer's hands stretched out to enclose the stone. The stone screamed. Ping knew that she could never let this man have her stone. She leaped over the side of the boat and into the foaming yellow water. The necromancer gave out a strangled, angry cry.

"Don't let her go," he ordered Jiang Bing.

The boatwoman didn't hesitate. She plunged into the water after Ping.

Ping couldn't swim. She felt the suffocating water all around her, eager to fill her nose and mouth and stop her from breathing. The swift current pulled at her, carrying her along as easily as if she were a leaf. She knew that she was going to drown. She didn't care. She'd much rather die than allow the necromancer to get hold of the dragon stone. Ping wasn't afraid of death. She felt a clear, strong emotion that she couldn't put a name to. Instead of feeling cold, this feeling filled her with warmth. She smiled. The boatwoman swam up to her, struggling through the water. Ping's smile faded. No one was going to have the stone but her.

She pulled up her left leg and kicked out as hard as she could. Her foot struck the boatwoman on the nose. Jiang Bing cried out with pain as blood mingled with the yellow water. She spluttered and her arms seemed to forget how to swim. The boatwoman disappeared beneath the turbulent waters.

Holding on to the stone with a grip like a vise, Ping waited for its weight to drag her beneath the irresistible waters. She didn't sink, though. The stone was floating, bobbing along through the water like an apple, carrying Ping with it. Ping strained to keep her head above the water. She discovered that the less she resisted, the easier it was. She felt the cool hardness of the stone in her hands and let her body go limp. She was a leaf. She would let the river take her wherever it wanted.

She had been carried only a few *li* when she and the stone were washed into a side stream with other floating things—branches, fish entrails, rubbish from Wucheng. She crawled through the dirty yellow froth at the river's edge and onto the riverbank. She wiped the scum from the stone. Its purple depths were still dull, but the brown blotches were fading. The red veins that ran through the gray swirls didn't seem quite as thick. It would be all right. She would find arsenic and red cloud herb and heal it.

Ping lay stretched out on the riverbank, holding the dragon stone close to her. She was alive and she still had the stone. She had defeated the necromancer and his accomplice. The sun was just above the horizon, sending out shafts of orange light in her direction. The world was a beautiful place. She sat up and watched the sky turn from orange to pink. Then she realized she had forgotten something. Something important. The dragon was still on board the boat with the necromancer. And so was Hua.

CHAPTER SEVENTEEN

STRENGTH AND WEAKNESS

Ping's head was spinning. Danzi and Hua were more important than the stone. They were her friends. Without Danzi she would still be at Huangling. Without Hua she would probably have died of misery years ago. But something inside her was telling her that the dragon stone was more important. If she went back to rescue her friends, the dragon stone would be within reach of the necromancer again. She stared into the stone's depths. She lay her cheek against its cool surface. She couldn't bear to lose it. And yet she couldn't leave her friends either. She would have to work out a way of saving them all.

She didn't have the chance to think of even the beginnings of a plan before the necromancer's boat came into view. He was standing at the stern, holding on to the rudder and scanning the riverbank. The dragon was splayed out on the deck in full view of any-one who happened to pass. Each leg was tied to the side of the boat as if he were an ox ready for slaughter. The necromancer probably thought that Ping had drowned like Jiang Bing. He was looking for the dragon stone. Ping jumped to her feet.

"Over here," she shouted, holding the stone above her head. "Is this what you're looking for?"

The necromancer looked at her in astonishment. Not only was she still alive, she was also offering the dragon stone to him. He leaned on the rudder and steered the boat toward the riverbank. The inlet into which Ping had floated with the rubbish from Wucheng was too shallow to moor the boat. The necromancer threw the anchor overboard. The boat was pulled up short. The current tugged at it, but the anchor held firm. The necromancer picked up the gangplank from the deck and lay it over the side. It was too short to reach the bank, but it reached the shallows. No sooner had it come to rest among the fish heads and melon rinds than the necromancer was striding down it toward the riverbank.

Ping didn't know what to do. She had managed to take the necromancer by surprise in Wucheng, and her anger had helped her focus her *qi*. Now she didn't feel angry, she just felt scared. She had no skills to beat such a powerful sorcerer, no weapon except for her bronze knife. She tucked the stone into the crook of her right arm, took out her knife, and held it firmly in her left hand.

The necromancer was standing in front of her. He laughed at her blade, which was no more than four inches long and designed for cutting vegetables. He drew a long, curved sword from a scabbard. Its edge glistened menacingly in the sunlight. The necromancer swung it in her direction. He was weak, she could tell. His tunic was soaked with blood. He had spent five days on the boat in the shape of a cat. She knew how shape-changing drained Danzi's strength. No doubt raising the sentry spirits had also sapped strength from him. Ping might not have had sorcerer's skills, but she was quick. She ducked out of the way. The blade dug deep into the muddy riverbank. The necromancer grabbed the sword hilt with both hands to pull it out. Something small and gray streaked down the gangplank. It was Hua. When he got to the end of the plank he leaped into the air, trying to cross the shallows and the mud in one leap. It was too far. As he started to fall toward the muddy bank, he spread his legs wide and glided to one side, hooking his claws into the nearest thing. It was the back of the necromancer's gown. The sorcerer turned and saw the rat running up his leg. He let go his hold on the sword and swatted behind him, trying to dislodge Hua. Hua saw the waving fingers and latched on to one of them instead. The necromancer's struggles had only embedded him further in the mud. His feet were buried up to the ankles. He tried to shake the rat off his finger. Hua wasn't going to let go. He bit deeper into the necromancer's flesh until blood flowed from the wound.

Ping remembered something that the dragon had said to her back in Chang'an. It had seemed meaningless at the time, but now it made perfect sense.

"Recognizing one's limitations is wisdom," he had said.

Ping's limitations were as clear as a mountain stream. She had no way of overcoming the skilled necromancer. He might have been weakened, but he was far from spent. He was refocusing his energies, and would soon free himself from the mud and overpower her. He would have the dragon stone. She had to escape.

Ping ran to the gangplank.

"Come on, Hua!" she shouted as she raced up to the boat.

The necromancer had pulled one foot and his sword from the mire. He tried again to shake the rat from his finger. This time he was successful. Hua sailed in a high arc, his legs scrabbling in the air. This time there was nothing for Hua to grab hold of. He landed in the water. The necromancer had now freed both his feet and was only three strides from the end of the gangplank. Ping placed the dragon stone gently in a coil of rope. She needed both hands. She lifted the boat end of the plank and threw it into the river.

The sorcerer hesitated momentarily at the water's edge, unwilling to wade into the water. Ping still had her bronze knife in her left hand. She hacked at the anchor rope. Hua was swimming toward the boat, his little legs paddling so fast they were a blur. Ping had kept her blade sharp. With three slashes she severed the rope. Hua was still an arm's length from the prow. Ping leaned over the side, but couldn't reach him. The necromancer dived into the water, trying to grab the end of the severed rope.

Now released from the tugging anchor, the boat swept eagerly into the current. The rope, slippery with algae, slid out of the necromancer's grasp. Hua bobbed helplessly as the boat passed him. The boat surged down the river. Ping ran to the stern, unable to do anything as Hua was engulfed by the boat's wake. Then something long and green flopped out over the stern of the boat and into the water. It was the dragon's tail.

The tip landed close to where the spluttering rat surfaced. Hua hooked his claws under the green scales. The dragon pulled his tail onto the boat. It slapped onto the deck. Hua lay next to it, wet and exhausted. The current whisked the boat away from the furious necromancer, still splashing in the shallows.

"Are you all right, Danzi?" Ping called out as she made her way to the dragon. The boat rocked and swayed. Ping was thrown to the deck. The dragon turned his head.

"Escape."

Ping crawled to the stern and grabbed hold of the

rudder. It took all of her strength to guide it away from the furious central current to a slower part of the river closer to the southern bank. Hua was not fond of water or of being hurled through the air. As soon as he had recovered his balance and shook off as much of the river water as he could, he clambered up Ping's gown and burrowed into its folds.

Ping had to keep both hands firmly on the rudder. Her arms were aching after only an hour, but she didn't dare stop to rest. She glanced back at the dragon, still tied onto the deck, stretched out like a sacrificial goat. She looked anxiously at the dragon stone nestled in the coil of rope.

"I can't stop, Danzi," she shouted. "We have to get as far away from the necromancer as possible."

The dragon made a low sound. It was just the faintest tinkle, like wind chimes stirred by the merest whisper of a breeze.

"The sapling is small, but none can defeat it," he whispered.

It wasn't much, but Ping knew that the dragon, although weak, was all right.

It was the longest day of Ping's life. The strength of the river's current meant that she couldn't let go of the rudder or she would lose control of the boat. In truth, the river had more control of the boat than she did. No matter how hard she tried to keep the boat close to the riverbank, it kept finding its way back to the middle of the stream. In the end Ping let the river have its way, but she still needed all her strength to keep the boat coursing along the central current. It was dangerous, but Ping was glad of the extra speed. The faster they traveled, the less likely it would be that the necromancer would catch up with them.

Ping had to keep her eyes focused on the river ahead. She would have liked to watch the bamboo groves and the villages on the distant shores, but she had to look out for rocks and other boats. She couldn't rest. She was hot and thirsty. She was tired and hungry. But she couldn't stop for food or water. Her arms ached with the strain of holding the boat to its course. She glanced at the motionless dragon, tethered to the boat.

She couldn't stop to free Danzi.

As the day wore on, the sun shone from a cloudless sky. It became harder for Ping to concentrate. She fell asleep where she sat at the rudder and was woken by the cries of men. She looked up and found that they were bearing down on another boat, which was fighting its way upstream with the help of four men with poles, two oxen on the riverbank roped to the boat, and a tall sail angled to catch the breeze. Ping wrenched the rudder and steered away from the other boat and its dismayed boatmen. She had to stay awake. She practiced counting up to a thousand. She sang aloud the only two songs she knew—a children's rhyme that she had learned from Lao Ma and a drinking song that Master Lan had been fond of singing.

At last the sun was low in the sky behind them. Ping allowed herself to believe that they had left the necromancer behind.

"I think it's safe to stop now," she called out to the dragon, though she had heard no sound from him for several hours.

Making the decision to stop was one thing. Actually stopping the boat was far more difficult. The anchor was still buried in the riverbed, back where she'd had her confrontation with the necromancer. Summoning her last *shu* of strength, Ping steered the boat toward the southern bank of the river. The current there was slower. Tall stands of bamboo arched over the river's edge, dipping and swaying in the breeze like bowing officials. Her hands were shaking from holding on to the rudder. Sharp pains were shooting up her arms. She forced herself to keep going. She steered with one hand. With the other she was just able to reach a length of hempen rope, neatly coiled on the deck.

Holding the rudder under her arm, she made a loop in one end of the rope and tied the other to the stern. She tried to throw the loop around the smaller stalks of bamboo, but the rope just slipped off the bending stems. She tried again and again with the same result. She waited for something more substantial to appear that she could throw the rope around—an overhanging tree, an abandoned boat, a protruding rock.

The sun disappeared, the light faded. Finally, a broken jetty loomed out of the twilight. The planks at the end had rotted away and the uprights were sticking out of the water. Ping threw her looped rope and missed the first one. She knew that this would be the last chance she had to tie up the boat before nightfall. She let go of the rudder. The current started to tug the boat away from the bank and toward the faster flowing center.

Ping stood at the stern with the loop of rope in her hand. As they passed the second upright, she threw it out. The loop of rope hung in the air for a second and then fell around the wooden stake. The boat continued on its way and then was pulled up abruptly. The wooden post leaned as the tugging boat threatened to pull it over. Ping quickly tied another rope to the prow and, jumping out onto the broken jetty, secured the boat.

Once she was sure the boat was firmly tied up, she hurried to Danzi. He didn't move. She untied the ropes that held the dragon's legs spread out. She pulled water from the river in a bucket and threw it over the unconscious dragon's head. Her own arms were shaking from the strain of holding on to the rudder all day. She forced open Danzi's huge mouth and trickled water into it. His long tongue was as dry as a strip of leather. She drank some of the water herself.

Ping continued to dribble water into his mouth and

gently scratched the dragon under his chin. Slowly he revived. Ping heard the familiar voice in her mind for the first time in what seemed like an age.

"Is stone well?"

Ping felt her way to the coil of rope where she'd left the dragon stone. She picked it up. The sky was black. The crescent moon was slender.

"I don't know," she said. "It's too dark to see."

Ping made a small fire. It seemed to take forever to produce a flame. Then she lit a lamp. She held the stone in the circle of lamplight. Its surface was dark purple. The creamy swirls in its depths could have been made from the missing piece of the moon. The red veins winding through it had turned a deep maroon. They only made it more beautiful. The dragon struggled painfully to sit up on his haunches. He held his great head close to the stone, peering at it as if he were trying to see through the stone into its center.

"It is all right," was all Danzi said.

They both sat staring into the stone's purple depths for some minutes. Then Ping turned her mind to food. There were stores of food on board—grain, dried fish, onions. She began to make a fish stew. She was just about to sprinkle in some of the dried leaves that the boatwoman had been fond of adding to her cooking, when Danzi reached out a taloned paw and stopped her.

"What is this?"

"It's some sort of herb."

Danzi picked up the jar of leaves and sniffed. He then threw the jar and its contents into the river.

"Why did you do that?"

"Chinaberry leaves," the dragon said. "Poisonous to dragons. Slows heart, makes weak and melancholy."

Ping groaned. This was more of the boatwoman's treachery. Ping had been fooled completely by Jiang Bing's false friendship.

"She put these leaves in all our food," Ping said. "There were some in the meal we had in Wucheng as well. The necromancer must have paid the innkeeper to do it."

Ping remembered how slow and vague the dragon had been. How easily he had given up the search for the dragon stone in Wucheng. How he had made little attempt to resist the necromancer on the boat.

"Why didn't the leaves have the same effect on me?" she asked.

"Small amounts give humans nothing more than upset stomach."

Ping recalled the queasy feeling and the stomach-ache she'd had that night at Wucheng.

Ping and Danzi ate their meal in silence. Hua ate some of the stew, even though he wasn't fond of fish. The dragon curled up and went to sleep immediately. Hua made his bed in the coil of Danzi's tail. Ping wished sleep would be as eager to visit her. She could have slept in the cabin, but chose to lie on the deck instead. Though the day had been sunny, once the sun disappeared it had grown cold again. She wrapped herself in the boatwoman's blanket and stared up at the clear night sky. The moon was making its way toward the fire star, which was the celestial dragon's heart. Ping remembered how happy she'd felt to be on the boat before they'd reached Wucheng just a few days ago. Before she'd learned that the boatwoman's friendship had been false.

Though she tried to keep them on other things, Ping's thoughts kept returning to Jiang Bing and how willing she'd been to trust the boatwoman. She would be much more cautious in the future. She would still be courteous to people she met, but she would guard her trust very closely.

CHAPTER EIGHTEEN

CHANCE MEETING

The dragon regained his strength more quickly than Ping expected. He wouldn't eat until the chinaberry was out of his system, but the next day he was strong enough to spend an hour or two in his old-man shape at the rudder. This gave Ping time to explore the boat. She found her reed basket containing the remains of the red cloud herb ointment and rubbed it into the dragon stone. Danzi wanted her to put some on the livid wounds on her arm where the crow had pecked her, but she refused to waste any on herself. She found a spare anchor and fishing equipment in a chest. Among the boatwoman's things were spare clothes and a bamboo sun hat. The necromancer had left more interesting things behind—a bamboo book, a bundle of yarrow sticks, and a gourd full of blood.

As they continued to travel east, Ping and Danzi took turns steering the boat. Ping had many questions that she wanted to ask the dragon.

"Why didn't you tell me that necromancers could change shape as well as dragons?"

"Didn't ask."

Ping smiled. It was good to have the dragon back to his infuriating self again. Hua was stretched out on the deck in the sun. Without the ginger cat on board, he seemed to be comfortable with sailing.

"Why did the necromancer want the dragon stone?" Ping had the stone in her lap.

"Can use for magic spells," replied the dragon.

"What sort of spells?"

"Nothing of interest to Ping."

Ping didn't believe him. The stone was changing. Not only had its colors altered, it was also bigger. It would only just fit in the basket now. There were also the sounds that she could hear in her mind along with the dragon's voice. Not the terrible, painful sounds she'd heard at Wucheng, but soft sounds like a cat purring. Whatever magical powers the stone had, Ping was sure it had some connection to her.

"Back in Wucheng, I had this . . . strength," Ping said, still hardly able to believe what had happened. "I'm not sure where it came from."

Danzi nodded. "Ping concentrated *qi*. Used its power."

"But I don't know how that happened."

"Anger."

"So can I only concentrate my *qi* when I'm angry?"

"No. Ping must learn to harness *qi* whenever needed, angry or not."

"How will I do that?"

The tinkling sound of a happy dragon drifted toward Ping. "Must learn to control breath, focus mind, and train body to strengthen *qi*. Danzi will teach."

They were on a quiet stretch of the river. Danzi could stay in his dragon shape for most of the time. He demonstrated breathing exercises that Ping had to learn and practice every morning.

"Best to do exercises at sunrise," he explained. "Air has most *qi* then. Turn to face east and take deep breaths. Fill body with golden *qi* from rising sun."

Over the following days, Danzi taught her slow movements of the hands that would enable her to concentrate the *qi*. There were other exercises involving slowly twisting her body and arching her arms.

"Must learn to focus mind," he told her as they sailed along the river. "Shut out all other thoughts."

No matter how hard she tried to concentrate on focusing her *qi*, she couldn't stop other thoughts creeping into her mind—what they were going to have for their midday meal, how many silkworms it took to make a silk gown, why boats didn't sink.

"Ping must be hesitant as if crossing thin ice, yielding as melting ice, blank as uncarved wood."

Danzi's instructions made no sense.

"I can't," Ping said.

"Must do exercises for mind as well as for body," Danzi said.

He told her to imagine a garden full of peonies and then count them. Ping remembered seeing peonies in the imperial garden at Huangling. They had died when the gardener forgot to water them one hot summer.

"What color should the peonies be?" asked Ping. She frowned as she tried to dispel the picture she had in her mind of the few wilting peonies at Huangling and imagine a garden full of flourishing flowers.

There were other exercises that she had to practice including counting backward from five hundred and imagining following the path of a beetle on a distant hill.

"Should feel tingling all through body," the dragon said.

Ping remembered experiencing that feeling when she had attacked the necromancer. The tingling feeling had rushed into her without her having to do any exercises.

"Can't you just do something to make me angry?" she asked.

The dragon shook his head. "*Qi* concentrated by anger is dangerous and difficult to control."

As they continued down the river, Ping practiced the breathing exercises and the body movements for hours each day. She concentrated on imaginary fields of peonies, distant beetles, and backward numbers, but she could summon nothing more than a faint prickling in her left thumb.

"Takes much practice," Danzi said. He was sitting quietly in the sun while Hua checked the dragon's ears for centipedes. After their recent adventures, the rat no longer slept in Ping's gown. He preferred to rest behind one of the dragon's reversed scales.

Ping had stopped worrying about the necromancer following them. She anchored the boat each evening well away from villages and harbors. She cut tender bamboo shoots from the soft muddy ground to add to their meal. Danzi searched for ginseng root, mustard leaves, and yellow pea flowers. These plants, he said, would help strengthen her *qi*. He also caught birds to roast.

"Will the birds strengthen my *qi*?" Ping asked as she picked the meat from the bones.

"No," Danzi replied. "But taste good."

After a week, Ping was able to focus enough *qi* to produce the tingling sensation in her hands. She could then concentrate the power and use it to move a chopstick across the deck of the boat. Danzi seemed impressed, but Ping thought it was going to be a very long time before she could harness enough *qi* to do anything useful.

The pace of the Yellow River was slowing. Steering the boat required less effort. The yellow waters were less turbulent, but were still carrying the little boat ever closer to Ocean.

"Why doesn't everyone learn to focus their *qi*?" Ping asked.

"Not everyone can do this."

Ping thought about that for a moment. She stared out at the bamboo plants that were crowded on the river bank like eager spectators jostling to watch a boat race.

"But I can do it," she said, feeling proud of her meager skill. "Just a bit."

The dragon nodded. "With practice will have control."

"Why can I do this and other people can't?"

Danzi's red lips softened as he made the tinkling wind chime sound.

"Ping is very special," he said. "Special, but slow to understand."

"Understand what?"

"Why Danzi chose Ping as companion."

"You didn't choose me. There was no one else . . . Lao Ma was too old and you certainly wouldn't have picked Master Lan to travel with."

"Chose Ping because she is Dragon Keeper."

"Me? A Dragon Keeper? Don't be silly."

"Remember Danzi said Dragon Keepers have attributes?"

"I remember."

"Dragon Keepers are left-handed. Hear dragon speech, can harness qi, and have second sight."

"What's second sight?"

"Ability to sense presence of certain people—friends and enemies—to read people's hearts, sometimes to foretell coming events."

Ping remembered how she'd known when Diao was nearby and how she had known that something bad would happen in Chang'an.

"But I couldn't read Jiang Bing's heart. I don't know what's going to happen tomorrow."

"These are skills that take lifetime to master."

"Anyway, you said Dragon Keepers were all from the Huan family or the Yu family."

Danzi nodded.

"But my name . . . "

"Ping doesn't know family name."

"Do you, Danzi? Did you know that I belonged to one of the Dragon Keeper families?"

The dragon shook his head. "Did not know. Chance brought Ping and Danzi together."

"But you saw the signs in me."

The dragon shook his head again. "Danzi also slow to understand. Couldn't believe Dragon Keeper was a girl."

Ping tried to take in what Danzi had just told her. It didn't make sense. How could she be such a special person, someone with skills that other people didn't have? They were passing a village and Danzi was in his old-man shape. People certainly weren't always what they seemed. But surely if she was such an exceptional person she would have known.

"I'm a slave," she said. "I can't be a Dragon Keeper."

"Attainment comes as a surprise to the humble."

"But you said they were always boys."

"True. Has never been female Dragon Keeper before."

Ping shook her head. "You must have made a mistake."

"Ping has all signs. Didn't trust signs at first, but Ping has proved herself. Saved Danzi from necromancer."

The dragon reached into one of his reversed scales with the talons of his right forepaw. He pulled something out. It was a bronze disc about the same diameter as a peach half. On one side there was a design etched into it. The other side was undecorated but so highly polished that Ping could see Danzi's reflection in it.

"All Dragon Keepers caring for Danzi have carried this mirror."

"How many Keepers have you had?"

"Many. Men's lives short compared to dragon's."

"Master Lan didn't have it," Ping said.

"Lan false Dragon Keeper. Even Wang Cao not true Dragon Keeper."

"But he was left-handed and he could understand you."

"But no second sight."

He held the mirror out. The design on the back was a dragon coiled around a central knob. The dragon had one paw out to grasp the knob as if it were a precious pearl. Ping reached for the mirror. The dragon pulled it back.

"If Ping accepts this token from Danzi, she will be bound to him . . . and his heirs."

"Of course I'll—"

"Decision should not be taken in haste," the dragon said. "Is binding for life."

Danzi tilted the mirror and the sun's rays deflected off it and into Ping's eyes. It was too bright to look at.

"Mirror can be used as signal. Dragons are hard of hearing, but if Dragon Keeper flashes mirror, dragon can see it from many *li* away."

Danzi held out the mirror to Ping again, the shiny side facing up. Ping could see her own reflection. There was nothing unusual about her face. Nothing that made her look any different from any other girl in the empire. But in her heart she knew the dragon was right. It was as if a secret place inside her that had always been closed, had opened. She felt pride swell her chest. A few months ago she had been a nameless slave; now she had discovered that she was a special person. She would accept the token. It was her destiny.

She was just about to say so to the dragon, when there was a terrible sound of splintering wood, and Ping was thrown forward. She skidded along the deck until she slammed into the cabin. Danzi was thrown overboard. Ping was winded. She got to her feet, holding her bruised ribs. A huge boat towered above her. The biggest boat Ping had ever seen. They had crashed into it.

Ping almost fell over again, because the deck was sloping sharply. The boat was sinking. She looked up at the other boat. It was ten times longer than their own small craft and as high as two houses. It was freshly painted shiny black and decorated with colorful flags and silk banners. It seemed to be undamaged. Ping didn't have time to admire the magnificent boat, though. The slope of the deck was getting steeper. The prow had disappeared below the water.

Ping quickly picked up the basket containing the stone and whatever else she could carry—the good cooking pot, her sun hat, a bag of lentils. The water was lapping over her feet. Danzi was back in his dragon shape, splashing toward the riverbank. Ping jumped over the side. The water was deeper than she'd thought. Her gown billowed up around her. Her feet couldn't find the bottom. The heavy cooking pot dragged her down. But she didn't want to let go and lose it. The water rose over her head. Then she felt hands under her arms, and she was lifted up out of the water and deposited on the river bank. She coughed up river water.

"Thank you," she said, though she had sandy water in her eyes and couldn't see who had saved her. "It was kind of you to pull me out of the river, but I'm safe now. You can let go."

She wiped the water out of her eyes. On either side of her were guards in red uniforms with leather caps and vests. They weren't smiling and they weren't about to let go of her. More guards were standing in front of her. They were all pointing swords or spears in her direction. Other guards were surrounding the dripping dragon with swords drawn. They stared at this creature, which had appeared like something out of a story. Danzi roared at them, a deep rumbling like metal being beaten. He tried to knock the weapons from their hands, but he couldn't summon the strength. The weapons were all made of iron.

Ping tried to concentrate her *qi* so that she could use it to throw the guards aside. She closed her eyes to picture a field of peonies, but could only conjure up an image of the few wilting plants at Huangling. She tried to count backward from five hundred, but kept losing her place and having to start again. A gurgling sound was distracting her. The boat that had carried them all the way along the Yellow River was stern up in the water. As she watched, air bubbled around the boat, and it disappeared below the surface.

"This is the sorceress of Huangling!" the captain shouted at the quaking guards. "She has stolen the imperial dragon. There's a decree that she is to be captured and beheaded."

The guards holding Ping tightened their grip. They took her basket from her shoulder. Ping tried to fight them off, but there were too many of them.

"We must capture the dragon as well," ordered the captain of the guards.

The guards surrounding Danzi stepped cautiously toward him. One of them had a length of rope. Danzi bared his huge teeth, threw back his head and let out a deep rumbling roar that sounded like thunder when a storm is overhead. He struck out with his talons. The guards all jumped back. One of them was clutching his arm. Blood oozed between his fingers as he tried to stop the bleeding from a deep cut. More guards appeared. They were carrying crossbows. They formed a circle around the dragon.

"Wait," said Ping. "You mustn't hurt him."

The guards didn't take any notice of her.

"Take aim," said the captain of the guards.

The guards pointed their crossbows at the dragon.

"No!" shouted Ping. "The dragon belongs to the Emperor. Killing the one remaining imperial dragon would be punishable by death."

The guards glanced at their captain.

An idea popped into Ping's mind. "I am on my way to return the beast to His Imperial Majesty."

The guards looked at the girl with the dripping hair.

"I'm not a sorceress," she said. "I am the Imperial Dragon Keeper. If you stand aside I will control the dragon."

The commander nodded to the guards, who lowered their weapons and let go of her. She took the coil of rope from the guard with the wounded arm and walked toward the dragon.

A rumbling sound came from deep in the dragon's throat. "What is Ping doing?"

"Just play along," she whispered. "I'll convince them I'm returning you to the Emperor."

The dragon's angry rumbling changed to a low growl. Ping made a loop in the rope.

"Lower your head, dragon," she said sternly.

Danzi lowered his head and Ping slipped the rope over it.

"That's very impressive," said a voice behind her.

Just as Ping turned to see who it was, the guard next to her slipped and fell forward on the path.

A young boy was walking down the path to the river's edge. Another guard also lost his footing and fell over. Ping looked at the stone path. It was particularly smooth and well made. She couldn't understand why everyone was tripping. The boy stood in front of Ping and Danzi, and stared at them in what Ping thought was a rather impolite way. He was about ten and five years old and should have learned better manners by now.

"Bow down before your Emperor," hissed the guard, who was still kneeling on the path.

Ping looked around. "I can't see any Emperor." She was getting irritated. "I'm dripping wet and cold," she said, "and I don't feel like arguing with an annoying boy."

"And I am in no mood to argue with a girl," said the boy. "I am the Emperor."

"You could get into serious trouble for saying things like that," she said. "If the real Emperor found out."

Ping looked around. All of the guards were kneeling with their foreheads on the ground. She and the boy were the only ones on their feet.

"I am the real Emperor," the boy said.

Ping stared at him. His face was clear and without whiskers, like any boy his age. A small scar cut through his right eyebrow. His lips were pinched together as if he'd just sucked a lemon. She was about to say something else, when the guard pulled on her soaked gown and dragged her down to her knees. She tried to look up, but the guard's large hand pinned down her head. All she could see was the hem of the boy's gown and his slippers. The hem was attached to a black satin gown. It was decorated with dragons woven in gold thread. The dragons were woven in such a way that they were raised from the surface of the fabric. They looked so real they appeared to be about to jump off the gown. The slippers were covered with embroidery in a swirling spiral pattern that resembled wisps of high cloud. Ping had seen a similar hem and identical slippers before.

They had belonged to the Emperor.

CHAPTER NINETEEN

ANOTHER IMPERIAL BANQUET

Several ministers hurried down the path, their ribbons of office fluttering from their waists.

"Who dares to offend the Emperor with such rudeness?" one of them said, out of breath.

"I'm sorry," said Ping, though it was difficult to speak with her face pushed into the path. "I didn't realize he was the Emperor. I thought emperors were all old and fat."

The boy's tight mouth widened into a reluctant smile.

"It is treason to speak to His Imperial Majesty in such a way!" said the minister with the most colored ribbons and a gold seal hanging from his waist.

Ping recognized the voice.

"Let me see the girl's face," he said.

The guard pulled Ping's hair back. She looked at the minister. She knew him. He also knew her.

"I have seen this wretch before, Your Majesty." It was Tian Fen, the Emperor's Grand Counselor.

The Emperor wasn't listening to his Grand Counselor. He was staring at the dragon.

"She is the sorceress from Huangling," Counselor Tian continued. "She stole your father's—"

"Your Imperial Majesty," Ping said, "I didn't steal the dragon and I didn't mean to crash into your boat, either."

"You cannot speak directly to the Emperor!" shouted the Grand Counselor.

The boy Emperor raised a hand. "It's all right, Counselor Tian. I will question our prisoner."

The young Emperor dragged his eyes away from Danzi and looked at Ping.

"Stand up."

Ping stood up. Water from her wet gown had formed a small pool beneath her.

"She claims she is the Imperial Dragon Keeper, Your Majesty," said the captain of the guards.

The Emperor looked Ping up and down.

"If you don't think I look like an Emperor, I don't think you look like a Dragon Keeper," the Emperor said.

Ping couldn't argue with that.

"Though the creature is tame in your hands." The Emperor stared at Danzi." You say it's an imperial dragon?"

"He is, Your Imperial Majesty," Ping replied. "The last surviving imperial dragon."

"I was with your honored father when this sorceress escaped with the imperial dragon, Your Majesty," said Counselor Tian.

"I'm not a sorceress. I am a slave," said Ping. "I served Master Lan, the Imperial Dragon Keeper. He was not a good man. He was going to sell the dragon to a dragon hunter for his own profit. I only wanted to stop him from killing the dragon . . . your dragon, Your Imperial Majesty."

"Why didn't my father tell me about this dragon?" the boy asked.

"Your revered father was not fond of dragons, Your Imperial Majesty," Counselor Tian replied. "And he had much on his mind before his fatal illness."

Ping shuffled nervously, hoping the Emperor wasn't going to question her about his father's death.

"She is a sorceress and cannot be trusted, Your Imperial Majesty," the Grand Counselor continued.

"But she has brought the dragon to me," replied the Emperor. "All the way from Huangling Mountain."

Ping nodded.

"What is your name?" asked the Emperor.

"Ping, Your Imperial Majesty."

"If you are a slave, Ping," the Emperor said, "then you belong to me, just like the dragon."

Ping opened her mouth to say something but changed her mind.

"Your father decreed that she should be beheaded

for her crimes, Your Majesty," said Counselor Tian.

The Emperor walked over to the dragon. Danzi growled, but the boy didn't flinch. He circled around the dragon, inspecting him from head to foot.

"It's a handsome beast," he said. "Does it have a name?"

"His name is Long Danzi, Your Imperial Majesty," replied Ping.

"Execution doesn't seem to be a suitable reward for returning my one remaining dragon, Grand Counselor," said the Emperor. "I think I will reverse my father's decree."

Counselor Tian bowed. Danzi's growl turned into a tinkling sound.

"He's making a different sound now," the Emperor observed.

"That means he's happy, Your Imperial Majesty," Ping said.

"Does he understand our speech?"

"Some of it." Ping glanced at the dragon.

The Emperor finished his circuit of the dragon.

"Welcome to Ming Yang Lodge, Ping." He turned to the guards. "Give the girl her basket and find her some dry clothing," the boy commanded. "When she is rested she can join me in the Hall of Cool Fragrance for the evening meal."

One of the guards handed the basket to Ping. She held it tightly to her.

"The dragon must be tied up in the stables," said the Grand Counselor.

Danzi started to rumble again.

"Can't he stay with me?" asked Ping. "He's very well behaved." She looked at the guard with the bleeding arm. "Most of the time."

The Grand Counselor shook his head. "No, the creature is dangerous. He must be safely confined."

The boy Emperor turned and went back up the path. The ministers hurried after him. The imperial guards, who were still holding on to Ping's arms, led her up the path. Danzi walked behind her on the end of the rope. Ping had a chance to take in her surroundings for the first time.

The ground rose gently from the riverbank. There were no fields, no forests. The slopes had been transformed into a beautiful garden, which stretched as far as Ping could see along the river's edge. A stone path zigzagged up the hill, weaving its way through garden beds and stands of cypress trees. Flowers crowded on either side of the path. Ponds and streams were cut into the hillside so that they didn't overflow. Cherry trees covered in blossom were scattered about the garden. At intervals, the path wound its way through grottos of misshapen, craggy rocks, which suggested the shape of lions or dragons or monkeys. There were also pretty pavilions. Ping would have liked to stop and sit in one of them, but the guards marched her past them, ignoring the garden's beauty. At the top of the hill was a beautiful house, bigger than any of the houses Ping had seen at Chang'an. It had a black terra-cotta roof just like Huangling Palace. It was two stories high and had a wide balcony that was supported on thick columns.

Ping went with Danzi to the stables. The stable hands glanced nervously at the dragon as they swept out a stall and put clean straw on the floor. She gave them instructions for the dragon to be fed on nothing but roasted swallow and milk, and for no iron to be within ten paces of him. She also insisted that they find some arsenic so that he could have a rejuvenating drink. As soon as the stable hands left to search for the dragon's strange requirements, she took out the dragon stone and hid it under the straw at the back of the stall. Fortunately, the Emperor and the guards had been so interested in the dragon, they hadn't searched her basket.

"Ping has plan?" the dragon asked.

"Not exactly," Ping replied. "Don't worry. I'll think of something."

She reached behind one of the dragon's reversed scales and lifted Hua out. He blinked as if he'd just woken up.

"Are you all right, Hua?" she asked, scratching the rat behind his ears. "You stay here with Danzi. I have to go and eat with the Emperor. We don't want you causing a fuss at another imperial meal."

Ping followed the guards to a large entrance hall. It contained finely carved tables each displaying a vase or a potted plant. Unlike the entrance hall at Huangling, its polished tables shone, the lanterns were free of spiderwebs and there wasn't a speck of dust on the stone floor. The guards escorted her through the hall and along a corridor to a beautiful room. It contained a bed draped with fine silk hangings. The walls were painted with scenes of tall mountains wreathed in clouds. There were latticed windows the shape of lotuses, which gave splendid views of the Yellow River as it swung in a curve below. Servants carried in a bath and started filling it with hot water from jars.

"I don't need a bath," Ping tried to tell them. "It's not even two months since I had the last one."

The servants took no notice and continued to fill the bath. It was late in the afternoon and Ping had been in wet clothes for over an hour. She was shivering.

"I suppose a hot bath would warm me up," she said.

Master Lan had had a bath similar to this one, a wooden tub, like a wine vat, but lower and wider. Ping had never bathed in a bath before. She took off her wet gown and climbed into the tub. The water was as warm as the hot spring pool. The servant had sprinkled dried rose petals in the water so the steam was fragrant. She lay back in the water and relaxed. If she had servants to fill a tub for her, perhaps she could get used to bathing regularly—possibly even twice a month.

When she stepped out of the bath, she found that her wet gown had been removed and a neatly folded clean one was in its place. This was not a gown for outdoors. It was made of fine blue silk woven with white flowers. She slipped the gown on. It was cool and light against her skin. It had deep sleeves that reached halfway to the floor. There were also clean white socks and silk slippers.

An imperial guard arrived to escort her to the Hall of Cool Fragrance, which was in the upper story of the house and reached by a flight of wide stone stairs. Ping was the first to arrive. The room was similar to the dining hall at Huangling, except that on the floors there were all sorts of animal skins instead of carpets. Ping recognized the pelt of a bear, the dabbled hide of a deer. The most beautiful skin was striped yellow and black. This, she guessed, was the skin of a tiger. She'd seen paintings of these creatures at Huangling Palace.

Before she had time to examine the paintings on the walls, the Grand Counselor entered, followed by the Emperor, two servants, and six ministers. The ministers looked at her suspiciously as they took their places. The ministers and the servants were all kneeling with their foreheads resting on the floor. Ping quickly knelt down and put her forehead to the floor as well.

"Come and sit over here with me, Ping," the Emperor said as he took his place on a large cushion, waving away his servants as they tried to assist him.

Ping stood up, tripping on the long sleeves of her gown. She stumbled over to sit at the Emperor's side. The ministers glared at her.

As soon as the Emperor was seated, servants brought in tables set with beautiful black and red lacquer bowls and ebony chopsticks with precious stones set in the ends. There were also wine cups that looked to Ping as if they were made of gold. The Emperor had his own table, just as the old Emperor had at Huangling. The ministers had to share tables. The servant set down a table next to Ping. She was to have one all to herself.

"I'm not really hungry," said the Emperor. "So I have asked for a light meal tonight. I hope there will be enough for you."

Ping was rather hungry. With all the events of the day, she hadn't had anything to eat since early morning.

The servants poured wine into the gold cups and then brought out the first course. Ping stared at the dish that the servant placed in front of her. It looked like a turtle shell. Ping had never heard of anyone eating turtle shell before. In fact she was pretty sure it would be like gnawing on old bones. The servant reached out to the shell, as if she could read Ping's mind, and was about to take it away. But as she grasped it the top came off.

The bottom half was filled with steaming stew.

"Turtle stew," the Emperor said when he saw Ping staring at it. "It's quite good."

The Emperor, despite his lack of hunger, eagerly started eating. Ping remembered how at Huangling everyone had waited until the Emperor had finished his first course before they started eating. Ping's stomach was rumbling urgently at the smell of the stew, but she waited.

"Aren't you hungry?" asked the Emperor.

"Yes, I am, Your Imperial Majesty," replied Ping, "but—"

"Eat then!"

That sounded like an imperial command, so Ping ignored the scowling ministers and started to eat. The Emperor concentrated on his own bowl of stew until his turtle shell was empty. Ping was glad to see that the young Emperor had better table manners than his father. She followed his imperial example. The turtle stew was delicious.

The next course was roasted meat. It didn't taste like any meat Ping had tasted before.

"It's panther breast," the Emperor told her.

The meat was served with lotus root and sprouted beans. Ping ate in respectful silence.

"You can talk to me, Ping," the Emperor said. "There's no need to be afraid of me."

Ping searched for something to say to the Emperor.

"Why are you out here in the country, Your Imperial Majesty?" asked Ping. "Instead of in Chang'an."

"I'm on my way to Tai Shan," the Emperor replied.

Ping had never heard of this place.

"It's the most sacred mountain in the whole empire," he explained. "I'm going there to ask Heaven to bless my reign."

"I'm sure you will be a very good Emperor," Ping said.

The servants brought out the third course.

"I've only been Emperor for a month," said the Emperor with a weary sigh, "but I'm already bored."

Ping's stomach was very full and she wished she hadn't eaten so much turtle stew. The young Emperor's face brightened when he saw the latest course.

"Baked owl with peony sauce," he said. "It's one of my favorite dishes."

Ping thought it would be impolite to refuse the Emperor's favorite dish, so she let the servant spoon some into her bowl.

The servants were already bringing out another course. Ping recognized this one. It was barley with peas and leeks. She could only manage to swallow a mouthful. Finally the servants brought out fruit—pears, plums, persimmons. The meal was over. Ping was so full, she didn't think she'd be able to stand up. Fortunately, the Emperor was in a talkative mood. He told her about palace life in Chang'an and asked her questions about her life at Huangling.

"It's good to talk to you, Ping," said the Emperor. "I only ever have old men around me."

She realized that though the Emperor was surrounded by people day and night, he never had anyone he could talk to. Ping smiled. It was a new experience for her as well to talk to someone around her own age. The ministers all stayed where they were, unable to leave until their Emperor did.

"The shamans say we must wait here at Ming Yang Lodge for an auspicious day to climb Tai Shan." The young Emperor leaned closer to Ping. "I've decided to spend my time here profitably. I've summoned scientists from all over the empire—alchemists, herbalists, geomancers," he said. "I haven't told my ministers the reason yet. That's why they're so grumpy."

He grinned, looking more like a cheeky boy than an Emperor. Ping glanced at the ministers. They seemed to be very annoyed that they couldn't hear what their Emperor was saying to her.

"I don't want to grow old and fat and greedy like my father," the Emperor whispered. "I want to be a better Emperor than he was. That's why I've invited the scientists here. I want them to create an elixir that will keep me young forever."

"I'm sure you'll be a great Emperor," replied Ping. She had only known the boy for a short while, but she felt in her heart that he would rule the empire well and justly.

"When will the scientists be arriving?" she asked.

"They'll be here tomorrow."

Though Ping wasn't sure that an elixir of youth was a good idea, she felt very privileged to be hearing the Emperor's secret plans.

"I suppose I had better retire for the night," he said reluctantly. "I must get up very early tomorrow. I have to begin the purification ritual so that I am fit to approach Heaven. I have to throw yarrow sticks, which the shamans will read to calculate the best time to climb Tai Shan."

"I must go and see how Danzi is," Ping said.

The Emperor stood up. So did all the ministers. Ping was relieved to find that, despite her extremely full stomach, she could do the same.

"Good night, Ping," said the Emperor. "I've enjoyed our conversation."

Ping went out to the stables. The stable hands told her they hadn't been able to catch any swallows yet, but they had given the dragon some baked fish from their own dinner.

Danzi was hunched in the horse's stall. The rope around his neck was fastened to the stable wall. Ping could see him looking at her new gown. She glanced guiltily at the wooden bowl that contained the dragon's half-eaten meal. The enormous dinner that she had just eaten was lying heavily in her stomach.

"Here." She held out a plum that she'd saved from her meal for Danzi.

The dragon ignored it.

Hua appeared from behind one of the dragon's reversed scales. He scurried over to Ping. His whiskers quivered as he sniffed the air. Ping was sure he could smell the food she'd just eaten.

"I couldn't bring anything for you, Hua," she said, though in fact she hadn't thought about the rat at all throughout the meal. "I'll save you something from breakfast. I'm sorry. You'll have to find your own dinner tonight."

The dragon made a low rumbling growl. "Too much color confuses the eyes," he said. Danzi was not in a good mood.

"You must be patient, Danzi. The Emperor will be meeting with a group of scientists tomorrow," Ping said. "We'll have a chance to escape then."

The dragon rumbled.

Ping had never slept in a bed before. The one in her room at Ming Yang Lodge seemed wide enough for a troop of guards to sleep in. It was raised about two feet off the floor and covered with a carved canopy. She stroked the silk sheets. It took her a while to work out why there were two—one to sleep on top of, and the other to cover her. Ping put on the sacrificial shift and slid between the sheets. They felt smooth and slippery. The bottom sheet was also warm. There was no fire in Ping's room, but the heat from a fire somewhere in the palace must have been piped to the bed. It was a cold night. There was a bearskin to cover herself with. She had never felt so warm and comfortable in her life.

CHAPTER TWENTY

THE GARDEN OF
SECLUDED HARMONY

The next morning Ping ate breakfast alone. There were only three courses. Ping helped herself to large portions of everything. She only ate a little, though. She put the rest in a bamboo bowl that she had hidden under her gown. Then she took the food to the stables.

"Look," Ping said, putting the bowl in front of the dragon. "I brought you some—"

Hua flashed out of his hiding place and had his nose buried in the food before Ping could finish speaking.

"Don't you want some, Danzi?" Ping asked.

The dragon reached out a paw and picked up a morsel of meat between his talons. He sniffed it and then put it in his mouth. He chewed it slowly.

"Have some more, Danzi," Ping pleaded.

The dragon shook his head. He'd hardly eaten since

they'd been in Wucheng. He was looking thinner. It was as if he didn't trust food anymore.

"There you are, Ping," said a voice at the stable door.

It was the Emperor. Ping quickly stuffed Hua behind one of the dragon's reversed scales before she turned to bow before the Emperor.

"I was just making sure that the dragon is eating enough," Ping said.

"I've spent all morning with shamans and ministers," the Emperor said. "I'm in need of some conversation. Come and talk to me, Ping. I've got a little free time before the scientists are due to arrive."

Ping looked at the dragon. She didn't want to leave him alone again. She tried to think of an excuse. "I was just about to take Danzi for some exercise, Your Imperial Majesty," she said.

"Excellent," said the Emperor. "I'll come with you."

Ping untied the rope and led the rumbling dragon out of the stables.

"My mother said that the Garden of Secluded Harmony is very beautiful at this time of year," the Emperor said. "I promised her I would visit it."

Ping remembered the thin, pinched woman she had seen at Huangling.

"Is the Empress well?" she asked politely.

"She is still mourning my father in Chang'an."

Ping was relieved that the Empress wasn't about to visit her son.

Ping and the Emperor stepped out into the crisp morning air. Ping shivered in her thin silk gown and slippers.

"We will need coats," said the Emperor. The servants, who were never far away, stepped forward. "And Ping will need some stronger shoes."

A servant bowed and went off to do his Emperor's bidding. He arrived out of breath with coats and shoes in less than a minute. He somehow managed to help the Emperor into his coat while remaining on his knees.

"I don't need you to accompany me on my walk," the Emperor told his servants.

It was their duty to stay with the Emperor at all times and yet they could not disobey him. They watched unhappily as the Emperor walked off down a garden path without them.

The path led behind the house and then continued to snake up the hillside. The morning mist hadn't yet cleared. The Yellow River was hidden from them. In fact they could only see a few feet of garden around them. The flowers were closed up, the trees dark with dew, the grottos of misshapen rocks looked even more like strange creatures looming out of the mist. Then they climbed through the mist and the top of the hill was in front of them bathed in sunlight. The path had snaked so gently up the hill that Ping had hardly noticed the climb.

At the top of the hill the ground leveled out.

"This is the Garden of Secluded Harmony," the Emperor said.

The garden was wrapped around the edges of a small irregular-shaped lake. Azaleas provided a pale purple border to the path. Above them, cherry blossoms rustled in a light breeze. A zigzag bridge led them from one side of the lake to the other. On a trellis overhead, a wisteria vine wound its way across the bridge. It was heavy with clusters of purple flowers. Wayward branches reached out and dipped toward the water. Huge orange fish circled lazily beneath the surface. Ducks bobbed and dived for food. The Emperor was peering into the water.

"What are you looking at, Your Imperial Majesty?" Ping asked.

"Why don't you call me by my name? It's Liu Che," he said.

"I don't think I could do that, Your Imperial Majesty," said Ping.

"I command you to call me Liu Che," said the Emperor with a smile.

Ping took a deep breath, glad that Counselor Tian wasn't around to hear her. "Why are you looking in the lake, Liu Che?"

"There are turtles in the lake," he replied. "Or so my mother says."

On the other side of the bridge, spring flowers—

sky-blue crocuses, daffodils, tiny snow poppies—were bursting from the dark earth.

"I've never seen such a beautiful place," said Ping.

This wasn't entirely true. She had seen such gardens in the paintings at Huangling Palace, but she didn't want the Emperor to know she had been sneaking around one of his palaces. Behind her Ping could hear a faint discordant sound, as if someone were impatiently striking a gong. The dragon was not enjoying the walk as much as she was.

They stopped and rested in a pavilion. It was a beautiful little building like a miniature palace. It was six sided and its tiny roof had six upturned corners supported by six columns. The guardians of the four quarters were painted beneath the eaves: the blue dragon of the east, the white tiger of the west, the black tortoise of the north, and the red bird of the south. There were no walls. The pavilion had been built solely as a place to admire one particular tree.

"What sort of a tree is that, Liu Che?" Ping asked.

The tree's slender branches were dark brown and damp. It had no leaves, but it had the largest blossoms Ping had ever seen. The buds were like pale hands clasped together. Some had opened to reveal beautiful, pure white flowers as big as goblets.

"It's a magnolia. Beautiful, isn't it?" the Emperor said. "This pavilion is called Watching Magnolia Buds Open Pavilion."

Ping smiled. It was a perfect name for the little building. Liu Che went over and picked one of the white flowers. He gave it to Ping.

As they walked, the mist below evaporated in the morning sun and revealed the countryside stretching off into the distance. The Yellow River snaked away to the east like a bolt of ocher cloth that someone had carelessly thrown out across the landscape. On the other side of the river, the flat plain was divided into fields—some green, some yellow, some brown. To the south, there was nothing but thick, dark foliage as far as the eye could see. The garden was designed so that the slopes of the hill weren't visible, just the vistas around it. It was as if the garden were floating on air.

Liu Che talked about his childhood in Chang'an.

"We have something in common, Ping," he said.

"We both had no other children to play with when we were young."

"Haven't you got brothers and sisters?" Ping asked.

"Yes, but my brothers were sent away to rule their own kingdoms. My sister was very young when she married and went to live with her husband's family. I spent most of my childhood with servants as my only companions."

"What about your parents?" Ping asked.

"My father was always busy with imperial business. My mother has poor health and found my childish games too noisy."

Ping found it hard to believe. In a way the Emperor had been abandoned by his family just as she had. Though she thought it was probably a serious crime to touch the Emperor, she slipped her arm through his. Liu Che didn't object. They walked around the edge of the lake, looking for turtles.

"I have something for you," the Emperor said. He pulled something from his sleeve.

Ping was speechless.

"It isn't a gift, Ping," Liu Che said. "It's yours by right."

Ping held out her hand and then pulled it back. She recognized the thing he was offering her.

"It's your seal of office, Ping," the Emperor continued.

It was the white jade seal that had belonged to Master Lan. It had hung from his waist by a length of greasy ribbon. On more than one occasion he had thrown it at her. Ping took the seal from the Emperor and turned it around in her hand. She had never had a chance to examine it carefully before. It was a slender rectangle less than an inch across. One end was flat and had characters carved in it. The other end had been skillfully carved into the shape of a dragon. The carving was so lifelike; she couldn't imagine how the craftsman had managed to carve each leg, each tooth, each scale with such precision. Master Lan's greasy ribbon had been replaced with a new purple silk ribbon.

Liu Che also gave Ping a small container of seal ink.

He showed her how to dip the seal into the thick, red ink. He looked around for something to make an impression on. He took the magnolia flower from her hand and pressed the seal onto one of its petals. Ping noticed that the skin around the Emperor's manicured thumbnails was chewed. The seal left a bloodred impression of two characters with a tiny dragon coiled around them.

"I can't read," Ping said sadly. "What does it say?"

"It says 'Imperial Dragon Keeper.'"

"But I'm not the Imperial Dragon Keeper."

"Yes you are. I have appointed you."

He handed the seal back to her.

"Thank you, Liu Che." Ping tied the seal to her belt.

They walked on through the garden. A breeze stirred the air and a shower of pink drifted down from the cherry trees. The Emperor looked at the pink petals resting on his sleeves and then shook them off.

"I wish I didn't always have to wear these black robes," Liu Che complained. "They're so dull."

The Emperor's gown was made of shiny, black silk, embroidered with gold. Ping thought it was beautiful.

"Can't you wear whatever you want?" Ping asked.

"No," Liu Che sighed. "I have to always wear imperial robes and everything imperial is black."

"Is that why palace rooftops are always black?"

Liu Che nodded.

"Why don't you change the imperial color?" Ping said.

"I can't do that. The imperial color has been black for a hundred years."

"But you're the Emperor, Liu Che," Ping replied. "Can't you do whatever you want?"

Liu Che stopped in his tracks. "I can," he said. "You're right, Ping. I am the Emperor."

He surveyed his empire. "What shall the new imperial color be? Something cheerful."

Ping looked around the garden. There were daffodils everywhere—in the garden beds, in between rocks.

"What about yellow?" she replied. "That's a nice, bright color."

Liu Che's serious face broke into a smile. "The daffodils come out in spring, bright and cheerful after a dreary, dark winter. It's the color of the sun, which shines on the whole empire. It's also the color of gold, a metal whose brightness never tarnishes. That's the perfect color to symbolize my reign!"

They walked on through the garden to the Pavilion of the Auspicious Nightingale. The view from this pavilion was different. It looked out to the south where there were dense trees that stretched from the edges of the garden as far as the eye could see.

"Ming Yang Lodge is the imperial hunting lodge," Liu Che explained. "My father built it so that he could hunt in that forest."

"What sort of animals did he hunt?"

"Deer, bears, tigers."

"Are there tigers here?" Ping said, looking among the trees anxiously.

The Emperor laughed. "Not here in the garden, but in the forest."

"Have you seen a tiger?"

"I've never seen one," the Emperor said. "I don't think there are many left."

"That's a pity," said Ping, though she was pleased they wouldn't be running into any.

"You can hear monkeys, though."

Ping listened. She could hear a distant chattering.

"I don't like hunting," the Emperor continued. "I've been considering turning the Tiger Forest into a park where it is forbidden to hunt. I'd like to bring other animals here—strange beasts from barbarian lands."

"That sounds like a wonderful idea," said Ping.

The Emperor turned to Danzi, who was crouched sullenly on the path, his great, green head sprinkled with cherry blossom.

"My dragon will be the first creature in my new pleasure garden," Liu Che said. "I'll have a special enclosure built for him with a lake. Dragons like to swim, don't they?"

"Yes," said Ping, trying not to listen to the anxious noises coming from the dragon.

"You will live here as well, Ping," Liu Che said.

"Oh," said Ping. "Thank you, Liu Che. I'd like that."

It wasn't a lie. She would like nothing better than to live at Ming Yang Lodge. She just couldn't.

Counselor Tian appeared at that moment so she didn't have to discuss the matter further.

"Ah, Grand Counselor," the Emperor said cheerfully. "Just the person I wanted to see. I am going to make an imperial edict. Two in fact! First, the Tiger Forest is now a park for animals. Hunting there is to be forbidden. Also, henceforth, the imperial color will be yellow. Please make arrangements for new robes to be made and for all the palaces in the empire to have yellow roofs!"

Counselor Tian didn't look at all pleased by these imperial pronouncements.

"Perhaps you might like to seek advice on these matters, Your Imperial Majesty," he replied.

"No, my mind is made up," Liu Che said cheerfully. "Now what did you want?"

"I came to announce that the first group of scientists has arrived." The Grand Counselor looked very annoyed that he still didn't know why the Emperor had summoned the scientists. "They are waiting in the Chamber of Spreading Clouds."

"Ping, come with me to meet these scholars," Liu Che said. "I'd like them to see me with my dragon."

Ping had been enjoying herself so much, she'd

almost forgotten about the dragon on the end of the rope in her hand. Danzi's rumbling annoyance was getting louder.

"Is he hungry?" asked the Emperor.

They walked toward the Chamber of Spreading Clouds. Ping's stomach suddenly went tight. The warm, peaceful feeling that had filled her as she enjoyed the pleasures of the garden and Liu Che's friendship froze inside her. There was someone that she knew in the chamber, but she didn't know who. It wasn't Diao, she was sure of that. Perhaps it was the necromancer. Surely Liu Che wouldn't have invited him?

Guards opened the doors to the chamber. Ping and the dragon followed the Emperor in. Ten and two serious-looking men were waiting in the Chamber of Spreading Clouds. The scientists stared at the dragon. Liu Che looked pleased that he had impressed the scholarly men. Ping searched their faces. They were almost all very old with long gray beards. There was only one younger man. A smile of relief spread across Ping's face as she realized who it was. It was Wang Cao. She was just about to rush over and greet him, when the dragon's rumbling changed to an urgent gonging.

"Ping must pretend not to know," said the dragon's voice in her mind.

Wang Cao looked at the dragon with interest, as if

he were seeing one for the first time. He glanced at Ping without any sign of recognition as he fell to his knees before the Emperor with the other scientists.

"I have to welcome my guests," the Emperor said to Ping.

Liu Che walked over to the scientists. Ping felt Danzi pull on the cord.

"Go back to stable," he said.

Ping led the dragon back to the stable and undid the cord around his neck. She looked at the dragon guiltily, aware that he hadn't enjoyed the walk to the Garden of Secluded Harmony as much as she had.

"How did Wang Cao know we were here?" Ping asked.

The dragon shook his great head. "He didn't. Wang Cao has no second sight."

"So he's here just by chance?"

"Net of Heaven is cast wide. Though its mesh is not fine, nothing slips through."

As usual the dragon's wisdom made no sense to her.

Ping left Danzi in the stable. She needed to think. She had to work out a way to escape. She walked back up the hillside to the Garden of Secluded Harmony.

Sitting in the Watching Magnolia Buds Open Pavilion, she realized that she didn't have to go all the way to Ocean to live like a princess. She imagined a life in this beautiful place. Being able to stroll around it every day, watching the trees and the flowers change with the seasons, listening to the birds and the distant chatter of monkeys, perhaps venturing into the Tiger Forest and glimpsing yellow and black stripes through the trees.

She toyed with the stone seal hanging from her waist. If she wished, she could choose that life. She could eat baked owl and persimmons. Liu Che would walk with her whenever he visited Ming Yang Lodge, asking her advice on imperial matters. The most important person in the empire would be her friend. If she escaped with the dragon, she would become a hunted person again. The Emperor would no longer be her friend.

A squirrel scampered down from a nearby tree. Its bushy tail twitched nervously, its bright little eyes darted from one side to the other looking for danger. Ping was sitting so still that it didn't notice her. She stood up and the startled creature leaped up the tree and was gone in a flash. Such a life wasn't possible for her. She had to get the dragon to Ocean.

The dragon was hunched miserably in his stall.

"Must think of way to escape," the dragon said.

"I've already thought of one," Ping replied.

Six roasted swallows lay on a plate in front of the dragon, untouched. Even Hua seemed to be off his food.

"We have to leave tonight," she said.

"Good," replied the dragon.

"We'll go through the Tiger Forest," she continued. "No one will dare look for us there."

"Good evening, Your Majesty," said Ping, kneeling and bowing her head to the floor as the Emperor entered the dining hall.

Ping wasn't Liu Che's only guest at dinner that evening. The visiting scientists were also there, all on their knees with their foreheads resting on the floor.

Liu Che was smiling happily. "It has been a very profitable day, Ping," he said, waving her over to sit next to him.

The scientists all took their places at a respectful distance from their Emperor. Ping sat down next to him, aware that Wang Cao was watching her.

"I have learned much from the scientists already," Liu Che continued.

Servants began to bring in the food.

"They already know a great deal about making elixirs to lengthen life. Did you know one of the alchemists is more than one hundred years old?"

He pointed to a man who didn't look a day over six tens. The sparrow broth that had been put in front of her smelled delicious, but Ping could only eat a few spoonfuls. Her stomach was churning nervously. The Emperor managed to eat and talk at the same time, telling her about the events of the day.

"They think that an elixir of eternal youth will only need a slight adjustment."

More dishes were brought in—roasted quail,

minced carp, crane eggs. Ping ate no more than a mouthful of each.

"They will begin working on a new elixir when they return to Chang'an. I have set aside a small palace for their use. In the meantime, I have to eat peaches and cranes' eggs and swallow a little cinnabar each day. Have you ever seen cinnabar, Ping?"

Ping shook her head, though she had seen cinnabar before—in Wang Cao's explosive mixture.

"Show Ping some cinnabar," the Emperor commanded the scientists.

They were all looking at Ping suspiciously.

"It's all right, gentlemen," said Liu Che as he helped himself to dried plums and water chestnuts. "No need to be afraid of Ping. Wang Cao, please go and get some cinnabar so that I can show it to her."

Wang Cao bowed to the Emperor and left the dining hall. He returned a few minutes later with a leather pouch. He knelt at the side of Ping's table. He moved aside her wine goblet and emptied out the cinnabar. It was made up of deep red crystals.

"They're beautiful," Ping said, not daring to look at the herbalist.

"Ping is the Imperial Dragon Keeper," Liu Che explained.

Wang Cao glanced at her sharply as he bowed in her direction.

"The scientists are very interested in my dragon,"

the Emperor continued. "They say he will be useful. Isn't that right?"

"Yes, Your Imperial Majesty," said Wang Cao. "Dragon scales would be an important ingredient in the elixir."

"Ping will get you some. Won't you, Ping?"

"Of course, Your Majesty," Ping replied, though she wasn't sure that Danzi would give her any of his scales.

"It might also be useful to examine the properties of dragon blood, Your Imperial Majesty," said another scientist.

Ping nodded to the scientist, though she had no intention of asking the dragon to wound himself.

The Emperor continued to tell her about his plans. How he would send an explorer into the west to find the Kunlun Mountains and search for the fruit of life. Ping drank the rest of her wine. Now that she had decided it was time to escape, she wanted to get it over and done with as soon as possible. She couldn't leave the dining hall before the Emperor, though. She stifled a yawn.

When Liu Che finally retired for the night, Ping went back to her chamber. The silk sheets and the warm bed looked very inviting. She yawned. How could she feel so tired with such an important task ahead of her? She took off the blue silk gown that she had been wearing for the last two days and laid it neatly on the bed. She put on her own plain gown (which had been returned to her clean and sweet smelling) and picked up her basket. She took a last look at the silk hangings and the wall paintings, which she could just make out in the moonlight, and left the beautiful room.

There were three imperial guards in the courtyard. Ping slipped past without their noticing. She walked through the garden toward the stable. It wasn't the shortest way, but she wanted to see the garden one more time. It was bathed in moonlight. The leaves looked as if they'd been splashed with silver paint. Each pond and stream contained its own rippling image of the moon. Only the low noises of the night—the call of a night bird, the flap of a passing bat, the rustling of small animals—disturbed the silence.

The moonlight hadn't found its way into the stable. Ping wished she'd brought a lamp. She moved slowly to the dragon's stall, feeling her way along the rough timbers of the walls.

She could just make out the dragon in the darkness. He wasn't alone. Wang Cao was with him. The two were huddled together. The herbalist was talking in a low whisper. The dragon was making contented tinkling sounds as if thin strips of metal were being stirred by a light breeze. Ping hadn't heard him make that sound for days. When they saw Ping enter, they stopped talking.

"Ping," said Wang Cao. "Who would have expected we would meet again!"

He sounded pleased to see her, but his face stayed stern.

Ping smiled. "It is good to see you, Wang Cao."

The herbalist had something in his lap. Ping looked closer. Her smile faded. He was holding the dragon stone.

"I can see you've been taking better care of the dragon stone," Wang Cao said.

"We are leaving tonight," Ping said. For some reason her mouth had trouble forming the words.

"So Danzi has told me."

Ping reached out and took the dragon stone from Wang Cao. She noticed that he had a leather bag over his shoulder. She felt the stone's cool surface beneath her fingers. A ripple of pleasure coursed up her arm and through her whole body. At the same moment the moon came from behind a cloud and cast a pale light on the stone. The purple color was rich and deep, the milky swirls only just visible in the dim light. She put the stone into her basket. It was a tight fit.

Ping felt dizzy.

"Is Ping sure she wants to leave?" the dragon asked.

Ping lifted the basket onto her shoulder and felt the stone resting on her hip. "I'm sure," she said.

"Emperor will be angry."

"I know. Liu Che will restore the decree that I am to be beheaded," said Ping sadly. "It can't be helped."

Ping untied the rope around the dragon's neck and

threw it aside. She checked that Hua was safely behind one of the reverse scales.

"Danzi," she said. "I have a favor to ask you."

She stroked the soft place under the dragon's chin.

"Liu Che's scientists want a dragon scale for the Emperor's youth elixir," she said. "Would you let me have one to leave for them?"

The dragon suddenly reared up on his back legs. Ping stepped back, startled. Then Danzi started to examine the scales on his belly with his front paws.

"These scales easier to remove," he said. "Grow back quicker."

Ping watched as he selected a scale. She remembered what Danzi had told her before about some of his scales having properties to do good, some to do bad.

"Make sure you pick one that is for good," she said.

She winced as the dragon yanked out the scale. It looked painful. He pulled out another and then another. He handed the three scales to Ping.

"If I could write, I'd leave him a note," Ping said. "Can you make sure he gets them, Wang Cao?"

The herbalist took the scales and nodded.

Danzi continued searching through his scales. He pulled out another one.

"This one for Ping," he said, handing her the scale. "May need it one day."

Ping didn't imagine that she'd have any shortage of dragon scales if she needed them, with a large dragon at her side. She took the scale, though. It was shaped like a small fan and fitted in the palm of her hand. It was hard like a fingernail and rough to the touch. The scales were green but the color had a strange quality that made her think that if she held one up to a bright light she'd be able to see through it. There was a speck of blood where the scale had been pulled from the dragon's flesh. Ping turned to Wang Cao.

"I won't be seeing you again," she said. At least that's what she tried to say, but her words came out slurred and incomprehensible.

She took a step, but lost her balance. She reached out to steady herself, but her legs crumpled beneath her before her hand reached the wall. The stables were fading. She saw the expression on Wang Cao's serious face change. She thought it must be a trick of the moonlight, but there was no mistake. He was smiling.

Ping's vision blurred.

Ping waited for her eyes to focus again. It took a few moments. She got to her feet and stood unsteadily. She didn't have to look for the dragon stone. She knew it was gone. Shafts of pale moonlight threaded through the bamboo poles that made up the wall of the animal stall. It was empty. The dragon had gone as well.

A terrible sound shattered the silence of the night. It was a scream of pain and betrayal. The sort of rending cry that makes anyone who hears it despair. Ping was on her hands and knees. Something small and furry scurried up her and burrowed into the folds of her gown. It gave her no comfort. Imperial guards appeared behind her, shining a lamp in her direction, but too frightened to come any closer. Their faces reflected the misery of the scream. The scream went on and on. It would drain all the happiness from the entire world. Ping had no connection to the body crouching in the straw. There was nothing but the scream. That was all she was. All she would ever be.

The guards parted and a smaller figure came forward in a white nightgown. Ping was only dimly aware of these movements. They were happening somewhere else, far away from where she was. Then the figure in the white gown took hold of her arms and shook her.

"Ping," he said.

The scream stopped and Ping leaned on the Emperor's shoulder and cried.

· CHAPTER TWENTY-ONE ·

HALFWAY TO HEAVEN

Ping was back in the warm bed between the smooth silk sheets. She was drinking something hot from a blue earthenware cup. It had been prepared by the Emperor's personal physician. The Emperor himself was standing at the end of the bed surrounded by guards, ministers, and servants. Though the Emperor was looking at her with concern, the others were staring at the source of that awful scream with frightened faces. Ping wished that she could consider the idea that she had just had a bad dream, but even that small comfort wasn't possible.

Ping felt like someone had reached into her chest and squeezed her heart.

"The dragon has gone," she said.

The Emperor nodded. "He is not the only one who has gone," he said. "Wang Cao, the herbalist from Chang'an, has also disappeared during the night. My guards discovered that the southern gate has been opened. They believe that the herbalist and the dragon have both gone into the Tiger Forest."

Ping's hands shook. The physician reached out and grabbed the cup before she dropped it. She sank back onto the bed.

"She needs rest, Your Imperial Majesty," said the physician. "This loss has greatly weakened her."

Other things were said, but Ping didn't hear them. The figures around her bed disappeared. She was only dimly aware of them leaving. Sunlight was seeping into the room. She covered her head with the silk sheet. She didn't want to see the brightness of the dawn. The outside world had become a ghost world that didn't really exist. The only thing she was aware of was the pain inside, as if she'd been stabbed. Lao Ma had told her stories of princesses who had been heartbroken. Ping hadn't realized that heartache was a physical pain.

Danzi had left her and he had taken the dragon stone with him. He had told her that she was a special person, a Dragon Keeper. He had held out the Dragon Keeper's mirror to her. She had reached out to take it. But it had never lain in her hands; she'd been distracted. She had spent too much time with Liu Che. The comforts of imperial life had seduced her. She had allowed herself to be diverted from their quest to reach Ocean by the friendship of someone close to her own age. Worst of all, she had accepted the seal of the Imperial Dragon Keeper. Danzi saw her take it from the Emperor and tie it to her belt. Wang Cao would have seen it hanging from her waist by its bright purple ribbon. Anger filled her when she thought of the herbalist. She remembered his hand passing over her goblet while he was showing her the cinnabar crystals. He must have put some sort of sleeping draft in her wine so that she wouldn't be able to follow them. The dragon hadn't trusted her. Danzi had chosen Wang Cao to go with him to Ocean instead.

She had failed the test.

Ping didn't move from the bed for three days. She didn't sleep much, but she couldn't think of a good enough reason to get up. Whenever she did doze, she dreamed about the dragon stone. She woke with the keening sounds she had heard at Wucheng ringing in her ears.

She didn't eat, and when one of the servants came to wash her and comb her hair, she pulled Hua from beneath the sheets. The servant ran from the room screaming.

The Emperor came to visit her every day. He sent musicians and performing monkeys to try and cheer her up. He had servants carry her into the garden. She showed no interest in anything.

"You have frightened the servants," Liu Che said when he came to visit Ping on the third day. "The servant girl who was supposed to care for you refuses to come into your room. She says you are a sorceress. Something about a rat in your bed."

Liu Che started as Ping pulled the rat from beneath the sheets. "This is Hua," she said.

Liu Che smiled as he watched her tickle the rat's stomach. "Do you make a habit of befriending pests?"

"Only this one," Ping replied.

The Emperor sat on the end of her bed and gingerly stroked the rat.

"Ping, I am leaving for Tai Shan tomorrow," he told her. "My shamans say that it will soon be the most auspicious day to climb its peak and seek the blessing of Heaven."

Ping didn't say anything.

"I want you to come with me," Liu Che said. "Tai Shan is beautiful, so I'm told. Perhaps the sight of it will cheer you up." The Emperor thought for a moment. "You can bring your rat."

Ping didn't object. There was no point in arguing with the Emperor.

It wasn't far to Tai Shan, a little over one hundred *li*, but the Emperor didn't have to walk there. He wasn't going alone, either. A whole caravan of people were accompanying him. Four men carried him in a sedan chair made of polished ebony, decorated with a fine design of swirling clouds, painted in silver and pale purple and inlaid with mother-of-pearl. Embroidered hangings hid the Emperor from view. The Grand Counselor, the ministers and the shaman who would conduct the ceremony all traveled in carriages.

A small army of porters carried the imperial baggage (including food, cooking equipment, boxes of robes, a portable bed, a tent) suspended from both ends of poles carried over their shoulders. There were also imperial guards, servants, and a cook. At the rear were fifteen goats that were to be sacrificed. They were attended by two scruffy boys.

When the Emperor insisted that she travel in one of the carriages with the ministers, Ping didn't object. She didn't have the energy to walk. She watched the flat fields pass by with little interest. The carriage bumped over the rough country roads, making it impossible to sleep through the journey. The ministers didn't speak to her. She was left to her own thoughts, constantly going over the previous weeks events and wishing she had done things differently.

As the imperial caravan lumbered through the countryside, peasants in the fields dropped their hoes and abandoned their plows. They fell on their faces as their Emperor passed. When the caravan stopped for the night, their camp was bright with lamps and noisy with activity. When they started off again in the morning, they left behind flattened crops, discarded fish bones, fruit peel, and ox droppings. Ping remembered how easy it had been to travel with the dragon. How little baggage they had. How swiftly they'd moved through the countryside. How few people had noticed their passing.

When the caravan stopped at the end of the second day, Ping climbed down from the carriage. To the north, south, and west, the countryside stretched out flat and featureless, but to the east it was different. To the east a mountain rose abruptly from the plain in a series of sheer gray cliffs. Its craggy peaks disappeared into clouds. The only vegetation was pine trees clinging to the mountainside in pockets of earth caught in cracks or crevices. The trees were small and twisted as they grew toward the sun. The mountain was majestic and strangely familiar. An image of Huangling suddenly flashed into Ping's mind. It wasn't that magnificent Tai Shan reminded her of the bleak slopes of the mountain that used to be her home. There was no comparison.

What Ping remembered was a circle of lamplight in the darkness. One of the paintings that she had seen on the walls of Huangling Palace had been of this very mountain. She had thought that such a steep and beautiful mountain only existed in the imagination of painters.

Ping had had no interest in where they were going until then, but now that she could see the sacred slopes of Tai Shan, she felt differently. She pulled Hua out to show him.

"Look, Hua," she said. "That's Tai Shan and we're going to climb it."

The next morning she didn't travel in the carriage. She walked alongside the Emperor's sedan chair. She kept her eyes on the mountain, watching as it grew larger and more imposing as they approached.

"Tai Shan is one of the five sacred mountains of my empire," Liu Che told her when they stopped for the midday meal. "It reaches almost to Heaven. It is the place where each Emperor goes to speak to his heavenly ancestors and seek blessings for a long and successful reign."

The Emperor chatted cheerfully as he ate, but Ping noticed that he'd bitten the skin around his thumbnails until it bled.

The caravan reached the foot of Tai Shan that evening. The porters put up the imperial tent. Liu Che's personal servants unpacked tables, the imperial bed, carpets, and cushions to furnish the tent. The cook unloaded stoves and cooking pots and began to conjure an imperial meal from baskets and boxes. The Emperor came over to Ping.

"We will rest here tomorrow," he said. "Then in the evening we will begin our ascent of the mountain."

"Why don't you climb during the day, Liu Che?" asked Ping. "I'm sure it would be much easier."

"If we climb during the night, we will arrive at Jade Emperor Summit at dawn. That is the most favorable time to address Heaven and my honored ancestors.

Only myself, the shaman, Counselor Tian, and a few attendants will be making the climb. You can stay at the camp, Ping."

"I would like to climb with you if I may, Your Imperial Majesty."

"Only I am permitted to stand on Jade Emperor Summit," Liu Che told her. "But you can climb with me to the South Gate, if you wish."

"Thank you, Your Imperial Majesty."

Liu Che looked at her. "Are you sure you are up to such a difficult climb, Ping?"

"I'm sure. I'm feeling much better."

They ate bear paw soup, roasted crane with plum sauce, pickled fish, and red lentils, followed by slices of orange, dried peaches, and hazelnuts. It was the Emperor's last meal before he ascended the mountain. He would have to fast all the next day.

"Once I have made the sacrifice to Heaven," the Emperor said, "I will consult my ministers and think about what we must do to recapture my dragon."

Ping didn't say anything. Danzi may have chosen to leave her behind, but he was free. She knew that she wouldn't be helping the Emperor catch the dragon.

The next day seemed twice as long as any other day. Ping was impatient to start the climb. Everyone else was busily preparing for the ascent, but she had nothing to do to pass the time. She watched the goatherd boys play among their charges, throwing a leather ball over the beasts' backs, chasing each other around their legs. Their cheerfulness was infectious. Ping couldn't help but smile. She didn't know why, but the thought of climbing Tai Shan made her feel happier than she had since the dragon had left.

That afternoon, Liu Che went into his tent with the shaman to perform a cleansing ceremony. Ping, the Grand Counselor, and the attendants ate a small meal by imperial standards, but it was still lavish compared to the simple meals that she and Danzi had eaten when they were traveling. There had been days when they had gone hungry because they could find nothing to eat. She smiled to herself when she remembered how pleased Danzi had been whenever he could catch a swallow to roast over a fire. She had developed quite a taste for swallow herself. The imperial food was very nice, but she would have given anything to be sitting with Danzi by a small fire after a long day's walk, with nothing to eat but nuts and berries.

Ping fed Hua as much as he would eat, so that he would sleep through the climb and not get restless.

After the meal, just as she was starting to get sleepy, one of the ministers banged a gong to let everyone know that the Emperor was about to start his journey up Tai Shan. The party making the ascent was much smaller. As well as Counselor Tian, the shaman, two imperial guards, and a servant, the goatherds were also going to drive the sacrificial goats up the mountain.

Liu Che came out of his tent dressed in a beautiful gown made of black satin, embroidered with silver thread and with precious stones sewn into it.

"Are you going to climb the mountain with me, Ping?" he asked.

"I'd like to, Your Imperial Majesty."

"It will take all night. Are you sure you have the strength?"

"I'm sure."

The Emperor had to fast until morning, but the cook packed millet cakes for those who were accompanying him up the mountain. An imperial guard led the way with a blazing torch. The shaman followed. Ping was expecting Liu Che to climb back into his sedan chair, but he didn't. He started to walk up the steps.

"Walk with me, Ping," he said.

Counselor Tian glared at her, but Ping did as the Emperor asked. The Grand Counselor took his place behind Liu Che, followed by the servant. Behind him were the goats and the boys herding them. At the rear was another imperial guard with a torch.

The climb was easy at first. Ping had nothing to carry and the mountain began with a gentle slope. The moon was up. As they passed beneath a painted gateway, Ping could make out carvings of dragons and *qilin*.

"That's the Journey's Beginning Gate," said Liu Che.

"Have you been here before, Liu Che?" Ping asked.

"No," the Emperor replied, "but my ministers have told me of the stages of the journey. Next we will come to the Cypress Tunnel."

Sure enough, after walking for half an hour, the moon suddenly disappeared behind a dark mass. Ping could make out tree trunks on either side of the path. The dark branches of the trees reached up and met over the path, interlacing with each other and forming a living tunnel. When they came out of the other side of the Cypress Tunnel, the path grew steeper. The goats behind her were complaining about the climb. The boys smacked them on their rumps to keep them moving and called the beasts rude names. The shaman started to sing a low chant.

Before long, everyone was placing their feet one in front of the other to the rhythm of the chant. Then the earth path stopped and Ping felt the rock of the mountain beneath her feet. She stumbled as her foot struck a step. She looked up and the moonlight lit up their path before them. It was made up of hundreds of steps, carved into the rock of Tai Shan. The flight of steps reached up the mountain as far as the weak moonlight allowed her to see.

"How many steps are there?" she asked.

"Seven thousand," replied Liu Che.

The Emperor sounded weary. He'd had no food all

day. Ping thought that she had better keep her questions to herself and let the Emperor concentrate on climbing. The steps were too narrow for her to walk alongside him now, so she fell in step behind him.

Ping started to count the steps as she climbed. She got up to three hundreds, five tens, and six and then lost count. She started again, but the rhythm of the shaman's chant made her sleepy.

She closed her eyes, climbing one step with each beat of the chant. Ping wondered if it were possible to sleep and walk at the same time. Then she woke from a dream in which Master Lan was shouting at her to get up. She realized she was lying sprawled on the steps. She had dozed for a moment and fallen. The goatherds were shouting at her to keep moving because she was holding up the goats. Ping hurried to catch up with the rest of the procession.

It was another hour at least before Counselor Tian called a halt and they were able to rest for a few minutes. She ate a millet cake and drank from a mountain stream. Liu Che sat in silence.

They walked on for several more hours. On a night march such as this, there were no magnificent views to reward the climbers. All that Ping could see were the black shapes of rocks by the side of the path, occasional twisted pine trees, and the endless steps stretching just in front of her. They passed under another carved gateway.

"Are we getting close to the top of the mountain?" Ping asked Counselor Tian.

He shook his head and pointed to the archway. "This is called the Halfway to Heaven Gate."

Ping's feet felt as if they were made of stone. The muscles in her calves were aching. She was so tired, she just wanted to lie down by the side of the path, even though the night had turned cold. She wasn't important to the ceremony. No one would notice if she wasn't there. But she didn't want to let Liu Che down by leaving him to climb on without her company. Though the peak of Tai Shan was visible as nothing more than a black starless shape against the night sky, she could feel it pulling her upward. The image of the towering mountain that she had seen during the day was still visible when she closed her eyes. She had to climb the mountain.

The next hours were a blur. The steps became as steep as a ladder. The path twisted and turned. Ping concentrated on placing one foot painfully in front of the other and was aware of nothing else. She lost sight of the guard with the torch and the dark figure of Liu Che. Then the steps stopped and the path became a gentle slope. It was as good as a rest after so many hours of climbing steps.

A sudden breeze blew across the path. Ping could make out the track in front of her, defined by small white pebbles that reflected in the pale moonlight, but both sides of the path were pitch black. She had just been able to see the rocks on either side when she was climbing the steps. Now the surrounding darkness had an endless, airy quality. The wind came up from below, billowing her gown. She sensed that there was a steep drop on either side and was glad she couldn't see. The goats had stopped some way behind her, bleating plaintively. They didn't want to cross the path.

Counselor Tian turned back to hurry the boys along. "Get those animals across Cloud Bridge before the moon is hidden by a cloud," he shouted.

Ping stepped onto the narrow bridge. She focused on the bright pebbles which marked out the way as clearly as if it were lit by thousands of tiny lamps. Then the moon disappeared behind a cloud and the pebble lamps went out. Ping stopped in the middle of the bridge. There was nothing but blackness ahead. She turned to see if the others were behind her, but the rear torchbearer was also out of sight, still climbing up the last of the steps. Ping could see no one. She was alone on the narrow path with blackness all around her, the chill wind rushing under her gown. The ground was far below on either side.

She turned back but lost her bearings. She wasn't sure which way to walk. If she stepped the wrong way she would plunge off the mountain. The wind whining through rocks drowned out the boys' voices and the bleating of the goats.

She called out but the wind caught her frail voice as soon as it left her mouth and carried it away into the darkness. Her heart pounded louder and louder in her ears until its beat drowned out the roar of the wind. Ping's legs trembled—from cold, from fatigue, and from fear.

A few days before, when the dragon had left her, she wouldn't have cared if she'd plunged to her death from a mountain. But she knew now she didn't want to die. She felt a new strength fill her. She didn't draw it from the darkness around her. It came from within. She remembered what Danzi had said about her having second sight. Instead of peering into the darkness to find her way, she closed her eyes. The path was clearer. She still couldn't see it, but she felt its solid rockiness. She took a tentative step and then another. Then she walked forward confidently, her eyes shut tight, until she felt the wind die and the weight of the rock rise up on either side of the path again.

She opened her eyes. The moon came out from behind the clouds. The moonlit pebbles outlined the path behind her. If she'd waited a few more minutes she would have been able to see the path clearly, but she was glad she had crossed Cloud Bridge in the darkness. The young goatherds enticed the goats over one at a time, no longer striking them with their sticks and calling them names, instead coaxing in soft murmurs.

The steps started again, curving this way and that

with the contours of the mountain. They became so steep that there was a rope looped through iron rings in the rock alongside the path to help climbers. As she pulled herself hand over hand up the steep steps, Ping wondered how the goatherd boys would get the goats up there.

At last she noticed that the blackness was fading to gray. The sky had the faintest pink tinge. The steps ended suddenly and the path leveled out as it crossed flat grassland. Another carved gateway arched over the path.

"We've reached the South Gate to Heaven," Counselor Tian announced with relief.

A small stream wound its way across the grassland and cascaded over the edge of the mountain. In the dim light Ping could see the shaman strapping a slender dagger around his waist. She could just make out Liu Che in his black robes preparing for the final part of the journey. Ahead was one last flight of steps.

For this last stretch of his journey, the young Emperor would be accompanied only by the shaman, the goats, and their herders. The beasts crowded up on the path behind them. The goatherds shivered in the pre-dawn air. Their faces were pale, frightened. One was crying. Counselor Tian gave the boys something to drink. Ping was surprised to see the Grand Counselor being kind to the goatherds. He didn't offer the cup to Ping. The drink seemed to calm the boys. Then the Grand Counselor stripped off their rough, greasy jackets and trousers, and replaced them with short black tunics.

The shaman said some words that Ping didn't understand, then Liu Che began to walk up the steps. The shaman followed him. The goatherds stopped shivering. Their faces became serene. Without a word from anyone, the two boys herded the ten and five goats up the last hundred steps toward Heaven. These steps weren't steep. After the trials of climbing up so far, so many steps, this last part of the journey would be relatively easy. The animals climbed the steps with nothing more than a pat on the rump from the goatherds. Liu Che didn't look back.

As the light increased, Ping saw that they were surrounded by a sea of cloud. The clouds turned luminous pink. Though they couldn't see it beneath the clouds, the sun had risen. The Jade Emperor Summit pierced this soft sea and rose to Heaven in the still morning air. On the very top of the mountain there was a shrine. The boys looked tiny, the goats like toys, as they reached the peak. Ping couldn't see Liu Che or the shaman. They had already entered the shrine. The building must have been big enough to house the goats as well, because one by one they disappeared from sight.

Ping was expecting to hear the panicked cries of the goats as the shaman slit their throats, but no sound disturbed the still morning. The sun peeped over the edge of the clouds and flooded them with golden light. The rays reflected on gold patterns painted on the shrine far above them.

Another hour passed. Two vultures started circling above the peak. Then a small figure appeared outside the shrine. He was alone.

"Where are the boys and the shaman?" Ping whispered to Counselor Tian.

"The final steps to Heaven can be trod by the Emperor alone," he replied. "The penalty for anyone else who does so is death."

Ping caught her breath. The cheerful goatherds who had shared the grueling journey with her had been sacrificed along with their four-footed charges.

"Did the Emperor kill them?" she whispered.

"No, that was the shaman's duty, before he killed himself."

The Grand Counselor looked at Ping's stunned face. "They are blessed," he said. "They will have a special place in Heaven."

As the Emperor descended, the sun's rays reflected off him. He was almost too dazzling to look at. The Emperor truly did look like a god. When he reached the last step, Ping could see the reason why he looked so bright. He had exchanged his somber black satin robe for a golden yellow one. The ministers knelt down before him. The guards and the servant had been lying on their faces since the Emperor first appeared. Ping belatedly knelt and lowered her head to the ground.

"Heaven has accepted my offerings," Liu Che announced. "It has blessed my reign and proclaimed that it will be long and prosperous." Ping glanced up. She saw him smooth his new robes. "It has also approved the change of the imperial color from black to yellow."

Liu Che staggered. Counselor Tian stepped forward and caught him before he fell.

"You can break your fast now, Your Imperial Majesty," he said.

He lowered the Emperor onto a rock. The servant gave him some millet cakes. Counselor Tian handed a gold cup to Ping. "Fill that from the stream."

Ping took the gold cup and dipped it into the frothing stream. She was about to take the brimming cup over to Liu Che when two conflicting emotions struck her like a double slap on the face. One was a feeling of joy, which she felt as a rush of warmth through her body and heard as a sweet high singing. The other was a feeling of dread that lay in the pit of her stomach like a rotting melon. She dropped the cup and looked around.

The scene about her had not changed, except that Counselor Tian was now shouting at her for being clumsy. Ping ignored him. The feelings inside her made her gasp. It was as if her own emotions were battling each other. It could have been exhaustion or lack of sleep or the thinness of the air that were making her feel this way. It wasn't, though. She closed her eyes. It seemed impossible, but she knew for certain that the dragon stone was nearby. And so was the dragon hunter.

BLOOD ON TAI SHAN

Ping didn't open her eyes. She let her mind seek out the source of the singing, allowed her feet to take her to it. She felt a chill dampness surround her and knew that she was descending into the clouds. As she breathed, the cold, moist air filled her. It surrounded her heart like ice forming around the edges of a pond in winter. It was like breathing in sadness. This, combined with the lump of sour dread in her stomach, would have made her lose heart—if it hadn't been for the singing. She was getting closer to it, closer to the stone. Then suddenly the singing turned to an anxious, high-pitched keening.

A terrible sound of crashing copper bowls filled the air, along with what sounded like two rusty blades scraping together, and the agitated sound of someone banging a small gong. These were Danzi's sounds of distress, anxiety, and urgency. She had never heard him make them all at once.

Ping opened her eyes. She no longer needed anger to trigger her seeking powers. She no longer needed to close her eyes to feel the threads connecting her to what she sought. Her path was as clear to her as if it were lit by torches.

Ping started to run without any thought for her own safety. She reached Cloud Bridge. The mist was clearing as she stood there. She could see that it wasn't a bridge built by men, but a natural formation, a narrow blade of rock no wider than three feet. The mist evaporated completely revealing a heart-stopping view. On each side of the slender path the rock plunged to earth. On one side the cliff fell to a wooded valley hidden within the mountain range. On the other side the sheer rock plummeted almost to the base of the mountain. She could see all the way to the plain far below. At any other time, Ping would have been sick at the sight of such a dizzying drop; she might have stopped to think of the danger she had faced crossing the perilous bridge in the dark. She didn't pause, though. She ran across as if it were as wide as an imperial road, with flat fields stretching safely on either side.

At the other side of the bridge, to the east, there was another pinnacle. It was smaller than the Jade Emperor Summit. Ping looked down on its top, which was flat, as if one of the gods had lopped off its peak in a fit of anger. There was a single pine tree growing on it, twisted and gnarled. Danzi was on this small plateau rearing up on his hind legs. Next to him was Wang Cao holding a bronze sword in one hand, clutching the reed basket containing the dragon stone with the other. It was too far away for Ping to see if the stone was all right. They were both facing a third figure. It was Diao.

Between Ping and this lower peak was a valley littered with large, sharp-edged rocks. None of the three figures were aware of her presence. Danzi suddenly lashed out at the dragon hunter. His talons slashed Diao's face. Diao swung his dagger at the dragon, but Danzi managed to get out of its way. He already had the purple stripe of a wound across his belly. Wang Cao didn't move. It was as if his feet were stuck to the rock. Ping scrambled down into the valley that separated her from the plateau.

The dragon hunter pulled his crossbow from his shoulder and trained it at the dragon's heart. Ping cried out just as Diao squeezed the trigger. All three pairs of eyes turned to find the source of the cry as Diao's bolt streaked toward the dragon. The sound of metal on rock echoed emptily against the cliffs of the higher peak as Wang Cao's sword fell to the ground. The herbalist looked down at the crossbow bolt embedded so deep in his flesh that only the feathered flight was visible. Ping's cry had made the dragon hunter miss his mark. He'd hit Wang Cao instead. Ping heard Diao curse as he pulled another bolt from his quiver without even glancing at his victim. Wang Cao crumpled to the ground. Diao put the bolt between his teeth. Reloading a crossbow was a job that needed both his hands. The dragon stone rolled from Wang Cao's grasp. Ping's mind was filled with the shrill sound of its anxious cry. She started running across the spill of rocks.

Ping leaped across the rocks as sure-footed as a mountain goat, until she reached the base of the lower pinnacle. She wished she had wings. It wasn't a tall cliff, no more than the height of four men, but it was sheer. She could hear Diao swearing above as Danzi attacked him again. Then she heard the sounds of the dragon's anger and distress ring out, echoing against the steep slopes of the Jade Emperor Summit. Ping couldn't see what was happening. She had to find a way up. Hooking her fingers into the shallowest of cracks, finding a foothold on the narrowest of ridges, she climbed up the peak like an insect.

Ping pulled herself up over the edge of the cliff. Diao's back was toward her. His foul smell turned her stomach. Wang Cao lay motionless, a bloodstain spreading beneath him. Diao had reloaded his crossbow and had it aimed at Danzi again. The dragon looked dazed, glassy-eyed, as if he didn't know what to do next. Diao was concentrating hard, unaware of Ping's presence. His finger moved to the trigger. Ping launched herself at Diao, knocking him to the ground, but not before he released the bolt from his crossbow. It pierced the dragon's hind leg and embedded itself in the trunk of the pine tree, pinning the dragon to it. Ping had hold of Diao round the neck. He elbowed her in the chest.

Close up, his ugly face was made more ugly still by fury. There were four deep cuts where the dragon's talons had raked his cheek. He threw Ping aside and crawled toward the dragon stone and picked it up in his free hand. He ripped it out of the reed basket and his ugly face broke into a terrible smile. Inside Ping's mind, the stone's anxious keening turned to a piercing shriek of terror. It seemed impossible that no one else could hear it.

Ping felt the power within her focus in a breath-taking surge. She was tingling from head to foot. She didn't have to count backward or imagine peonies, it was there at her command. She thrust out her arms and the power shot out through her fingertips, knocking the crossbow from Diao's hand. A smile as bitter as apricot kernels crossed Ping's face as she strode toward the dragon hunter. She was just a slave girl and she was a full head shorter than Diao, but he had fear in his eyes.

The dragon hunter struck out at Ping with his ugly iron dagger. She turned the blade away with her invisible power. It was harder to direct the *qi* power at close range. She needed more space. Diao struck out at her again. Ping blocked the blow with her arm. His arm quivered with effort as he tried to force her to the ground, but she could match the dragon hunter's strength. Just as she was about to overcome him, he kicked her in the stomach. Winded, Ping staggered back. She was on the edge of the little plateau where it curved over to become a sheer cliff. The rock had been worn smooth by wind and rain. Ping's foot slipped. The soles of her shoes, worn from so much walking, wouldn't grip. She lunged forward, clawing at the rock, trying to find something to grab hold of. There was a tuft of wiry grass that had managed to find enough earth in a cleft of rock to anchor its roots. Ping grabbed hold of it with both hands. Diao had his dagger raised again. He aimed it at Ping's hands. Ping looked down. It wasn't a long drop compared to some she'd seen on Tai Shan. Just far enough for the fall to break her neck.

As the dagger blade was falling toward her, a gray blur shot out of the folds of Ping's gown and ran up Diao's leg. The dragon hunter yelped in startled pain as Hua dug his teeth into Diao's already wounded cheek. Diao dropped his dagger as he tried to get the rat off him. It clattered down the side of the mountain. He still had hold of the dragon stone with his other hand. The roots of the grass that Ping was hanging on to were being pulled out by her weight. Her feet scrabbled on the sloping rock surface, trying to find a foothold. Diao let go of the dragon stone. The sound of it hitting the rock made Ping wince. It started to roll toward the edge. It was about to plunge off the peak and smash on the rocks below. Her right foot found a tiny ledge. She levered herself up, gripping the rock with her knees, and reached out toward the dragon stone, grasping it with the tips of her fingers just before it rolled off the edge of the plateau. Diao was screaming as he tried to pull the rat from his face. Hua's teeth were still buried deep in the dragon hunter's cheek.

Ping felt the dragon stone beneath her fingers. Her heart soared as its terrible shriek changed to a singing. She hugged it to her. Diao grabbed a club from his belt and struck Hua with it, even though the blow must have crushed his own cheekbone. Hua fell to the ground, a chunk of Diao's cheek still in his mouth. Ping saw the club arc through the air toward her. Still on her knees, she thrust out her left hand and the *qi* power coursed out of her, even more powerfully than before. The dragon hunter was lifted off his feet and carried backward across the plateau. He landed on the opposite edge. He looked behind him, saw that there was nothing but air separating him from the rocks below. He frantically tried to regain his footing, but his feet slipped on the smooth surface of the rock. He fell over the edge, his arms flailing uselessly. Ping waited, calm and coldhearted, until a bone-crunching thud told her he'd hit rock below.

Ping didn't know which way to turn. Danzi was bleeding, speared to the tree by the crossbow bolt. Hua was lying motionless on the rock, blood oozing from a wound on his head, one of his legs twisted at an unnatural angle.

She turned to the dragon and grasped the crossbow and wrenched it out of the dragon's leg. Blood flowed from the wound. Ping pulled a handful of moss from the earth beneath the pine tree. She staunched the wound with it. She untied the seal from her waist. With the purple ribbon she bound the moss to the dragon's leg. Then she went over to Hua and picked up his small, limp body. She held him up to her face, felt his warm fur against her cheek. Tears filled Ping's eyes.

"Rat not dead," said a voice in her mind. It was the first time Danzi had spoken.

Ping looked at the rat's broken body, but she knew the dragon was right.

Ping was suddenly aware that she was being watched. The golden figure of the Emperor was standing at the edge of the Cloud Bridge. Counselor Tian, the guards, and the servant were with him. They were motionless, staring in her direction. Liu Che shouted out an order to his guards. They leaped into action, running across the Cloud Bridge toward Ping and the dragon.

"Danzi must leave," the dragon said.

"You can't walk to Ocean with a wounded leg and a

gaping hole in your belly," Ping said.

The guards were across the bridge and clambering across the rocks.

"Don't have to walk," replied the dragon. He opened out his wings. "Can fly."

Ping's red stitches were still there, but they had done their job. The tear in Danzi's left wing had healed completely.

"Are you strong enough to carry passengers?"

The tinkling sound of wind chimes filled the air. Ping gently placed Hua behind one of the dragon's reversed scales.

The dragon turned toward the Jade Emperor Summit. "Emperor will be pleased Ping has saved his dragon from Diao," he said. "Ping will be honored if she stays."

"I'm not staying with the Emperor, Danzi," she said.

The seal of the Imperial Dragon Keeper lay on the rock at her feet. She picked it up and traced the beautiful carved dragon with her fingertips. Then she raised it above her head, ready to hurl it into the distance. She looked across the valley to Liu Che. She lowered her hand and put the seal in her pouch. Though Liu Che didn't realize it, she was doing what was best for the dragon. She was still the Imperial Dragon Keeper.

Ping could hear the guards at the foot of the cliff, trying to find a way up.

"Are you sure you can carry me?" she asked.

"Sure."

Ping heard a groan. She turned to Wang Cao. She hadn't given him a thought. She kneeled at the herbalist's side. The pool of sticky blood was widening around him.

"I didn't have the courage to fight Diao," he whispered. "I failed Long Danzi again. You are the true Dragon Keeper, Ping."

He reached out to the dragon stone, but his hand fell back before he touched it.

"He who tries to take carpenter's place, always cuts his hands," the dragon said softly. "Danzi's fault."

The imperial guards had found an easier ascent. The first one was easing himself up onto the plateau.

"Must leave," said Danzi. "Get Wang Cao's rope."

Ping took the coil of rope that was tied to the herbalist's waist. She also took his leather bag and the reed basket. The imperial guard scrambled to his feet and ran at Ping with his sword raised. She easily knocked him aside with her *qi* force.

Ping climbed onto the dragon's back. The dragon took five steps and flapped his wings. The sixth step took him off the edge of the peak. He didn't fall, he didn't lose any altitude at all, his beating wings carried their combined weight easily.

"Have long way to fly," the dragon said. "Ping must secure herself and stone."

Ping put the stone in the basket. She had to push it hard to get it in. Then she hung the basket from Danzi's horns. She wrapped the rope around the horns as well and then twice around her waist before she tied the ends in a firm knot.

Danzi soared up and around Jade Emperor Summit. Ping looked down at Liu Che. He was watching them escape, his hands on his hips. Ping could see his face clearly. His mouth was pinched in the same angry expression as when she had first met him. She had enjoyed being the Emperor's friend for a short while, but she had rejected his friendship and stolen his dragon. Now the Emperor was her enemy.

CHAPTER TWENTY-THREE

OCEAN

Ping watched the figure of the young Emperor shrink to a golden dot as the dragon flew away from Tai Shan. The mountain receded and the plain lay beneath them checked with squares of yellow and brown. Some of the brown squares were striped with green where the spring crops had begun to grow. The hedges and walls between the fields stood out like embroidered seams so that the landscape resembled a blanket sewn from squares of different fabric. Ping had many questions to ask the dragon. The first was the most important.

"How is Hua?" She had to shout to make herself heard over the rush of air and the rhythmic flap of the dragon's wings.

"Can feel his heartbeat." The dragon's voice in her mind was as clear as ever.

Ping smiled to herself. She'd known in her heart that the rat was still alive, but she still didn't trust her second sight.

"How far is it to Ocean?"

"Not far now. Will reach it today if wings hold."

"What were you doing up on Tai Shan, Danzi?"

"Escaping from Diao," the dragon replied. "Must have had spy among imperial guards. Knew we were in Tiger Forest. Was waiting when we emerged."

"What happened?"

"Diao wounded me. We escaped, but Diao followed. Wang Cao said wings were okay to fly, so we climbed Tai Shan for altitude and to escape Diao."

"I'm sorry about Wang Cao, Danzi," Ping said. "I was too slow to save him as well."

"Is Danzi who must apologize, Ping," said the dragon. "Wang Cao was jealous of Ping. He wanted to be Dragon Keeper. I listened to his bitter words and allowed him to convince me that Ping was not true Dragon Keeper. I am sorry."

It was overcast. Danzi continued to climb higher. At first the clouds were no more than wisps, like steam from a kettle. Then they grew denser until Ping and the dragon were enveloped in a cold, white fog. Danzi was buffeted by gusts of wind but he kept climbing. Suddenly they broke through the clouds and were in the sunlight again. All Ping could see beneath her was an expanse of undulating white stretching in every direction, as if they were flying over a world of ice and snow.

She could hardly believe it, but soon they would

reach Ocean. After all their trials, all the diversions, all the people who had tried to stop them, they were finally going to Ocean, and this last stretch required no effort from her at all. Ping yawned. She wanted to watch the clouds change shape beneath her, but she hadn't slept for two days. She was glad of the rope securing her to the dragon. The dragon stone, encased in the basket, made a pillow for her head. She closed her eyes and allowed her body to slide into sleep.

When she woke, Ping was cold. Her body was stiff. She guessed she had slept for several hours. The clouds were bright with sunlight, pink tinged. Through gaps in the cloud the landscape below looked dark and uninviting. The flap of the dragon's wings had slowed. His breathing was labored.

Ping was just about to ask how much farther they had to go when she noticed that the basket holding the stone had a tear in one side and the stone was showing through. Its color looked different in the steely light. It was a darker purple, like ripe plums. The maroon veins, which had just been thin threads before, were thicker. Ping took the stone carefully in her hands, afraid that the basket would tear right open and the stone would fall out.

The bank of cloud below them suddenly ended and the miniature world was visible again. It was no longer patterned with tiny fields. Instead it was blanketed with low, green hills. Something on the horizon reflected the sunlight like a band of polished silver. As they drew closer, the band became wider. The dragon's breathing grew hoarse, his wings beat more slowly, the distance between them and the earth below decreased. The hills gave way to flat land. The silver strip grew wider and wider and turned to blue as they got closer to it. It wasn't solid, its dimpled surface was dipping and rising. Ping couldn't imagine what sort of place it was they were going to. The land ended in a sudden cliff and then there was just a thin strip of pale earth between the land and the surging blue. Where the blue met the earth there were tiny rolls of white. Ping realized that what she was looking at was water. It stretched as far as she could see to the north, to the south, and east until it merged with the sky. Its size terrified her.

"What is that?" said Ping.

"Ocean," replied Danzi.

"But I thought Ocean was a place, a country, a province."

"No. It is the water that surrounds all lands."

Ping's image of Ocean, a garden paradise, dissolved. "But you told me—"

"Cannot describe Ocean to one who has never seen it."

"It's so big."

"It is greatest thing in the world."

Ping watched the Ocean continue to grow until it seemed to surround them completely and there was nothing but blue.

"Are you going down into Ocean?" Ping asked, thinking that the dragon's goal might be below the waves.

"No. Must find place to rest."

Danzi swung back toward the land. Gray clouds had appeared on the horizon. The air around them felt alive. It made Ping's skin prickle and her hair seemed to move of its own accord, floating and crackling when she tried to smooth it down. It was eerily quiet. Danzi glided round in a circle as he prepared to land. A sudden gust of wind blew back the dragon's wings and Ping's stomach lurched as he dropped almost a *chang* before he recovered. The clouds moving in from the east were thick and black. There was no sign of the sun and it was as dark as dusk.

The wind grew stronger. The clouds were lit by a blinding flash and there was an earsplitting crack. Water started to pour from the sky as if someone had opened a hatch in the clouds. The air went from being dry to drenched in a few moments. Ping held the stone tight to her chest. Another flash of lightning lit up the underside of the clouds. The wind grew so strong, Ping was afraid she would be blown off the dragon's back even though she was tied on with rope. She couldn't see for the rain in her eyes. She clutched the stone tighter.

Danzi's fragile wings were tossed around by the wind like autumn leaves. Ping was afraid they'd be blown right off. He was heading for the pale flat strip between Ocean and the land. The dragon couldn't control his descent. The ground accelerated toward them. As they got closer, Ping could see that it wasn't entirely flat. There were rocks scattered across it. The rain made it hard to see. She leaned over to get a better view, searching for a safe place to land. The wind buffeted the dragon, blowing him around like a kite. The dragon banked steeply, trying to aim for a spot with no rocks. The wet dragon stone slipped out of Ping's grasp. She cried out as she saw the purple stone fall.

She fumbled with the knots securing her. She wanted to fall after the stone and save it. She watched helpless as it crashed onto the rocks below. Moments later the dragon hit the ground with a bone-jarring thud. He plowed into fine white sand, making a furrow several feet deep. Ping was winded for a moment, then she undid the rope, leaped off, and ran to the dragon stone.

It was lying between two rocks. She knelt and picked it up and turned it over. There was a large crack running along its length. The weather at ground level was as wild as it had been in the air. The wind threatened to lift her from her knees. Lightning flashed overhead, followed immediately by booming thunder. As she watched, more cracks split off at angles to the central fracture. Water started to seep out of the cracked stone. The crack grew wider, the flow of water from the stone increased until it was gushing out over Ping's hands. It was warm. It seemed impossible that the stone could contain so much liquid.

"Danzi, I've broken the dragon stone."

The exhausted dragon crawled over to Ping's side.

Ping looked at the ruined stone in her hands. A final gush of warm water split the stone in two. The two halves lay in her hands. The wind died. The rain slowed. The sky became lighter. There was something inside the half stone in her left hand, something the same purple color as the stone itself. It wasn't solid though, not crystalline as she'd expected. It was like a strange purple vegetable covered in a sticky substance. It slithered out into her lap. No, it was more like sodden fabric scraps wound around each other into a ball. As she watched, the mass twitched and one of the purple strands unwound itself and flopped onto Ping's knee.

It was soft and limp and frayed at the end. Another purple strand unwound from the shapeless mass, then another. In all, five strands unwound themselves. They were flexible, soft and sticky with mucus. Four of them had frayed ends, the fifth ended in a point. She was about to brush the ugly thing off her, when the last part of it unfolded. This strand was thicker, more solid, not so shapeless. It raised itself up. It had a certain symmetry. There were two circular bulges, two pinpoint holes. At the end of the strand, a larger hole opened moistly.

Inside the hole were two rows of tiny white spikes. Ping gasped as she suddenly saw the thing as a whole for the first time. It wasn't a vegetable, it wasn't a ball of scraps. It was alive. The spiky hole was a mouth; the smaller holes, nostrils; and the bulges, unopened eyes. It was a creature with a head, four legs, and a tail.

Danzi carefully lifted the creature from her lap and licked off the mucus with his long red tongue, then placed it on the sand. It balanced for a moment on its fragile legs and then collapsed onto its belly. Ping saw that the little creature was covered in fine purple scales—shiny and smooth like fish scales. There was a row of soft spikes running down the length of its body from its head to the tip of its tail. The frayed edges at the end of each leg were tiny toes. It was a baby dragon.

"Danzi," Ping whispered. "Why didn't you tell me the dragon stone was an egg?"

When the baby dragon heard Ping's voice, it turned its head toward her. Its eyes opened for the first time. They were green. It made a high purring sound. Ping stared at it in wonder. It wasn't ugly at all. It was beautiful. She picked it up and held it to her.

"Didn't want to make Ping anxious."

"But I could have broken it!"

"Did break it."

"I mean before it was ready to hatch." She couldn't take her eyes off the little creature. "Was it ready to hatch?"

Danzi inclined his head.

"Is it a boy or a girl?"

"It is boy. Can tell by straight nose."

"What will it eat, Danzi?"

"Milk at first. Then insects. Later small birds."

Ping looked alarmed. "What sort of milk? What kind of insects?"

"Ewes' milk very good. Goats' milk good too. As for insects, moths and dragonflies are best. Caterpillars also good. Nothing with hard shells, nothing that stings."

Ping had ten thousand questions to ask. Danzi's voice in her mind was faint, hard to hear over the constant purring of the new dragon voice. The sun appeared in the narrow space between the clouds and the horizon. The baby's newly dried purple scales glistened in the orange rays. Ping dragged her eyes from the baby dragon and looked at Danzi for the first time since he had plowed into the beach. The old dragon looked exhausted. His scales didn't reflect the sun. They looked dull and faded. His eyes had developed the yellowish cast they'd had when he was living in the dragon pit at Huangling.

Ping gasped. "Hua!" she said. "I forgot about Hua!"

Danzi reached behind his top reversed scale and lifted out the rat. Ping placed the baby dragon in her lap. It curled up and went to sleep. She reached out and gently took the motionless rat from Danzi's talons. He lay draped over her hands like a rag. She held him closer. His small chest was moving a little as he took in tiny breaths of air.

"He's still alive," Ping whispered.

"May not survive," Danzi said.

"This is my fault," Ping said, tears filling her eyes. "Poor Hua."

"Darkness soon arrive. Must find place to spend night."

Ping suddenly felt overwhelmed. She had a newborn baby, an aged dragon, and an injured rat to care for. They had no shelter, no food. An image of the beautiful bedchamber at Ming Yang Lodge came to her mind. She remembered the smell of the Emperor's banquet. Just for a second she wondered if she'd made the right decision. She looked at the little dragon in her lap. If she'd stayed with Liu Che they would have all been more comfortable, but the baby would be facing a long life in captivity. She gently put Hua back behind the reversed scale and transferred the baby dragon to the crook of her right arm. She stood up. She had work to do.

CHAPTER TWENTY-FOUR

PERHAPS THERE IS NO END

Ping searched the cliffs for a cave, but there was none. She walked along the beach in both directions, looking for somewhere to shelter for the night. At last she found a strange construction made from the skeleton of an enormous sea creature. Its head and tail had been removed, leaving just the creature's body. Its rib cage was so big that Ping could walk inside it. The dried skin formed a perfectly weather-proof covering. Inside were signs that it had once been a fisherman's home.

Before it got dark, Ping collected firewood and rain-water, and found some small fish and crabs trapped in a rock pool. She started a fire. In Wang Cao's bag there was a cooking pot, some lentils, and grain. It also con-tained a jar of the red cloud ointment, some of Danzi's herbal mix and a small packet of tea. Wang Cao had prepared well.

Ping cooked a meal for herself and Danzi, but the old dragon ate little.

"What about the baby?" Ping asked. "I haven't got any milk."

To Ping's surprise, Danzi stretched out a talon and pierced the wound in his chest which had only just stopped bleeding.

"What are you doing?"

Danzi collected some of his purple blood in a seashell. The baby dragon lapped it up.

"Can survive on blood for few days," Danzi said.

Ping laid the baby dragon in a bed of dried seaweed when he had finished feeding. He was soon asleep. She made an herbal brew for Danzi and put ointment on his wounds. When all her charges were sleeping, she went out onto the beach and looked at the massive Ocean shimmering in the moonlight. Waves of water crashed onto the beach only to be sucked back again by some invisible force. She drank some of the water, and spat the salty liquid out again. Ocean was nothing like she'd imagined it to be.

The next morning, Ping woke early and rekindled the fire. The baby's legs were stronger. He was able to totter around the beach. Danzi still looked faded and tired. Ping managed to catch a seabird, which she roasted for him. She fed a few drops of fish broth to Hua.

"You lied to me about the waters of the Ocean, Danzi," she said. "It's too salty to drink and I don't believe it has any magic powers."

"Ping is right," Danzi replied, "but could not tell you your task back then. Ping wouldn't have been able to comprehend."

"So here is the Ocean," Ping said. "Why have we traveled all this way to get to it?" She looked at his frail, scarred body. "Will the waters heal you?"

"No. Must cross it to reach Isle of the Blest."

"Why must you go there?"

"If stay here in the Empire, will die. On Isle of the Blest is stream of the water of life. This will heal me."

She peered out toward the horizon but could see no sign of land.

"How far away is it? Will you be able to carry us that far?"

"Only Danzi going."

Ping couldn't believe her ears. "You're going to leave your baby behind?"

"Wanted to take dragon stone to Isle of Blest, so baby would be born away from world of men."

"You can still take him."

The dragon shook his head. "World without dragons would be sad place. Will leave him here with Dragon Keeper."

Ping realized he meant her.

"But I don't know how to look after him."

"Young dragons usually spend first hundred years with mother." Danzi sighed sadly. "Ping must take place of dragon mother, Lu Yu. Do as she would have. Nurture him, but do not tame him. Shape him without controlling him." Danzi touched the little dragon's head with one taloned paw. "Ping will know."

Ping wished she had as much confidence in her ability to raise the dragon as Danzi did.

The old dragon clambered slowly up the steep path to the top of the cliff.

"Must leave now."

Ping picked up the baby dragon and followed him.

"But you haven't got any food. You'll need fresh water."

"All will be provided."

"Won't you get lonely?"

"Will take Hua as companion. He also requires water of life to survive."

"How will I manage without you, Danzi?"

"The path is easy if you avoid turning off it."

"Will you be able to fly so far?"

"Who knows how things will end? Perhaps there is no end."

Ping knew from experience there was no point in arguing with the dragon. She placed the baby in a nest of grass and took Hua out from behind the reversed scale. She held his soft, warm fur against her face for the last time. Hua turned his head toward her. He blinked but didn't make a sound. She carefully placed him back. Danzi gave Ping all the gold and other things that he had hidden behind his reversed scales, things that she didn't have time to examine. He handed her the Dragon Keeper's mirror. It flashed in the sunlight.

"You are the last Dragon Keeper, Ping."

"The last?"

The dragon nodded wearily. "The last and the best."

"The baby isn't the last dragon, is he?"

"He is the last and the first."

Ping didn't know what he meant.

"Last imperial dragon. First to live free with true Dragon Keeper."

Danzi opened his wings.

"Wait!" Ping said. "What is the baby's name?"

The dragon thought for a moment. "Call him Kai Duan, which means Beginning," he said. "Long Kai Duan."

Before Ping had a chance to say anything else the dragon flapped his wings and took three paces off the edge of the cliff. He was so thin that the strong wind carried him easily over the breaking waves. He flew off without a backward glance. His life had been full of hardship. Ping hoped he would find peace on the Isle of the Blest. It seemed impossible that his fragile wings could carry him over such a distance. Ping watched him until he was too small to see. She prayed he'd have the strength to reach his destination.

She looked down at the baby dragon standing unsteadily at her feet. Would she be able to live up to

Danzi's expectations? In the past weeks she had achieved impossible things. She had found her name. She had gained the friendship of an Emperor—and lost it again. She had helped a dragon.

"Come on, Kai," she said, picking up the little creature. "We have to find a she-goat."

She was no longer the timid girl who endured a miserable life of slavery rather than venture into the unknown. She was responsible for the last dragon. She turned her back on Ocean. Her path lay a different way, and she was looking forward to the journey.

GLOSSARY

CASH
A Chinese coin of low value with a square hole in the middle.

CHANG
A measure of distance equal to about seven and a half feet.

CINNABAR
A bright red mineral whose chemical name is mercuric sulphide.

CONFUCIUS
A Chinese philosopher who lived around 500 B.C.E.

FIVE CLASSICS
Five Chinese books, more than 2000 years old, that formed the basis of knowledge in ancient China.

FOUR SPIRITUAL ANIMALS
The dragon, the *qilin*, the red phoenix, and the giant tortoise. The ancient Chinese named four constellations after these animals.

HAN DYNASTY
A period in Chinese history when the emperors all belonged to the Han family. It lasted from 202 B.C.E. to 220 C.E.

HAN FOOT
A measure of length equal to about 9 inches.

JADE
A semiprecious stone also known as nephrite. Its color varies from green to white.

JIN
The measure of weight for gold.

JUJUBE
A name for the fruit known as the Chinese date.

LI
A measure of distance equal to about three tenths of
a mile.

MOU
A measure of land area one pace wide and 240
paces long.

PANGOLIN
An animal with a scaly skin and a long snout that
eats ants.

QI
According to traditional Chinese beliefs, *qi* is the
life energy that flows through us and controls the
workings of the body.

QILIN
A mythical Chinese animal with the body of a deer,
the tail of an ox, and a single horn.

RED PHOENIX
A mythical Chinese bird that looks a lot like a pea-
cock.

SHEN
According to traditional Chinese beliefs, *shen* is the
spiritual energy that drives our mental and spiritual
activities. It is sometimes translated as the soul.

SHU
A drop; a very small amount.

GUIDE TO PRONUNCIATION

The Chinese language includes many sounds unlike any sounds in English. The Chinese words in this book are written in pinyin, which is the official modern method for writing the sounds of Chinese characters using the Roman alphabet. The pinyin system was introduced by the People's Republic of China in 1958, and has since been adopted worldwide. In pinyin, words aren't always pronounced the way you might think. Here is a guide to help you pronounce them properly.

Diao	Dee-ow (rhymes with *now*)
Hua	Hwah (rhymes with *pa*)
Huangling	Hwang-ling
Jiang Bing	Jahng Bing
Lao Ma	Low (rhymes with *now*), Ma (rhymes with *pa*)
Liu Che	Lee-oo (oo as in *loop*), Chuh (as in *church*)
Long Danzi	Lung (u as in *butcher*), Dan-za
Long Kai Duan	Long Kai (rhymes with *buy*), Dwahn
Ping	Sounds just like it looks
Tai Shan	Tai (pronounced as *tie*), Shan
Tian	Tee-en

Wang Cao	Wahng Tsow (like the end of *cats* and the end of *now*)
Wei Wei	Way Way
Wucheng	Woo-chung
Wudi	Woo-dee

This story is set in the year 141 B.C.E., the first year of the long reign of Emperor Wudi. Long Danzi's words of wisdom were inspired by the *Dao De Jing*, an ancient Chinese work written more than 2500 years ago. The Dao forms the basis of the Chinese philosophy known as Daoism and encourages people to live a simple, honest life, interfering with nature as little as possible.